THE CASTLE OF SPIRIT AND SORROW

BRIARWOOD WITCHES, BOOK 5

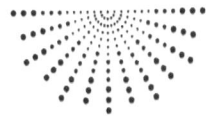

STEFFANIE HOLMES

BACCHANALIA HOUSE

ISBN: 978-0-9951111-8-9

Can't get enough of Maeve and her boys? Get *The Summer Court* – a Briarwood short story – for free in *Cabinet of Curiosities*, a Steffanie Holmes compendium of short stories and bonus scenes. To get this collection, all you need to do is sign up for updates with the Steffanie Holmes newsletter.

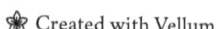 Created with Vellum

For Sam,

Thank you for ginnanigans and introducing me to My Dad Wrote a Porno, and also for being the only other person I know who appreciates the genius of Chelsea Wolfe.

Miss your face.

1

MAEVE

*C*orbin's lifeless head lolled back against the stake, and my heart crumbled to dust.

He can't be dead. He can't be.

But my rational mind fought against my protests. Corbin wasn't moving or crying out. The bone knife was buried in his side right up to the hilt. It would've struck organs. He'd been bleeding internally for Athena knows how long. I hadn't seen him since he'd locked Rowan and I away in the priest hole.

Blood pounded in my ears. The world around me faded – the angry villagers, the triumphant grin on Daigh's face, the horrifying stakes rigged up to accept their sacrifices all blurred into white noise as Corbin's glassy eyes shattered the universe around me.

The remains of my heart sank through my chest cavity, settling over my organs like crystalline tears. My body lost form and function, toppling forward through the void of the world. My head slammed into the ground and bounced, wrenching my neck so hard stars danced in front of my eyes. I didn't feel any of it.

Corbin's dead. Dead, dead, dead.

Pain tore at my body as the familiar, numb horror of grief settled in. *Corbin's dead and it's all my fault.*

I made the decision to drop the barrier and allow the humans into Briarwood. *I* trusted Daigh and Aline against all the evidence that warned me otherwise. *I* kept secret what Aline and I had done and allowed Corbin to walk into that battle unprepared. *I'd* hidden away in that priest hole like a coward while he sacrificed his life for us. I should have known as soon as he shoved Rowan and I in there that all was lost. *Corbin would never allow us to lose Briarwood without a fight, even if it meant...*

... if it meant... I choked on the dust of my shattered heart.

I gulped in a breath, trying to force myself back to the present. But the grief bit into me and I couldn't think. Numb, I watched Daigh pace in front of his troops, his lips curled in a smirk, his eyes cold and focused. He yelled something that made the villagers cheer, but the words were without meaning.

Maeve, can you hear me?

Blake's voice roared inside my head, snapping me back from my grief. Cold dirt bit my cheek. Fresh grass tickled the back of my neck.

Maeve, I know you're hurting, but you've got to focus. We need to get everyone else away from here before they end up joining Corbin. I don't think even the villagers are safe. I have a way, but I need your help.

At the mention of Corbin's name, another wave of pain rocked my body. I reeled, pulling my mind back to the present, to Blake, to Arthur and Flynn and Rowan and Kelly – the people I loved who were still alive but in terrible danger. I was still the High Priestess. I was still responsible for them.

Two of the fae stepped forward, looping their bows over

their backs as they grabbed Corbin's legs and arms and dragged his body toward the roaring bonfire. Behind me, I was faintly aware of the villagers yelling. *They're going to get their burning witch tonight.*

But they won't get us all. The Briarwood coven will survive. I'll make sure of it, even if means I die on that fire myself.

I tested my magic, calling up the pillar of power that flared inside me. It sizzled as it slid under my skin, but when I tried to push the energy out of my palms and fingers, it resisted, bouncing back at me and shooting hot energy back into my veins. I was definitely blocked.

I lifted my head and sent a thought back to Blake. *Okay. I'm here. My magic is blocked but I'm ready to push as soon as it's free. What's the plan?*

There's going to be a distraction. I'm hoping it will break the spell that prevents us from using our powers. When it happens, I need you to do whatever it takes to get to me. We're going to have to break that annoying moral code of yours and force all the fae back into the underworld, and then rewrite the memories of the villagers so we're the good witches saving them from the evil magical fae.

It took me a moment to realize what he was talking about. *Compulsion.*

As witches, Blake and I should never be able to perform compulsion – it was fae magic through and through. Just as well, because like Blake said, the idea of messing in other people's minds was a bit ethically wobbly to me. But Blake's childhood under Daigh's ruthless tutelage had given him the ability to transcend his spirit powers, and he could perform basic compulsion that – when teamed up with my heightened powers of projection and dreamwalking – meant we'd once been able to tell a whole bunch of fae to fuck right off, and off they'd fucked.

Apparently we were going to do it again.

I can do that, I thought to Blake. *We are the good witches.*

3

I could practically hear Blake's smirk. *If you say so, Princess.*

Let me take Daigh, though. I'll feed him nightmares until his head explodes.

Much as the thought of watching you kill Daigh excites me, Princess, you can't. Not tonight.

Why not? You saw what he did—

I saw. Even inside my head I could hear the darkness in Blake's words. *But this won't be over just because Daigh dies, and right now his connection to you might be the only leverage we have.*

He was right. I hated that he was right. If Daigh died, the Slaugh would still come. And even if we defeated them, the fae would come again, and again. We needed a permanent solution.

What kind of distraction can you do without your magic?

You'll know it when you see it. Just stay alive for another couple of minutes.

I'll do my best, I promised.

Blake's voice went dark as the fae tossed Corbin's body into the fire. The flames leapt over his body, capturing his limbs and tangling through his dark hair. High, keening wails pierced the night, stabbing into the cavity that had once held my heart. I recognized the voice, even though the sound was like nothing I'd ever heard before.

Rowan.

This was breaking him. It had broken me. His pain pierced the night as the flames charred and peeled Corbin's skin.

I couldn't cry, couldn't feel. Daigh had taken everything away from me.

Daigh strutted down the line in front of his fae warriors, his emerald eyes glittering under the moonlight. *My eyes.* I hated him with the fire of a thousand suns.

"Why have you done this?" I yelled at him, my voice

ringing clear and hard over the crackling flames. "We would have aligned with you and given you back your wild places. We would have helped you oppose Liah. Wasn't that what you wanted?"

Daigh's eyes flickered to mine. "What I wanted was *you*, daughter. Your magic will bring the world to its knees. These pointless witches stifle you. They rein in your destructive power and force you to bed them in order to channel but a fraction of your true skill. You and I will rule over this world together, with every fae and witch and human slave in our thrall."

"Nothing you do will make me rule alongside you now."

"I don't believe that's true. When you brought Aline back for me, for us, I knew that in your heart you wanted us to be together. You gave me no choice. I could see you wouldn't join me while these humans were still alive. Now you'll see your *real* family."

"If you think this is the way a family behaves, then you know even less than I thought."

"True enough. But I need them all gone. I need to show my fae I will be ruthless in the face of my enemies, and any witch who refuses to swear fealty to me is useless. It does well for me to have the humans weasel out the rest of your kind. Once word spreads across the world about what went on at Briarwood tonight, none of the covens will be safe."

Cold horror settled on my chest. I couldn't let Daigh get into people's heads. I knew how convincing he could be, even without compulsion. He'd light the world up with witch burnings once again.

You're brilliant, Princess, Blake's voice boomed in my head. *Keep him talking.*

I glared at Daigh. "If this is about witches, then let Kelly go. She's not even one of us."

"No, but you love her. I'm hardly going to share you now,

am I?" Daigh snapped his fingers and two other fae stepped out of formation to approach Kelly. They grabbed her arms and dragged her to her feet.

"Kelly!" I screamed, my vision swimming.

Her eyes flew open. "Maeve, help me!" she cried.

I bucked and thrashed, trying to break through my bonds. My magic pulsed and twisted inside me, desperate to be free. It slammed against the wall again and again. I can't. *I can't I can't I can't.*

You can, *Princess.* Blake's fierce voice pierced my mind. *I won't let anyone else die tonight. But you have to keep it together just a bit longer. Distraction inbound.*

"Time to hoist up the annoying one." Daigh snapped his fingers again. Two soldiers by the fire poked Corbin's body with two long poles, rolling his corpse out of the flames. They heaved him up and shoved him onto the stake.

A sickening *CRACK* pierced the night as the stake broke through Corbin's chest. His blackened corpse slid down the wood. His head lolled back and the whites of his eyes caught the flames. I knew that for the rest of my life I'd never be able to close my eyes without that vision burning my eyelids.

Someone was screaming. It took me a moment to realize it was me.

"Maeve!" Kelly yelled. I tore my eyes from Corbin. Kelly thrashed against her kidnappers, kicking her legs the way she used to do when we were kids and I had a toy she wanted to play with.

"Kelly, hold on!" My hand wriggled a little in my bonds. I tugged at the knot, my magic humming in my veins. Someone kicked my hands, but I ignored them. No physical pain could penetrate my shattered heart.

They're almost here, Princess, Blake's voice echoed in my head.

"I'm so sorry!" Kelly sobbed. "I said such horrible things, and I didn't mean any of it. I don't care about the witchcraft or the guys or any of it, just please, please… Maeve? MAEVE!" Her words dissolved into screams as the fae dragged her towards the fire. They lifted her into the air and my body dissolved into dust and they swung Kelly back and she screamed and screamed and screamed and I screamed and there was nothing I could do—

"Hello, everyone!" A bright voice sang over the meadow.

Kelly's captors dropped her on the ground and grabbed for their bows.

One distraction, signed, sealed, delivered, Blake sung inside my head.

Daigh's head whipped around. I forced my neck muscles to engage and shift so I could see, too. Aline stood uphill from the stakes, her wavy hair whipping around her face. Blood streaked the white fabric of her dress, and she carried one of the swords from the Great Hall in her hand. Beside her stood a small crowd of people. I recognized Clara, her black shawls wrapped around her tiny shoulders. A large red fox wound its way around Clara's ankles, its thick tail held high and alert. On the other side of the fox was Obelix, who sat his plump ass on the grass and washed his face as if he didn't have a care in the world.

But… Aline betrayed us. She conspired with Daigh to break the protective charms around the castle. So why is she here now with Clara and… and…

My chest swelled as I recognized other faces. Beside Clara was Gwen and Candice from the Avebury coven, dressed in their white druidic garments. Behind them stood Isadora, her six-inch spiked pumps sinking into the soft earth. There was Jane, lifting a cricket bat in her hands with a menacing glint in her eyes. Next to her was Corbin's dad Andrew, and a woman with dark hair and kind eyes I

7

assumed was his mother. There were a couple of other people I didn't recognize and… and…

A hunched figure gripped Aline's arm as though it were the only thing holding him upright. He raised his head, and the moon caught his handsome features.

It was Robert Smithers.

What is going on? If Aline is working with Daigh, then why is she here with all of these people? Are they all working against us?

The villagers howled and cursed as they recognized Aline. "I told you she was a ghost!" cried one.

"No, not a ghost. Look, she's holding that man upright. A ghost couldn't do that."

"She's a zombie innit! Quick, someone cut off her head!"

"Look at her, she hasn't aged a day. What beauty serum is she using?"

"Arrest her!" someone yelled to Officer Judge.

"No. Get her skincare secrets first!"

"I can't arrest her for being *alive*," Officer Judge shot back from somewhere behind me.

"Vicar, *do* something!"

But the vicar had fallen to his knees in front of me, his voice high with fear as he prayed for salvation at the top of his lungs. Aline's presence was too much for him. He was out of this fight.

"What are you doing, my love?" Aline called down to Daigh. Her tone was casual, as if it didn't much bother her what his answer was. A fresh wave of hatred rolled through me, but I couldn't hold on to it. I was too surprised to see her there and with all those people. How had she collected them all? The last time I saw her was only an hour or so ago on the roof, when we were betraying the coven…

Maeve, Blake called inside my head. His magic thrummed against the edges of my mind. *They're weakening. I need you to get to me.*

"The only thing I *can* do to save both our races from an irradiated death," Daigh said. His face remained. He didn't look as if he was weakening to me. "I'm securing possession of the witches."

I tested my power again. It went a little further before it was pushed back. The guy holding me down yelped as a tiny piece of my magic seared him, but it wasn't enough to get him off me. *Keep trying*, Blake urged me.

"You know that's not true," Aline patted Smithers' arm. "*I* told Rob about that dream, for I had it night after night after night starting from the time you entered his head. He painted the dream from my descriptions. You didn't get this vision from Blake. You'd already seen it through Rob's eyes, through his brush. Because it is your vision. It is *your* future, Daigh, not ours. You've changed it – corrupted it with your broken magic – and given it to our daughter."

What?

"My future... Liah's future... Maeve's future... It's no matter," Daigh waved a hand. "They are all the same. Tonight I have put a stop to it. The world cannot die if the witches are already gone. You are here and Maeve is here. I see you have already gathered a coven to join us. As soon as the rest of these witches are dealt with, we can get on with our business."

"I'm not here to join you, Daigh. There are a million other ways to stop this vision coming true than killing our daughter's coven. We're here to stop you."

What?

Daigh's smirk froze on his face. He honestly hadn't expected Aline to stand against him.

My mind reeled. I hadn't expected it, either. *Was Aline telling the truth? Why had she run off to collect everyone on her own? Had she known Daigh was lying all along? Why didn't she tell me?*

Maeve, Blake roared inside my head. *Stop worrying about Mother Dearest and her lover boys. Break your magic free.*

I pushed again, forcing my mind to focus on the magic pulsing against my skin. But once more, it slammed into the invisible wall.

It's not breaking! I cried at Blake.

It will, my love. But you must be ready. A voice that wasn't Blake's cut through my head, light and lyrical. Aline. How did she get inside my head?

"You can't stop me," Daigh said, his voice dark. "The humans have spoken – the world does not want these witches. The Slaugh will come in three days to scour the earth of anyone who opposes me. They are unstoppable. Under my rule, the fae will have our territories once again. We will tear down the iron fortresses and rebuild our world in earth and leaf and stone."

Aline tipped her head to the side. "One thing we both know about humans is that they can change their minds on a whim. And as for these fae who still follow you, what will they do when they learn your secret?"

"I have no secrets from my fae," Daigh said, his chin high.

"I suspected you of planning something the day we spoke through the mirror in the forest. But I knew our daughter wasn't yet able to trust me, so I had to keep my fears secret from her. When you came back to speak to Maeve, I knew you were lying. I have studied the wards of the castle when I discovered what you'd done to Rob. I know you cannot cross them, not even to speak through a mirror. The only way you could have achieved that was if you are no longer fae."

What?!

Blake's voice screeched in my head. *Bloody hell!*

A gasp rocked through the fae legions. The two soldiers dropped Kelly and glared at Daigh.

I zeroed in on Daigh's face. His casual grin did not falter, but the firelight caught his eyes. He blinked. That blink – the only sign from Daigh's chiseled features that anything fazed him – told me everything I needed to know.

Holy shit.

It was true. I didn't know how or why, but Daigh was no longer a fae.

ARTHUR

"... S peak through a mirror." A familiar singsong voice called me back from oblivion. "The only way you could have achieved that was if you are no longer fae."

My head throbbed as I raised my neck toward the bright fire. Grass tickled my face. It took me a couple of moments to realize where I was. I thought I must've accidentally set the meadow alight. Panic caught me as I tried to shrug off my coat so I could smother the flames, but my arms wouldn't budge.

Thin memories stretched across my mind. Standing on the staircase raining fire down on the compelled villagers. Corbin racing down the stairs, sucking all the air from the room and dropping them like flies as they gasped for breath. Corbin yelling at me to run. Corbin and I sprinting for the meadow and crashing into a phalanx of fae soldiers. My sword clashing against bone blades as arrows flew past my head. Losing sight of Corbin in the fray, my vision blurred with green and red – fae and human blood and the blinding force of my own rage. My feet stomping on the fallen bodies of my enemies as I forced my way across the field, knowing that if I broke through I could run to Raynard Hall for help, or maybe I'd just stand on the crest of the hill and burn them all to dust. My sword plunging into a fae's stomach. Green blood spurting across its green uniform. The fae collapsing against me, trapping my sword between us. Trying to shove him back so I could yank my blade out, and hearing a crack as something hard slammed into my skull.

Then the pain came, and nothing else.

I spat dirt out of my mouth. Even with the pain throbbing behind my eyes, I got the gist of what had happened since I'd been out. The villagers had tied me up and immobilized me. I lay on my stomach, my hands bound and a heavy weight on my back, holding me down. I kicked out with my leg – my boot made contact with bone. My captor grunted in pain, but didn't loosen his hold.

A few feet to my right, my sword blade glinted as it reflected the orange flames. If I could get to it…

But any plans for escape were halted as the rest of the situation came into view.

Behind the bright fire, six stakes lined the highest point of the meadow. *Just like in Maeve's vision.* I turned my neck to the side, and saw Maeve and Flynn and the others tied up and held down by the villagers. Daigh paced in front of an army of fae that faced up the hill, arrows drawn but not yet loosed. Kelly lay tied up on the ground between two warriors. She curled her body up and tried to wriggle away. They barely seemed to notice her, their attention drawn to a figure on the top of the hill.

Aline.

If it wasn't for her long hair whipping around her face, I'd have thought it was Maeve. She *radiated* power, magic pouring off her in waves and rolling down the hill. Behind her, figures remained in shadow, but I swear I heard a cat yowl.

I craned my head toward her. *Did she just say what I think she said... that Daigh isn't a fae anymore?*

"Don't move, witch," a voice hissed in my ears. I flattened the backs of my hands, palms facing up at my captor, and forced my magic through my body, building a great ball of fire. It wasn't hard. I was angry enough to torch the world.

I fired the ball.

Instead of leaping through my skin, it slammed against my palm and bounced back, shooting hot fire through my body.

Shite, they've blocked our magic again.

I focused on what was going on around me – on Daigh, frozen in position in front of his army. On the villagers, their attention not on the fae but on a gaggle of people on top of the hill. The crowd surged forward. Behind Aline, I recognized Jane, Clara, Corbin's parents, Gwen and Candice from Avebury, and from his picture in Maeve's art book, Robert Smithers. Obelix was even sitting by his feet, gazing down the hill with a bored expression only a cat could master in the middle of a massacre.

What's going on? My vision narrowed in on Aline. *She betrayed us. So why is she here, looking like she's facing off against Daigh? Did she mean what she said about Daigh?*

Daigh's face remained frozen in his ghoulish grin, but I'd been around Blake long enough now to know that the fae would laugh on the way to the guillotine. But Aline's words shuddered through the army – bows rattled, feet shuffled, fae bent toward each other in whispered conversation. In front of the fire, his two fae generals stepped over Kelly's prone body. They narrowed their eyes at Daigh. One raised his hand. "Does she speak the truth?" he demanded.

Daigh laughed, the sound ringing clear across the

meadow. "You think I've lost my powers, Regin? That would be ludicrous," he said. "I am here, am I not? Just as I am."

"Robert can't see my thoughts, Robert can't do his tricks," Smithers chanted.

"Shut up," Daigh snapped.

"The best as I can guess, you gave your powers over to a demon so that you might have the means to speak with Maeve through the castle mirrors," Aline said. "I gather you intend to return to the underworld with all the fae on your side and get your magic back somehow, perhaps in exchange for the spirits of these witches. Demons do so love the taste of a witch."

Aline held up her hand. The corner of her mouth curled up into a smile that looked so much like Maeve's it hurt. Daigh opened his mouth to answer her, but all that came out was two lines of some ghastly pop song. I recognized it as a song Aline had been playing on repeat ever since Flynn showed her how to use the system in the Great Hall.

Daigh snapped his mouth shut, his eyes blazing. He lurched forward, his hands raised as if he intended to choke the life out of Aline. Instead, his hand flew up and he slapped himself across the cheek.

What... the... fuck?

Another shudder rippled through the fae. Behind Aline, Clara stifled a laugh behind her hand.

"You can't do that," Daigh gasped, staring at his hand in shock. "That's fae magic."

Bloody hell. Aline just used compulsion. That's... not possible. Blake's the only witch who can use compulsion, and not on a fae...

"Can't I?" Aline lifted her hand higher, a serene smile playing across her lips. "It seems that when you made the binding between us, Maeve wasn't the only one who got a piece of your magic. I've been carrying this spark of you with me for twenty-one years, and now it will be the spark that is your undoing."

"Binding?" The fae soldier named Regin growled. "You're bound with those witches? You told us you mated with her, but not that there was a binding."

"She's lying, obviously. She wants to turn you against me!" Daigh yelled. He slapped his other cheek, then kicked his feet out in a merry jig. Clara couldn't hold in her mirth any longer, and her peals of laughter carried over the meadow.

Regin's fingers tightened around his bow. "If you are still a fae, then you must show us. Cast a glamour."

"I do not dance like a trained monkey for my court," Daigh retorted. Aline waved her hand and Daigh hopped about, scratching his armpits and making monkey noises. He smashed his foot down on Kelly's shoulder. She screamed and rolled over.

"Kelly, get away!" I yelled.

Sobbing, Kelly caterpillar-crawled across the dirt toward me. I shoved my feet back and dragged my body forward half a foot. My captor grunted in protest as he was carried along with me. Rough hands grabbed me and tried to force me back down, but I shook them off, spurred on by Kelly's desperate cries.

Regin raised his bow, holding the string beside his cheek. Daigh opened his mouth to say something, but his words turned into a moan as an arrow buried itself into his thigh.

Daigh's face twisted into an ugly scowl. He gripped the shaft in his leg, his hands shaking as he tugged it. With every movement, his body sagged and he bellowed louder.

"If he were fae, the poison would not hurt him," Regin cried out. "This is irrefutable. Daigh is no longer a fae."

How is that even possible?

Kelly wriggled around the bonfire. From where I lay I had

a good look at her face. She was petrified, her skin white and covered with cuts and bruises, but there was a grim determination in her eyes that reminded me of her sister. I shoved off the ground and inched forward, sending another fireball at the annoying guy on my back. The fire hit the invisible wall again and slammed back into my body.

Maeve, if you can hear this, I need you. I need your power now.

"I command you to come down here and suck this poison out of meeeee…" Daigh slurred. He gripped his leg above the knee, but the forward movement caught him off-balance. He toppled forwards, his forehead cracking against the dirt.

Regin spat on his head. "He's no king of mine."

The second fae removed the bow from his shoulder and threw it at Daigh. The heavy wooden weapon bounced off Daigh's back, buckling his body. Others stepped out of formation to spit and kick their king. Regin tore the crown of bones and vines from his head.

"No," Daigh raised a hand to grab the crown. "I'm still… your king…"

Regin wrenched it out of reach. "We will bring this to Liah," he called, raising the crown above his head. "She will lead us in our triumphant march across the reclaimed earth."

"Noooooo…" Daigh wheezed. He grabbed Regin's leg, but the soldier kicked him off.

Regin stared up at the wooden stakes. I noticed a dark shape pierced through on the end one, and a cold fear settled between my shoulder blades. *Is that a person? It can't be, we're all here…*

"This isn't our work," Regin said, his words sending a clatter of agreement from the ranks of the fae. "Let the humans have their witch burnings. They have the stomach for it more than I. We'll be back in three days time to claim the earth for ourselves."

He tore something from around Daigh's neck and tossed

it into the fire. Daigh howled. The earth cracked and splut-
tered. A crack split the meadow, running between me and
the stakes. Inky tendrils rose from the crack, calling the fae
back to the realm of the dead.

"What the fuck?" The guy on my back cried.

"Get back!" The female cop, Officer Judge, yelled. "That's
the same stuff that was at the church!"

The crack split through the meadow, severing the
bonfire. Kelly screamed as the ground beneath her buckled
and the inky gloom crept over her skin.

"Kelly!" I yelled as her face disappeared behind a wall of
darkness. Fear and rage welled up inside me. *They are not
taking Kelly, too.*

A fireball shot out of the end of my hand, blasting the guy
off my back. He screamed as he rolled across the grass,
pounding his sleeve into the dirt in an attempt to staunch the
flames.

Got my powers back.

I roared in triumph as the wall around my magic broke
free. I sent a fireball into the ranks of the fae as they raced
for the crack. Green-clad soldiers leapt out of the way as one
went down screaming, flames devouring his clothes and
blackening his skin.

Something heavy jumped on my back. *Not this shite again.*
I flung my body to the side and kicked out with my boot.
"Oof!" someone moaned, and a dark shape behind me went
down. Light glinted off something on the ground.

My sword.

I used my feet and stomach muscles to shuffle forward
like Kelly had done, twisting my body around so I came in
sideways. My hand clasped around the hilt of my sword,
fingers stroking the leather the way I touched Maeve's body.
I swung around and wrenched my arms back, slamming the
hilt into the guy's cheek. He screamed and went down. I

shuffled my body so I could slide the rope over the blade, and just like that, my hands were free.

I stumbled to my feet. For the first time I could properly see the rest of the coven. Flynn shot jets of water into the villagers, sending them cowering toward the blazing castle. Blake had already freed himself, and was working on untying Rowan's bonds. I couldn't see Corbin anywhere, but the field hung with thick smoke and black fog, obscuring places not touched by the light of the flames. Aline and her motley army moved across the meadow, firing spells to shake the earth beneath the fae and spray the weapons from their hands. A tiny red fox leapt from behind Clara's skirts and bit a fae soldier's face, sending him down.

Maeve rolled onto her back and kicked her legs at Officer Judge. Waves of spirit magic radiated from her body as she poured her nightmare magic into the cop's head. Officer Judge dropped to her knees, clutching her temples and screaming for help. But the villagers were too terrified to care about us witches anymore.

"Arthur, get Kelly!" Maeve screamed.

Kelly's shriek tore through me. The crack formed a barrier between Kelly and I. It was too wide for me to jump now, and even with Aline's baptism, I didn't want to risk falling in. I ran along the edge of the crack, ducking and dodging around the black fog. Here, the crack split into smaller fissures, and I leapt between them with all the grace of a ballet-dancing porpoise. My feet landed on the grass on the other side, and I dived into the darkness, led by Kelly's screams.

Acrid smoke burned my lungs. I bent low, gasping for air, and barreled forward. The fog slid over my skin, leaving burning trails that sucked precious breath from my lumps. My foot caught on one of the stakes and I fell to my knees, my hands brushing something wet. I turned to see what it was, and hot rage rose in my throat as my eyes captured the outline of the body in the gloom.

Corbin.

He lay at the foot of the stake, the wood piercing his chest. Charred skin peeled from his bones, and his head slumped against his shoulder like he was sleeping. Blood smeared the stake where he slid down its smooth surface. A deep wound in his side still trickled with blood – likely the wound that killed him.

At least, I hoped it killed him. I hoped he hadn't been alive when they did this.

Dead. Corbin's dead.

The news hit me like a cold shower, shocking my body. Corbin was a force of nature in life – as strong and immovable as the walls of Briarwood – and to see him reduced to this degradation was more than I could bear. I didn't want to leave him here to suffer further humiliation, but I was out of time. I had to get Kelly away from the fire and the fae, or we'd both be joining him.

I scrambled across the shuddering earth, and made it to where Kelly lay. "Untie me," she begged. I sliced through her ropes with my sword. Black fog licked my shoulders, searing my skin with every caress. I threw Kelly over my shoulder and ran up the meadow, looking for a good spot to jump back over the crack. My eyes watered from the smoke and pain, and I stumbled as my foot caught the edge of the fissure.

"I'll take her," a voice yelled. Jane crashed into me. Through the fog and smoke all I could make out of her was two eyes blazing. I flung Kelly at Jane, who drew her arms around her limp body and hobbled up the hill toward the circle of witches.

I made to follow her, but fresh rage bubbled inside me. *Corbin.* Was I just going to leave him there on the battlefield?

Like fuck I was.

I turned back to the carnage. The inky blackness obscured much of the battle, but from the shouts and cries I knew the others also had use of their magic. A fae sprinted from the darkness, falling on me with bone blade raised. I stepped forward and opened a deep wound in his belly. He fell to his knees and collapsed in the dirt as I jerked my blade free.

I plunged into the blackness, ignoring the sting of the fog as it slid over my skin and tried to draw me in. I knew it couldn't drag me down with it because of Aline's baptism. I stumbled blindly in the direction of the stakes. I wouldn't dishonor Corbin's memory by leaving his body in the hands of the fae. I would give him this last honor, for everything he had given me.

A body brushed against my arm. A fae yelled out. I twisted my body and felt my sword slide home. Fire boiled in my veins as I took another life. Red welts circled in the blackness.

The fae killed Corbin. I wouldn't rest until I bathed in their blood. I swung wildly, not caring who or what I hit, living for the screams and the acrid scent of their blood in the air. I didn't even stop to watch them go down. I hacked and slashed and burned my way through their ranks as I fought to reach my friend.

My arm brushed against a hard object. A spike. No longer able to see, I felt down its length, but it was empty. I stepped over it and moved to the next one.

Here he is. My hand brushed Corbin's head. Cold, dry skin flaked away in my fingers. I lifted his body up, sliding it off the spike. The wood pulled at his flesh, trying to keep him. But I was stronger. I slid his body off the end, lifted it over my shoulder, and ran.

No one stopped me. Fae leapt out of my way as I barreled

through their ranks and vaulted over the gaping fissure, no longer afraid of its murky depths. My boots slammed into the earth, and I kept on running. Villagers screamed as I sprinted past them. My sword arm itched for more blood.

I'll make them pay. I'll make them all pay.

3

MAEVE

The fae moved through the panicking villagers, slicing them with their vicious bone knives. Behind them the black fog swirled. Dark tendrils curled toward us, seeking new victims.

Flynn tugged at my arm. I knew I had to get to Blake, but my body froze as the black fog swirled higher, completely obscuring the fire and the stakes behind it. *Corbin's back there. And Kelly.* The numbness settled over me, pinning me in place.

"Maeve, we have to... Mary Mother of Jesus," Flynn breathed.

A huge shape barreled out of the fog. Light from the fires flickered across it, illuminating black clothing torn and splattered with green blood, and features twisted in wretched vengeance. A dark shape like a backpack hung over its shoulder, and above its head, moonlight caught the edge of a steel blade.

Arthur.

He moved like a giant from mythology crushing his foes beneath him. Sparks trailed from his sword as he swung at the fae, and an orange aura encircled his body – his rage manifesting as blazing skin. Never before had I seen a person look so out of time, so not of the earth.

"Get everyone behind the wards," Arthur yelled, lunging forward on one knee to slice through a fae's arm. Screams followed in his wake as he cut down the fae with one hand, the other holding that bloody lump over his shoulder.

He has Corbin's body.

I couldn't bear it. A sob escaped my throat.

Blake's hand clamped around mine, jolting me out of my grief. We dived into each other, casting out with our magic. Arthur's wrathful image burned in my head, and I took his rage into myself and forced it outward, hunting out the fae one by one and gripping their minds with my own.

Leave this place, Blake commanded through my mind. Images slammed into me – flashes of life in the fae realm, of Daigh leering over me while pain rocked through my body, of revels and orgies and dreams of green places without barriers. The images swirled and changed – the bright forest and green meadow of Tir Na Nog replaced by dark hallways lined with wooden doors and harrowing screams, of fae burning in a black cauldron as their souls were captured to unleash the Slaugh, of dark creatures made of shadow and nightmares, reaching through the fog for me.

You're not welcome here, Blake hissed. The thought slammed into the connected minds, and they, and I, turned around and fled to the crack, and in a hundred splintered fractures of thought I, and they, leapt into the gloom. Blake threw his arms around me and held me still so I wouldn't follow them, but my mind tipped over the edge a hundred times. As the void swallowed the fae, their minds uncoupled and spun free, severing their thoughts and memories until finally there were none left.

My mind spun from the emptiness. I rocked on my feet,

struggling to remain upright. Blake's voice faded, pulling me out of the darkness with him. "Now the villagers," he whispered. "Maeve, can you do it again?"

I nodded. Blake gripped my hand and pressed his lips to mine, feeding me his energy. I sucked in a breath, dropped through space again and into the minds of the villagers around us. It was even easier than finding the fae – the villagers were too scared to notice our presence tapping on the edge of their conscious. Blake fed them thoughts of trust and safety. *Follow the witches and everything will be okay.*

I tried to close my mind from the images that assailed it, but there was no stopping the torrent of fear pouring into my mind. My throat closed as I *lived* the fear of the villagers, long simmering and deep rooted. Every unexplained phenomena and personal misfortune jokingly attributed to 'the witches up at the castle,' until it wasn't a joke anymore, but a belief. Fears of parents that their kids would be sucked into a cult and forsake their futures, that they'd all die in some silly ritual like all those people did twenty-one years ago. Deep personal distress that by acknowledging the coven they would be cast out of the village as well. Small minds and small hearts that smiled politely while they wallowed in doubts and nightmares. Our faces flashed in a blur of terror – Flynn's twinkling eyes suddenly menacing, Corbin's bookish interests becoming reclusive obsession, Arthur a dangerous warrior out of time, Rowan's anxiety and skin color a reminder of the other lurking in the shadows, Blake's cool beauty utterly frightening.

That's not what we are, I cried into the onslaught, but the thoughts and images kept coming, again and again painting us as the architects of horror. Every tragedy, every evil thing, every unexplained coincidence in the village had built a mountain of evidence against us. We were the scapegoats for grief and hatred and woe.

For the first time, I understood the true, awesome, and destructive power of *belief*.

Hopelessness settled on my heart, burrowing deeper with every fresh horror flashing front of my eyes. Even if we triumphed against the fae, what hope did we have of living a peaceful life amongst such hatred?

Blake pushed his voice through my thoughts, and they, and I, felt his authority rumbling in our chests. *Trust the witches. Follow them to the castle and you'll be safe.*

It's not working, I cried.

Of course it won't if you don't believe it, Princess!

Through the jumble of images and memories and sensations, I found my own mind – the one voice of dissension against a tide of hate. I tore up every good feeling and every true emotion the guys had given me, every kind word and every hug and every secret they'd trusted to me and every piece of their pain they'd shared with me. I bundled up those pieces of them and I shoved them into a tiny, hard ball and I fired their *spirit* into the villagers.

The images changed. Flashes of the boys in the village – Corbin chatting with the butcher, Flynn and Arthur helping an old lady lift her groceries into her car, Rowan dropping off a tray of seedlings for the kindergarten garden, his face hidden behind a curtain of dreadlocks. Blake at the pub trying to break up Flynn's fight. Me looking like my mother reborn, my terrified face pinned to the window of my taxi as I drove through Crookshollow for the first time.

Around us, people gasped and cried out, and the images swirled and swelled, becoming a flood of beautiful acts and everyday kindnesses and simple truths. They *saw*. They saw my boys as they truly were – the witches in the castle who had no one else but each other, who loved fiercely and fought on the side of what was good and right and true, even when they fought alone.

Trust the witches, Blake screamed over the images. *Run to the castle. They will save you!*

They ran. Screaming and crying with the force of the emotions I'd pushed through them, they surged toward the small meadow gate, heading up toward the blazing castle. As each passed through the gate their minds unhitched, taking with them tiny pieces of my love.

My emptying mind reeled as it was plunged into darkness, no longer seeing the battlefield and the burning castle beyond through the eyes of the villagers. I kept my own eyes clamped shut and flung myself around, searching for something to lift the darkness.

"I got you, Princess," Blake's voice whispered in my ear. His warmth wrapped around me, bringing me back to the present. I opened my eyes, seeing the meadow through my own mind, my retinas burning from the pain of it all. Black tendrils curled toward us. They'd completely engulfed the bonfire and the stakes. I could no longer discern the lights of Crookshollow in the distance, nor could I see Aline or Smithers or any of the others.

Blake and Flynn grabbed an arm each and yanked me forward. I forced my legs to move, slipping and sliding over the long grass as I ran with them up toward the castle. My chest burned. My feet pounded against the path as we ducked through the trees. The villagers fell in step behind us, winding up the narrow meadow path and collapsing in the wide parking area outside the portcullis, where the taxi driver had dropped me off on my very first day at Briarwood.

At the edge of the parking area we caught up with Rowan. He collapsed against me, his whole body shaking. I buried my head in his shoulder, letting his long dreadlocks hide my face from the fire.

The four of us huddled together, bracing ourselves

against a wall of heat. Power slid from my body, and with it the strength to remain standing. I collapsed on the sloping lawn, bringing the guys down with me. My eyes flew open, and the breath fled my lungs.

Fire leapt from Briarwood's windows, tainting the night air with the scent of burning furniture. The night rang with exploding glass and cracking beams, and sparks rained down from the battlements like Fourth of July fireworks.

I tried to crawl toward the castle, but the wall of heat slammed into my body, knocking me back like it was an actual barrier. The whole castle glowed like a fairground ride.

Just like the Ferris wheel that took my parents. Everything I love burns.

The boys wrapped me in their arms. Flynn tried to turn my face away, but I wasn't going to hide while my castle burned. Flames tore through the Victorian stables, and I knew they would have reached the Great Hall, rendering that beautiful ancient room to ashes. The lintel above the ticketing office collapsed, bringing a wall of stone down with it. Each stone hitting the ground punched me in the gut.

Beside me, a body knelt in the grass. Aline placed her hands to her face and wept. I knew I should be able to summon the same tears. After all we'd fought for and all we'd achieved, a castle that had stood for centuries as a last bastion against the fae would fall tonight. But the same numbness that infected me after my parents' deaths clung to me now. There was no emotion left inside me. Corbin's death had stolen the part of my soul capable of feeling.

Arthur appeared from the shadows, his face streaked with blood and filth, his eyes dark and unreadable. He collapsed on his knees, sliding Corbin's body from his shoulder and laying it out reverently in front of him. I flung myself toward him, but Flynn grabbed my waist.

"Maeve, you don't want to see."

"Don't tell me what I want," I screamed, tearing away from Flynn and draping myself over the body. The last of my spirit magic hummed through my hands. I pressed my palms to Corbin's cold, charred cheeks and pushed and pushed and prayed and prayed that it would somehow bring him back but there was nothing, no spark of life for me to cling to.

He's gone.

"Corbin... Corbin!" A voice screeched. Corbin's mother dropped down beside me. I slid back as she embraced her son's body, tears flooding down her cheeks.

A warm hand fell on my shoulder. I looked up. Andrew's eyes flashed at me with the same sad intensity I knew from his son. "Get back, Maeve," he said. "This isn't your fault. We'll look after him now."

"No," I whispered. Hands grabbed me under the shoulders, dragging me away. "No," I said again. I kicked out, but my limbs slowed, dragging through the air like they were underwater. I had nothing left to fight with.

I let them pull me away. The guys surrounded me, pressing their bodies against mine, trying to bring me back from the dark, numb place. But it was an illusion. We were all untethered now, all of us living with the horror of what we had made.

Sirens whirred as two fire engines careened up the winding drive. The first engine stopped at the gatehouse – too tall to fit under the arch. The firefighters leapt out and unrolled their hose up the drive. The second engine was smaller and managed to make it through. Glass shattered as one of the enormous windows in the Great Hall blew out. Jane and Clara stood closer to the front of the house, directing the villagers to get back, to stay safe.

It didn't matter. None of it mattered now that Corbin was gone.

Two police cars pulled up, sirens wailing. Detective Inspector Wallace got out of the passenger seat and stormed toward Officer Judge. "Thank god you got here," she cried. "I'm trying to secure the scene and—"

"You let this get out of control," Detective Inspector Wallace yelled, pointing to the squad car behind him. "Get in that car and turn over your badge immediately. I don't want to see you on this scene."

Officer Judge's face whitened. She slunk off to the car. The villagers huddled together, their eyes haunted.

"Everyone stay back." DI Wallace waved his arms in an invisible line we weren't allowed to cross. "No one leave this area. You'll all be held for questioning. Where are the castle tenants?"

"We're here," Flynn called out.

"Not all of us." Arthur barreled up to the DI with fire in his eyes. "They killed our friend."

Wallace bellowed as the topiary behind him spontaneously burst into flames.

The firefighters spread out, shouting orders at each other as they unrolled their hoses and went to work putting out the blaze. My boys gathered around me, pressing their bodies against mine. I buried my face into Rowan's chest, watching flames leap through the Great Hall windows through a curtain of his dreadlocks. Like some great Viking funeral, Briarwood's legends burned to ash, her legacy rising into heaven on a trail of smoke.

Everything good in the world burned along with it.

4

MAEVE

"...*D*amage isn't as bad as we feared. The Victorian addition is toast, but we managed to save the eastern wing of the house and most of the Norman keep. It looks as though structurally she won't need much work, but smoke and water damage will have destroyed some of the interiors."

The firefighter's words filtered through my ears. I knew they were happening but I didn't register any of them. Over his shoulder, his squad fired jets of water through the broken Great Hall windows.

He has no idea. My numb heart pattered against my chest. *This damage is forever. We can't ever repair what's been broken tonight.*

I sank against a wall of warm bodies, allowing my boys to hold me upright. Pulses of magic fed through my body – Arthur's heat tempered by Flynn's coolness, Rowan's deep, rich earth and Blake's sizzling spirit. I registered the energy but *felt* none of it.

"We can go back in?" Flynn asked, wiping a strand of red hair from his face.

The firefighter shook his head. "Not for a while yet. As soon as it's safe, the SOCO team need to go through and collect evidence. We gather a serious crime was committed here, so you'll need to give a statement to the police before you leave tonight. You'll also need to have a structural engineer look at the building as soon as possible. I'll go over some information with you on what to do next, but for the meantime, I suggest you find somewhere safe to sleep for the night."

"They'll be staying with us," Clara said, hitching her black shawl up her shoulder. I looked around for Ryan but couldn't see him. The red fox still twined around her legs, curiously unafraid of the burning castle or the hordes of people.

Faces flicked in my vision. Clara. Isadora – brushing dirt and fae blood off the hem of her silk dress. Robert Smithers – his eyes focused, his face surprisingly calm for his first jaunt outside the institution in twenty years. Aline...

My mother stood off to the side, her arms around Corbin's mother and her head bent toward Andrew as she spoke in hushed, hurried tones. How had she pulled this off? How had she got so many witches here so quickly? My mind swam down a dark river, but I wasn't going to get answers tonight.

Thick arms wrapped around me. "It's over, Maeve," Arthur whispered in my ear. He smelled of sweat and smoke and blood.

Inspector Wallace called us over. Unlike his interrogation at the church when he'd all but accused us of having something to do with the black fog, his voice choked with empathy. He wanted to know about the villagers attacking the castle, the stakes, the last time I'd seen Corbin alive. We didn't have a plan like we had back at the church, a script of what to say to avoid revealing the secrets of our powers. Corbin was the one with all the plans. I talked, but I didn't hear the words I said. From the look on Wallace's face, I gathered I wasn't making a lot of sense.

The next thing I knew, I was walking through an unfamiliar hallway, my fingers tracing over faded Victorian wallpaper and stuffy gilt frames. It looked like a museum. Flynn and Blake held me between them, and we trailed after Ryan, who gestured into rooms and spoke words I didn't hear. Obelix weaved around our feet, his fluffy tail swooshing against my bare legs as he darted between the rooms, his nose twitching with exciting new smells.

We're at Raynard Hall. I had no recollection of getting in a car, of stepping out and seeing the impressive manor from the outside. But it must have happened.

Another moment passed. I sat at the island in a gleaming modern kitchen, a plate of hot stew in front of me. I stirred the food with my fork, contemplating my options – lift fork to lips, chew, swallow, or pick up bowl and toss it against wall. I could also tip it over my head, but that might cause burns. I was already burned out on the inside.

The idea of lifting the fork to my mouth seemed foreign, a thing not of my knowledge. A bald man in an immaculate black suit set down steaming bowls in front of everyone else. Flynn and Arthur scraped hungrily at theirs, but no one else touched the food.

Another moment. Kelly with her arms around me, sobbing into my ruined Blood Lust t-shirt. Her hair smelled of soot and sandalwood. I patted her back and said some words about everything being okay that neither of us believed.

It would never be okay again.

Another moment. The boys in an enormous walk-in rain shower, pulling off my clothes, holding me under hot water, sponging me down, rubbing shampoo through my hair. Arthur wrapped me in a fluffy towel and hoisted me into his arms. He carried me somewhere and settled me on a soft bed, sliding up beside me and cradling my body in his. The others piled on top, tangling their limbs around me, cocooning me in their warmth. They spoke in soft murmurs, but the words didn't register.

Rowan wrapped his body around me. I lifted my neck so he could slide his torso beneath me like a pillow. My ear rested on his chest and his heartbeat thudded in my head, fast and furious and wrecked with pain. His tears pattered on my hair. He would cry a river for both of us.

I already knew enough about mourning to last a lifetime. I knew I wouldn't cry. I couldn't. It had taken a kiss from Arthur to wrest open the floodgates after my parents' death, but now I wasn't sure even that would do it.

My fingers groped for Corbin's reassuring body – the one in my coven I always turned to for an explanation, for leadership. They found only Obelix's furry body curled up against Arthur's chest. *How can we carry on without him?* The idea of our coven still fighting, still existing without Corbin seemed ridiculous. It was like trying to drive a spaceship without arms.

Sleep must have come to me during the night, because I fell into a dream world. I walked down a wide, vaulted hall, the walls made of dark, veined stone that hummed with stored energy. There was magic in this place, wherever I was – built into the very fabric of it. My feet kicked up clouds of dust and sand as I jogged on and on and on, looking for a way out, for a reason why I was there, for another soul to talk to. But there was nothing except locked doors flying by on both sides and endless swirls of dust around my feet.

The hum of the magic drowned out all other sounds. I couldn't hear my feet hitting the ground, or the pounding of my heart – nothing except that low, discordant hum. Until…

Maeve... a voice rasped. The sound boomed inside my head, driving back the hum and lighting up the dark world.

From behind the doors came such terrifying screams and shrieks that I broke into a full run to escape them. A creeping sense that something followed me spurred me onward. The voice rasped my name.

The voice was coming for me, and if it caught me... I'd be thrown into one of the locked rooms and the screams would be mine. I just *knew* I had to run.

If I can just find an exit, a way out of this labyrinth, I'd be safe. The hum rose again, and the screams rose with it, the two competing for my attention. My chest heaved, and cramps arced along my leg. Every step was agony, but I had to keep going. I couldn't let it catch me. I couldn't...

The hallway turned a corner, but all I could see were more doors. Screams pounded inside my head, driving out rational thought. I slowed to a hobble, dragging my cramping leg behind me, and flung myself at the next door. *I'll take the torture over this horrible chill creeping down my back. Just let me in!*

The door didn't budge. The rasping voice drew closer. The hum roared in my ears. Panic rose in my chest, and I slammed into one wall, then another. The voice loomed over me, closer, closer...

Maeve...

My hands groped in the dim light, tugging at the locks, scratching at the walls, tearing at my own skin. *Get me out get me out get me out...*

Maeve... the voice boomed between my ears, so loud it made me jump. It was right behind me.

Terror clung to my chest. I had to face it. I had to know.

I spun around. "Go away!" I yelled. The words came out as a tiny whisper. Something slammed into me, its weight knocking the breath from my lungs. My body slammed against the stone wall. A thick, heavy smell invaded my nostrils. Musty books. Ink. Leather. *Home.*

Corbin.

He grabbed my arms and held me upright so I didn't fall. He looked exactly the same as the last time I'd seen him alive, his black t-shirt clinging to his tight muscles, his dark hair falling over his right eye. The creeping, itching sensation surged down my spine, and I twisted away from him. His hands gripped my arms like a vise.

"Hi Maeve." Corbin kissed me on the forehead, his lips brushing my bangs – so warm, so real. He bent down to press his lips to mine, devouring me in a breathless kiss. Fire shot through my body, burning up the last of my doubt. It was Corbin. No one could kiss me like he did. My hands moved of their own accord, wrapping around his strong body. My fingers brushed a bone handle sticking out of the edge of his t-shirt, and the open wound underneath...

The wound that killed him.

It all flooded back, slamming into my body like a cold blast. *This isn't real. It's a dream. Why did my stupid subconscious have to feed me this dream tonight, of all nights?*

I pressed my hands against Corbin's warm chest, my fingers touching where his heart should have been, but where nothing now beat. I shoved him with all my might, breaking our kiss as he staggered back and slammed into one of the doors.

"Get away from me," I cried.

"Is that any way for a High Priestess to greet her loyal servant?" Corbin pulled himself up. The knife blade in his side jiggled as he moved.

"You're dead," I wailed.

"Damn right I'm dead," Corbin grinned. He gestured to the walls of doors behind me. "I'm in the underworld, and right now, so are you."

"Why are you doing this to me?" I moaned. "Why did you have to die?"

"Don't worry, it was all part of the plan." Corbin's grin widened. "And before you get pissed at me for not telling you, I had to do it this way because you wouldn't have let me do it otherwise. And before you think of blaming yourself or anyone else for my death, remember that even if you'd all held me down or locked me in the priest hole I still would have found a way to get myself here."

"Why?" I sobbed. Why did my head have to conjure up this image of him? Why did he have to talk like he was still alive, like this was all some clever plan of his?

"Because this is our shot, Maeve. If we play this out right we can stop Daigh and the fae for good." Corbin ran a hand through his dark hair. "And then you can bring me back."

5

ROWAN

*S*omeone shook me. I sank into the bed, cowering from the darkness of my dreams. I was back in my last foster home, the one I ran away from. My foster mother held my head against the cold edge of the bath, and *he* was behind me. The heavy sting of his belt buckle against my back was nothing to the pain I knew was coming, to the pain that was a knife sliding up inside me, splitting my body in two—

"Rowan, wake up."

My eyes flew open. Sweat streaked my skin. I recognized the voice. Female and kind. *Maeve.*

She drew me back to the present. I wasn't in that home any longer. I was at Briarwood, with the coven, and I had her and Corbin and the guys, and everything was finally okay…

It all came flooding back to me. The attack. Briarwood burning. The villagers pulling me and Maeve out of the priest hole and dragging us to the meadow. The fae with the stakes set in the ground. Corbin's body thrown on the fire and then slid on that stake like a barbecue skewer.

Corbin's dead.

Since Maeve showed up at Briarwood, since the first time Corbin kissed me, I'd never known it was possible to be so happy. I'd thought I'd live out my days at Briarwood, content with the amazing life Corbin had given me, content to watch him from a distance as he soared like the beautiful avenging angel he was, content to stay behind when he finally went off to a university and got his degree in a gazillion dead languages and married Maeve and started a family of his own. Content just to be a small part of his life. But for a few glorious days he and Maeve had given me a glimpse of another life, a future I couldn't have dreamed of. And then the fae ripped it away and burned my happiness along with my home.

"Rowan, please. I need to talk to you."

I dragged my eyes open and looked up at Maeve. I expected to see my own despair reflected there, but what greeted me was even worse. The sparkle had left her eyes. She was cold and dead inside. Tears streaked her cheeks, but I knew they were my tears, because she hadn't cried. Her eyes took up half her face – wide pools of deep hazel that glinted with no hint of pain, no hint of anything at all.

"I just had a dream," she said, her voice steady. Her hands stretched across the bed and stroked Obelix's thick fur. "Corbin was there."

The words pierced through my grief, battering me around the head with their sweet implausibility. Corbin's body burned up in the fire, and then that stake plunged through his chest. This wasn't like Aline whose body was never actually discovered because she somehow took it with her into the painting. Corbin's body couldn't just be re-sculpted.

I clung to Maeve, my body trembling. Anxiety prickled at the back of my neck, creeping down my spine and filling my body with ice. The horror of seeing Corbin's death would never leave me, and for the rest of my life I'd wonder what I could have done to stop it.

"Please..." I moaned into Maeve's hair. "Don't make me think..."

I didn't think it was possible, but Maeve's eyes grew wider, like a manga girl. Her shoulders slumped, and the first flicker of grief jolted through her irises. Her fingers tightened around Obelix. He yelped in protest and jumped down off the bed. "It's all my fault."

"No, it's not..."

She sighed. "I broke the charms and let the humans inside the castle. Daigh came to me in the mirror and he told me all these things..."

Arthur sat up and narrowed his eyes. "Codswaddle. You told us everything Daigh said and it was nothing about the charms."

At the end of the bed, Flynn and Blake lifted their heads, their eyes questioning. My skin crawled and badgers gnawed at my stomach. I searched the room for something to count. There wasn't much. Ryan had very modern, minimal tastes. I settled for our shoes lined up beside the door, each one streaked with dirt and green-tinted blood. *One... two... three...*

"This was tonight. Daigh said Aline and I had to keep it secret, or the fae would use their compulsion and read your thoughts. I thought we were helping, but I just played right into his hands."

"This was when you went to the bathroom?" Arthur growled. "What did that bastard say to you?"

"He told us about the secret passage and..." Maeve shook her head. "It doesn't matter now. It was all lies. I should have seen through it. Aline did, and she's the only reason we're all still alive. I should have realized that Daigh no longer had his powers."

Four... five... shite, I ran out of shoes.

"You can't blame yourself." Arthur squeezed her shoulder. Maeve stiffened. "No one could have predicted Daigh would bargain away his powers. I think that's what he was counting on. Besides, this whole bloody thing is *my* fault. We were fighting the fae and I lost sight of Corbin. I let him get captured. I could have saved him if I hadn't let my temper get control again."

"Sorry, Arnold, you don't get to be the scapegoat." Blake piped up, reverting back to his pet name for Arthur because he knew it would piss him off. "You were the hero out there, getting Kelly out and Corbin's body and taking down all those fae. If you want to blame someone, blame me. *I* didn't understand what those two voices compelling the villagers meant. If I'd have figured out that Aline was the second voice sooner, we might've been able to—"

"It's my fault," Flynn added. "I'm Irish."

"I let Corbin hide us in that priest hole," I whispered. "I huddled in the dark while he died on his own. I should have been fighting. I would have fought for him."

I would have died for him, for Maeve, for all of them. It should have been me in Corbin's place.

"In my dream Corbin said that even if we'd all held him down he'd have found a way to do it anyway," Maeve said. "That's so like him."

"Is it…" I tried to keep the hope from rising in my voice. "Could he be alive still, sending us a message…"

Maeve shook her head. "Premonitions and precognition aren't real, and tonight proved that. I don't believe the dreams I had about the stakes were any kind of sign from the future. The stakes were there, just like in the dream, but there was no irradiated earth, no burning sky, no briar bushes as high as the castle walls. And even if it was the same, the fact that we stopped Daigh before all of us ended up on the stakes means that it wasn't a premonition. Because the future was never set in the first place. It's all about quantum—"

"If we could skip the quantum lecture for now, Einstein," Flynn stroked her hair. "Rowan doesn't look like he can take it."

Maeve's hand gripped my shoulder, her fingers tightening around my skin. The anxiety tickled down my back again as she said, "I think Daigh planted this vision of Corbin in my head in order to get me to follow him. It's just another one of his tortures. He makes me believe Corbin is still alive and then he makes a bargain to bring him back and I fall for it because I'm a complete fucking moron."

"Daigh gave up his powers," Blake whispered. "He can't affect your dreams any more than cheese."

"Mmmm, cheese," Flynn pretended to drool.

"Then this dream is just my subconscious reacting to my guilt and grief. We can't go reading it as a sign that Corbin's... that he..." Maeve sucked in a breath. "We all saw what happened. This isn't like Aline. You can't come back from that."

Everyone fell silent. I knew we were all picturing Corbin's body sliding down the stake. I counted the shoes again, my fingernails tearing the expensive cotton sheets.

"All the same, if you have it again," Flynn said, "try to pull us into it."

Even though I wasn't looking at her, I could feel Maeve's eyes in the back of my head as she said, "I don't want to hurt you guys. If you see him like that... it's so real. I hoped for a moment, but then I woke up, and it was horrible. I don't want you to hope for something that can't be."

"Even you have to admit that you don't understand everything about magic, Einstein. If there's even a chance something about this dream is Corbin reaching out for us, then we all need to see it."

Arthur and Blake nodded their agreement. I tore my gaze away to look at Maeve. She shook her head. I took her hand and squeezed it.

"I just want to grieve," she said, yanking her hand away and pulling the sheets up over her head. "I don't want to hope. It's like losing him all over again."

The four of us exchanged a look. Maeve wasn't going to talk about it anymore. But it was still the middle of the night. If she wanted to keep sleeping, then that was what we'd do, too. Maybe if I closed my eyes I'd get drawn into her next dream and I could see Corbin for myself.

She said not to hope, but my heart was already soaring with the stuff.

I remembered Corbin's face when he shut us into the priest hole. He wasn't afraid. His jaw was set, his eyes bright. He had a plan.

And one thing I knew about Corbin – he'd never, ever failed the people he loved.

Corbin hid Maeve and I away in part to keep us safe, but mainly because he didn't want us to see what he was about to do. He knew we'd try to talk him out of it, or worse, throw ourselves into it alongside him.

Maeve was wrong. She couldn't see past her scientific model of the world. She'd had prophetic dreams before, like the ones about all of us being with her, but she couldn't read them as such.

I *knew* it with every fiber of my body that Corbin showing up to speak to her tonight wasn't just her grief-soaked subconscious talking.

Somewhere, somehow, Corbin was still alive.

6

MAEVE

*S*unlight streamed through the open curtains, falling across the bed, warm and inviting. I cracked open an eye, reveling in the simple beauty of Rowan's arm across my waist, his long fingers cupping my breast – dark skin against my milky white. Arthur's barrel chest rising and falling. Flynn and Blake spooning each other. Corbin's... Corbin...?

Then I remembered.

Corbin was dead.

The room came into focus – soft cream walls and modern furnishings. A huge picture window overlooking an unfamiliar garden. No sign of the desk piled high with astronomy books and the huge beeswax candle Arthur made me and the giant cosmos made of metal leaves from Flynn. Even the bed under me suddenly felt foreign.

We weren't in my tower room at Briarwood because Briarwood was destroyed. We were in Raynard Hall, and I was being haunted by dreams of my dead lover.

"Maeve." A voice from the door startled me out of my thoughts.

I sat up, pulling the edge of the duvet over my naked breasts. Rowan's arm flopped off my stomach, and he stirred awake. Arthur was already grabbing for a t-shirt.

Clara leaned her tiny frame against the high doorframe. "Please, don't mind me. I used to be in the Soho coven – I've seen it all before. Good morning, boys. I'm sorry to do this to you all now. I know how badly you are suffering. But we all need to talk."

I rubbed my eyes. The last thing I wanted to do was get up and face the world, but Clara was right. So much happened last night that we needed to understand, and this was so much bigger than Corbin and Briarwood.

"Wait for us," I said. My voice echoed in my head, hollow and strange. I shook Flynn awake. Clara waited for us to pull on clothes – someone had left a pile of new jeans and t-shirts at the foot of the bed (and taken away our torn, soot-stained clothes, I noticed) – and we followed her down the hallway. I remembered the hallway from last night; the drab portraits and cluttered, old-fashioned furniture. She led us into a bright, airy drawing room decorated in pale blue and cream. For the first time I realized how stark was the contrast between the modern rooms we'd seen and the dark, gloomy hallway.

Eyes followed me as I entered the room. Faces turned to me, rent with pity and pain. Too many faces. Too many people counting on me.

Ryan stood at the head of the room, one arm leaning against the fireplace. Paint flecks splashed across his black t-shirt and tight blue jeans and stuck to the ends of his red hair, the colors matching the vibrant painting of frolicking foxes on the wall behind him. Gwen and Candice settled into a cream sofa, cups of tea nestled in their laps. Clara bustled over and plopped down beside them. Isadora perched on a wing-backed chair across from Ryan, her elegant legs crossed at the ankles and her hands folded in her lap like she was a model in a photoshoot. Absent was Corbin's mother, but Andrew sat on the floor at Gwen's feet, his back against the sofa and a hollow look in his typically bright eyes.

Aline stood by the window, her long hair swept off her neck in a messy bun. Beside her, Robert Smithers slumped in the window seat, his eyes fixed on the ceiling. My mother met my eyes, and I fell into her icy-blue pools, mesmerized by the pain that reflected back at me. My arms itched to wrap around her and hold her close, but my grief kept my legs glued to the floor.

"Please," Ryan indicated the empty sofa and chairs around the room. "Simon will pour you some tea."

"Where's Daigh?" Arthur growled, his hand rested on the hilt of his sword. His whole body stood rigid, every muscle poised for attack.

"He's secure," Ryan said. Clara nodded, reaching out to touch Arthur's hand. His arm relaxed a fraction. But he didn't let go of his weapon. "Smithers and Isadora dragged him off the battlefield before the fae could take him. Aline was able to extract the poison from the fae arrow, so he'll live. More's the pity. I figured we should get everyone up-to-date and strategize before we made any attempt to question him. Especially..." his eyes flicked to Smithers, "...given the present company."

Smithers' eyes rolled back in his head. "Robert is in a box. Robert-in-a-box. Turn the handle and he'll pop up again."

Rowan slipped his fingers in mine. His hand trembled as he pulled me toward the sofa. I sat stiffly, not even registering the fabric against my bare legs. Blake slid down on the other side of me. Flynn took a seat closest to the table where Simon was laying out some scones and cream. Arthur remained by the door, still gripping his sword and casting furtive glances over his shoulder as if he expected to be stabbed in the back at any moment.

Simon held out a teacup and I accepted it, bringing the hot drink to my lips. Usually I hated tea unless it was the raspberry and vanilla one Rowan made for me, but this one tasted like nothing and it gave me something to do with my hands, so I sipped and tried to pretend I wanted to be here, that every thought wasn't about Corbin.

"Briarwood?" I asked, my voice tiny in the cavernous room.

"I spoke to the police this morning," Clara said. "They're going to allow you back in later today. That nice Inspector Wallace says he's arrested several villagers in relation to the arson and Corbin's death. There are others being treated for superficial wounds before they're questioned. Simon's already spoken to an engineer from Crooks Worthy who isn't superstitious. He's going to join you when you go back and give you an overview of the repair work to be done. If you're not ready to deal with that, I'm sure Simon will be happy to go with you. He's done enough work on this place for Ryan that he knows all the traps."

"We'll manage," Arthur growled. I knew what he was thinking – he didn't want anyone else there when we went back to Briarwood, especially not a bald butler we hardly knew. It was ours and we needed to mourn it together.

"I've also spoken to that lawyer of yours, Emily," Clara said. "Apparently, the villagers tried to get information about your witchcraft from her. She was trying to warn you, but they locked her in her office, took her mobile, and cut the phone line. She says she doesn't care if you're a barbershop quartet of singing badgers as long as you pay her retainer. She'll sort you out with any money you need for restoration work from the Briarwood Trust. You will have your home back before you know it."

Rowan's hand tightened around my wrist. *We'll never have our home back now.*

"Thank you." The words were wooden, devoid of meaning. The voice that spoke them didn't sound like my own.

"Maeve, sweetheart, drink your tea," Aline cooed, like I was a child with a scraped knee instead of a grown woman with a broken heart. "Let me explain what happened."

"You used fae magic against Daigh," Blake said. "I'm impressed."

"It was you who gave me the idea," Aline said. "When I learned you had the use of some fae powers from Daigh's tutelage, I wondered if there were ways other than binding that fae powers could pass to witches. I realized that maybe when Smithers trapped me in the painting after I'd been using Daigh's power as a glamour that *somehow* the power left in the necklace had been fused into me."

Oh nope, she's not getting away with that explanation. "If powers are genetic traits, then you're talking about your DNA being changed, and that's not possible."

"That you know of." Aline gave me this sweet smile, as if decades of genetic research could just be swept under the rug because she said so. "I was also trapped inside a painting for twenty-one years, which isn't something science can explain."

"If Daigh's really just throwing around his powers like candy on Halloween, then how come I don't have any?" I demanded. "Shouldn't I be able to glamour and talk in mirrors and compel people and manipulate dreams?"

"You *can* do all those things, Princess," Blake said quietly.

"No. I can't."

Blake held up his long, slender fingers and ticked off his points one by one. "You spoke to Daigh in the castle mirrors without Aline present. You can pull people into dreams at will and use dreams to travel into the fae realm."

"Daigh spoke to me! And going to the fae realm was all witchcraft! I'm a dreamwalker. It's my spirit power."

"Or maybe it's a power that manifests in witches with fae blood," Clara mused. "Very little is known about spirit magic, even less about dreamwalkers. It would make sense that it was a fae power, as dreams are a form of glamour. Maybe there are more bindings between our people than we think."

"I don't have fae powers!" I yelled.

"You've compelled hundreds of fae simultaneously," Blake flicked down another finger.

"*You* do that! I just give you more power!"

"Do you think if I could control the minds of the fae like that I'd have stayed in Tir Na Nog for so long?" Blake smirked. "Face it, Princess, you've got all the gifts. You were always so greedy."

"This isn't funny!"

"No, it's not." Aline's voice rose. "I'm so sorry I did this to you, Maeve. These powers are my curse. It's only fair that I find myself with them as well. I found out when we first spoke to Daigh through the mirror. Like calls to like. The clay steals the clay. I thought Blake might realize that I was using fae magic to call him, even though I told you all it was a witch's spell."

"Daigh never showed me that particular trick," Blake replied.

"Why didn't you tell me?" I demanded.

"I wanted to." Tears stung the corners of Aline's eyes. "But you already didn't trust me. What would you do when you found out I also had fae powers?"

She had a point. If she'd demonstrated fae powers, we never would have allowed her inside Briarwood's walls. And she might never have saved us last night.

While I ate a cardboard scone Aline explained how she concocted her plan. After Daigh had spoken to me in the mirror at Briarwood, she'd realized that he was lying about everything. She'd used her powers to contact the other witches through their own mirrors and beg them to come to Crookshollow in secret. Andrew had cancelled a lecture, Gwen and Candice had shut up their gallery shop and broken Smithers out of the institution, and they'd arrived just in time.

"It's not every day a dead witch appears in your bathroom mirror and begs for your help," Gwen smiled, patting Candice's knee. "Of course we came as quick as we could to help our Briarwood friends."

"It was a shock to see Aline again," Andrew said, rubbing his hollow eyes. "But I didn't want Corbin to fight this battle alone. Not again. I just wish I hadn't brought Bree along. She didn't need to see..." His voice trailed off, and he gulped, holding in his grief.

Two sons dead. It was too much to ask a parent to endure. If I believed in a kind and benevolent God, then staring into Andrew's broken eyes would've cured me of that nonsense.

Flynn glared at Isadora. "I thought you didn't like to meddle in the affairs of other covens? Wasn't that what you told Maeve?"

Isadora patted her mouth with her hand, as though the whole conversation bored her. "When I discovered how much of a mess you lot made of things, I had to step in to protect the Soho coven."

"Come now, Isadora," Clara smiled sweetly. "We all know that's not true."

Isadora's lips pursed, her eyes flashing. Something about the exchange tugged at me, some mystery to unravel. But the grief shadowed over it. I didn't care about Isadora and her secrets. I didn't care about anything.

But Clara clearly did. She stared at the intimidating witch

with such a self-satisfied smirk on her face. She was bursting to tell whatever secret Isadora was protecting.

Isadora shot Clara a withering look. "You ungrateful little hussy. I took you and that wretched son of yours off the streets and gave you a home and a livelihood, and you repay me by stealing from me and now you try to undermine me. I am a High Priestess here, and you are just an ignorant rustic hedgewitch—"

"I wouldn't speak to my mother like that in my home." Ryan's voice took on a weird, gravelly tone. As I watched in fascination, his face moved, the bones and skin rearranging itself into a very different shape. Reddish hair pushed through his skin, and his nose elongated into a muzzle. He rolled back his lips to reveal rows of sharp canine teeth.

Okay, I am not *seeing this. Ryan's face did* not *just transform into a fox.*

But everyone else saw it, too. Flynn yelped. Rowan moaned under his breath. Arthur growled and crossed the room, drawing his sword from its scabbard and pointing it at the creature that had previously been Ryan. Clara tapped his leg.

"Don't you wave that thing around in here, son. You'll put someone's eye out."

"He's using a glamour. That's a fae trick," Arthur shot back.

Ryan growled at Isadora. It didn't seem to scare her, which was ridiculous, because my heart pounded a mile a minute. Isadora waved a manicured hand at Clara, wrinkling her face in disgust. "Can't you control that beastly son of yours?"

Ryan's fur retracted back into his skin, and his face rearranged itself back into human features. He shook his head, puffing out his cheeks and scratching his paint-flecked hair. My heart leapt into my throat. That… whatever it was… had woken me up from my grief-induced stupor.

"What the fuck just happened?" Arthur demanded.

"Oh dear." Clara frowned. "I'm sorry. Ryan didn't want you to know his secret, but sometimes when shifters feel their pack being threatened, their natural instincts take over."

"Shifters?" Flynn squealed. "You mean, shapeshifters? They actually exist?"

Ryan nodded. "I'm a vulpine – a fox shifter. I am part human, part fox. It's why I don't leave the house. The shift can be difficult to control, especially when you're excited. Or angry." He said this last glaring at Isadora.

"There was a fox running around on the meadow," I remembered. "It bit a fae in the ankle, and he fell back into the void. That was you?"

"I can still taste his blood."

I remembered something else, too. Corbin showing me an image from Isadora's book of an orgy that contained half-human, half-animal creatures. He'd called them shapeshifters. I hadn't wanted to consider the possibilities at the time, and Corbin seemed to think it was a conversation for another day. He was more interested in that rusty ampulla on his library shelf. I was surprised to find myself accepting the evidence of my eyes, but there were so many unanswered questions. I had to *know*.

"How does shifting even work? Is your human skin an exoskeleton? How do you change your size? That matter and energy must go somewhere – it can't just disappear and reappear when you transform back. What do you eat? Do you—"

Ryan laughed. "This is exactly why I don't associate with other humans."

"I'm sorry, but you can't just drop a bomb like that and

expect us to just accept it, no questions asked. I need to understand and—"

"Yes, yes, it's all very interesting." Clara leaned forward. "Shouldn't we hear from Isadora now?"

It came back to me then, the strange thing Isadora had said when Corbin and I visited her in London. She knew a secret that would help us, but she refused to tell me. Ryan forgotten, I studied the witch as she glared at Clara from her chair, her blood-red nails tapping against the rim of her teacup. In London with her perfect outfit and brusque manner, she'd been terrifying. Now, even though she wore sharp tailored trousers and a silk shirt and her hair and makeup were perfect, the way she sat under Ryan's fox painting all alone, she appeared different somehow. Almost… vulnerable. I wondered what my mother had done to convince her to come to Briarwood.

Isadora looked to Aline, her face pleading, but Aline merely nodded.

"Very well," Isadora sighed. She set down her teacup and uncrossed and crossed her legs. "I've known about Daigh's plans for some time, but I've been unable to work directly against him because of a pact we made many years ago."

What? Anger gnawed at my gut. The way she treated us when we'd gone to speak to her… *she met Corbin and she knew information that could save him and she kept it to herself and now he's dead, dead, dead.*

"A pact which his forfeiture of his powers has now freed you from," Clara said, a little too gleefully. "Go on, Isadora. We're all curious to hear about this pact you made with Daigh."

Isadora sighed again. "Some years ago, he loaned his magic to assist me with a little problem. In return, I vowed that I would find out what really happened to his daughter."

7

MAEVE

*W*hat?

My breath caught in my throat. Isadora had a pact with Daigh about *me?* She acted so cold in London and all this time she…

"Oh, Isadora," Aline sighed, her eyes filled with pity.

Well, she could pity that nasty woman if she wanted. I needed answers. "What in Athena's name would have possessed you to strike a deal like that with the king of the Unseelie Court?"

Isadora held her chin high, her gaze unrepentant. "Because he gave me something I couldn't get from anyone else, and that's all I'll say on the matter. All you need to know is that Daigh did me a service many years ago, and he called in his favor."

"And what was his favor?"

"Some months after the ritual where both Moore girls were *supposed* to have died," Isadora glared at Aline. "Daigh's face appeared in my bathroom mirror. He said he could not talk long, for he had only the power for a few minutes. He said that he wasn't certain that Aline hadn't tricked him, that his daughter might still yet live. He wanted me to find out what I could. I did a little investigating, but I'm not a police detective," she wrinkled her nose as she said this, as though we'd all suggested she was a toad.

"Aline is tricksy," Smithers sang out. "She tricked tricked tricked that nasty Robert, but then he stopped talking to me and I had no friends."

Isadora frowned at Smithers, then continued. "I found nothing, and told him so. Daigh wasn't satisfied but he had no power, so what could he do? He didn't bother me again until a few months ago. He appeared in my bathroom mirror. He said his daughter's twenty-first birthday was approaching. If she was still alive then she would come into her spirit magic and inherit Briarwood Castle. He wanted me to investigate again, and he threatened to come after my coven if I didn't give him a real answer. He had power once more, and I was afraid for my girls. So I used the resources I had – an MI6 intelligence officer is my exclusive client. It took him less than fifteen minutes to hack into your solicitor's office and discover the presence of Maeve Crawford in Arizona. I gave this information to Daigh, and he declared my debt paid."

Horror dawned on me as I realized what she was saying. I'd been safe in America as long as Daigh believed I'd died in the ritual. Everything that had happened in these last few months only came about because Daigh found out I was alive and wanted to bring me back to Briarwood.

My hands balled into fists. Isadora was the reason my parents were dead.

White welts danced in front of my eyes as rage burned through me. My palms prickled with flaring magic. I imagined shoving my hands against Isadora's temples and dragging out her nightmares, giving her a taste of the grief and guilt I'd felt at her hands. What was that cold bitch even afraid of? I'd find out and I'd give it all to her.

Beside me, Flynn's hand clamped around my knee, grounding me and – judging by the pressure he applied – deliberately holding me down. I tried to slide out from under him, but he threw his other hand across my chest, yelping as he caught a flare of my spirit magic.

"Blake, a little help? She's going to fry Isadora's mind."

Blake's face remained impassive, but his eyes blazed with violence. "If Maeve wants to fry a few brains, she's justified."

I wrenched Flynn's arm off me and stood up. Aline gasped when she saw my face, but no one stepped in to stop me. I stepped toward Isadora, and Corbin's face flashed in my mind.

You can't blame Isadora.

Damn him. The one imagined glimpse at Corbin's smiling face was all it took for the fight to leave me. Corbin wouldn't want me to use my magic to hurt Isadora, even though she deserved it for that defiant glare in her eyes as she stared me down.

It was Daigh's orders that sent the prince Kalen to America to light that fire. Daigh killed my parents and revoked my scholarship. Daigh's ridiculous plan forced me to move to England and start the chain of events that ended up with all of us in this room. Isadora was weak and selfish, but she's not evil.

I slumped to my knees on the thick carpet, and pressed my head to the ground. Tears prickled at the corners of my eyes, the first signs that the flood of grief would soon break. A heavy hand fell on my back, and then another, and another as my boys surrounded me.

"This is the only thing you've done to help Daigh?" I heard Clara ask through my shield of guys. "There's been nothing else?"

I lifted my head. Isadora tossed her hair over her shoulder

and glared at me. "Only a few weeks before the ritual that bound his powers, he – and by him I mean that man over there—" she pointed at Smithers, "came to me with the gift of a painting. In exchange for the canvas, he wanted information about binding. The Soho coven curates one of the finest witchcraft libraries in the world, containing many rare volumes, not the provincial cabinet you cobbled together at your castle, you understand?"

Anger at her insult to Corbin's greatest joy rushed through me. Beside me, Rowan stiffened. "Don't make me *understand* your face into a new shape," Arthur growled.

"If you want information from me, you'll obtain it only when you stop acting like barbarians."

"Isadora," Clara warned.

The witch sighed. "Daigh asked that I not tell Aline he was possessing that fool of a painter or that he came to me for advice about binding."

"Rob was no fool," Smithers chirped up. "Rob knew the birds from the trees from the flowers from the bees."

"Do keep the monkey quiet," Isadora frowned.

I snorted. "You call Smithers a monkey when you were the one dancing for Daigh's amusement? Daigh got himself one sweet deal when he found you – a weak witch willing to do his bidding for the chance to lick his boots."

"Oh no, I received more than sufficient payment for my services," Isadora smiled, baring a row of white teeth, "although the painting was wretched. It had no touch of Daigh's magic. When I took it into Sotheby's, they laughed me out the door. I finally managed to sell it online, but for a twentieth of the price Daigh promised me it was worth."

My head snapped up. I remembered something Hendricks, the guide at the National Gallery, had said about a final Robert Smithers portrait that hit the market just before he was institutionalized, and how it seemed as though the painter had lost his talent overnight. It was too much of a coincidence. Isadora had seen that last painting. Maybe it would tell us something that could help us understand how this binding had affected me and my magic.

Flynn sensed it, too. His grip on my arm tightened. "Did you keep a copy of it?"

"Of course not. It was ghastly."

"Can you remember the details? Was there anything in it that could link it to the fae or—"

Isadora wrinkled her nose. "One cursory inspection was all I needed to ascertain the artist had lost his talent forever. I never so much as glanced at it again. I cannot even remember the subject of the portrait."

I slumped back on the rug. "It's buried in a private collection somewhere. We'll never see it, and it could have been an important piece of Daigh's plan."

"Don't be so sure." Ryan gestured for Simon to lean down. He whispered something in the butler's ear. Simon left the room. When Ryan didn't volunteer any further information, I sat back on my knees and glared at Isadora.

"In London, you said to me that you knew a way to stop Daigh."

"I did say that, didn't I?"

"Tell me," I growled.

"You already have the answers, thanks to Clara's sticky fingers. You need nothing from me."

"Tell me!"

"I won't," she shot back. "There is little point in dragging up what is past and what is done. Daigh has no power. You have magic enough to defeat the Slaugh. If you want to torture and kill the fae king for his crimes, I won't stop you. As far as I'm concerned, this matter has entirely resolved itself."

"But the fae—"

"The fae will continue to be a thorn in our side, as they have been for centuries. After the Slaugh they will be forced back into their realm and they won't be able to emerge again for some time. It will be as it always was."

"Don't you get it? We can't go back to how it always was. The fae have tasted victory. They *killed* twenty-two people and turned a whole village against us. They have Liah to lead them, and she has none of Daigh's earthly attachments to witches. Briarwood's magic has been broken. Even if we defeat the Slaugh, we're unprotected. We can't—"

Simon entered the room, carrying a square canvas in his arms. He leaned the painting against Ryan's legs. Ryan turned over the image and held it up, his face beaming in triumph. "Was this what you wanted to see?"

I scrambled to my feet and squinted at the painting, trying to sort out what I was looking at. It was a portrait all right, but it took me a few moments to figure out of who.

It was Daigh, but not as I'd ever seen him. The fae king's angular features had been rendered in long, lurid strokes. Instead of the cruel indifference that shone in his emerald eyes, here the irises were tinted with fear. His mouth hung open – a crooked, gaping maw from which issued a curling tendril of smoky darkness – like a snake who'd been chewing on too much licorice. His face seemed to sink, dripping toward the edge of the page. The slick varnish on top of the canvas only added to the illusion that the whole portrait melted under a cruel flame.

I turned the image this way and that, but I couldn't make sense of it. "Flynn?" I angled the painting toward him. "You're the artist here. Is that…"

"…a piece of shite? Why yes, Maeve. It is."

Ryan laughed. "Excellent spotting, Flynn. That was exactly what caught my eye about it. This painting is bad—"

"Hey!" Smithers cried.

"—but it's *deliberately* bad. Look at those brushstrokes – that's that fine work of a classically-trained artist. See the structure of the face – it's as perfect as any of the old masters. But then why has the artist deliberately distorted it and made it look so grotesque?"

"Because Daigh didn't paint it," I said, realization hitting me. "Robert Smithers did."

All eyes in the room flicked to Smithers. He rolled his eyes at the ceiling and flashed a vacant smile.

"Honey, did you paint that picture?" Aline asked, patting his arm. "Did you do it yourself, without any help from Daigh... I mean, from Robert?"

Smithers clicked his tongue. "Robert wanted a portrait. He said I needed something to remember him when he left. I wanted to carry a piece of him with me always. He hated it but it was too late. Ha ha!"

Smithers' barking laugh echoed around the vast room. I stared at the painting again, and for the first time I noticed something at the edges. A shadow that seemed to flicker across the paint. "Clara, can you come here?"

She heaved her body off the couch and stood beside me.

"Could you sense if there was magic inside this painting?" I asked. "Like there was in Aline's portrait?"

Rowan had felt Smithers' earth magic last time, but right now he was so messed up I didn't expect him to have any kind of control. And I couldn't ask Smithers, because I'd never get a straight answer. Even though Clara was a spirit witch, I felt certain she knew how to sense something inside the painting. Sure enough, she pressed her hands against the paint. Her eyelids fluttered closed as she searched the pigments. A moment later, her eyes flew open, and she tore her hands away.

"Yes," she whispered. "And it's fae magic."

My heart pattered in my chest. A new idea was forming in my mind, a sense of exactly what Robert Smithers might've been trying to do. I took a deep breath and turned to Isadora. "When Smithers came to you with this painting, what did he want to know about bindings? Tell me *exactly.*"

"I don't have a photographic memory for conversations that happened two decades ago," Isadora snapped.

"Well, you better start remembering," Arthur growled, waving his sword in front of her face.

"I said, I don't know! Something about the lore witches had around bindings, if the children were viable, and what magic they would possess. He wanted to know who kept the children of bindings in myth – the fae or the witches, and if there was some magical connection between the child and the parents – if a child could sense who their true parents were through magic, or some such ridiculous thing."

"That's what I thought." I slid back onto the sofa, my mind reeling. It wasn't Daigh asking, it was *Smithers.* He knew Daigh was leaving him, and his addled mind had cobbled together a plan, and not just a plan to save Aline, to save the world, but to save me.

He wanted to be my dad.

"You look like Obelix after Arthur gives him a sneaky bowl of cream," Blake said, patting my knee. "Spill the secret, Princess."

"I think..." I turned over the ideas in my head. "I'm not certain on a lot of points, but I think we owe Smithers here a lot more credit. Daigh lived in his head for all those months, and I think Smithers heard and understood more about his plans than even Daigh realized. Smithers knew that there had been a binding, and that Daigh wanted to take Aline and Maeve back to the fae world with him. We assumed he'd placed Aline in the painting because he thought she was in love with Daigh, but I think what he really did was create Aline's portrait in order to save her from what Daigh planned. And he used *this* painting to trap some of Daigh's power so that he wouldn't be able to return for me or Aline. Does that sound right, Rob?"

"Robert thought he was tricksy, but I was tricksy, too," Smithers sang, beating his fist against his knee. "Tricksy, tricksy, tricksy!"

Ryan leaned the painting against the mantle, standing back to admire it. "I knew it was special as soon as I saw it. I think it might be your finest work, Rob."

Smithers beamed. Aline placed her arm around his shoulders, burying her face in his neck so she could whisper something in his ear. A pang of something shot down my side. Pride, tinged with sadness.

Daigh's desire for Aline had robbed her of years of happiness, of the life she could have had with a non-crazy Smithers, of raising me and being my mother. Even though Daigh was still taking and taking and tearing our lives apart, at least we'd given her back this tiny piece of the future she should have had. Maybe she could have it again.

I turned away from them, my eyes darting back to Smithers' painting. This time, the ugliness of Daigh's features struck me as hilarious. How he must've started when he saw it! I snorted at the image of Smithers painting away merrily while Daigh screamed protests inside his head. It really *was* genius.

"So we've got a painting that contains some of Daigh's power," Flynn whistled. "Isn't that a bargaining chip? We dangle the promise of a smidgeon of power over his head to get him to tell us what he's chancin' with this scheme of his."

"We already know what he wants – Maeve and Aline, and the rule of the fae and human worlds." Arthur glared at the portrait. His hand stroked the hilt of his sword. "Now he's got none of those things, and he's locked up. All we need to do is finish the job."

"Agreed," I said.

Kelly raised a tentative hand. Beside her, Jane reached over and rubbed her knee. The gesture was so tender it drove a stake through my heart. It was the kind of movement Corbin would've made. "Um... I know I'm just a human and I don't have any magical powers—"

"That's correct, you do *not*." Isadora wrinkled her nose.

"—but why are you all so eager to kill this guy? I know he's kind of the evil super villain, but right now he's defenseless. Isn't that like, against your witch code or whatever?"

"No," I said, at the same time Rowan whispered, "yes."

"Daigh killed our parents, Kelly. He killed Corbin, and he was going to kill you. Even as a human with no powers, he's dangerous. He's been stripped of his power before and he managed to come back."

"I get it. He's a bad dude." Tears spilled down Kelly's cheeks. "But if he turns my sister into a murderer, then as far as I can see, he wins."

"This isn't about me," I snapped. "It's about the whole *world*. We have to put an end to this, and that means putting an end to him. If we don't stop Daigh he'll just come back again, like he did before. Next time we might not be able to stop him."

"We could turn him over to the fae," Blake piped up. "Let them kill him. Problem solved."

"That's not any better!"

"Yeah, and I want to do it myself," Arthur growled, lifting his blade an inch out of its scabbard.

"Murder is never okay," Kelly sobbed. "Who are you people? Maeve, think about Mom and Dad. I know they wouldn't care that you're a witch. They'd still love you. But they wouldn't want you to be a murderer. It's one of the ten commandments and your immortal soul—"

"Maybe I have to think about more than just myself and my immortal soul, which I don't technically believe exists, anyway. Maybe I have to make the hard decisions to protect you, because that's my duty. Maybe I have to do a horrific thing for the greater good of humanity."

"Don't you think that's exactly what he wants?" Kelly cried. "If he really is this crazy fae who'd sell out his own powers just so he could talk to you, don't you think he'd allow himself to be killed if it broke up this coven?"

"That's ridiculous. Then he wouldn't be alive to gloat over his victory," Blake drawled.

"But he would! I mean, you know now there's some kind of life after death, because that's where he came from, isn't it? He came from Hell? So he can gloat all he wants."

"It's not Hell, it's another dimension," I snapped. "And you don't know Daigh—"

"Of course I don't know Daigh!" Kelly yelled. "You lot didn't trust Jane or I enough to tell us anything, and I ended up being captured by a fairy and Jane had to hear the whole story from your previously-dead mother."

"Don't yell at Maeve," Arthur snarled, his voice dripping with malice.

Fresh tears flooded down Kelly's cheeks. "And don't threaten me, Arthur. Why are you so full of hate? When I met you I thought you were the nicest guy I'd ever known, but now you're just a brute."

"My best friend is dead!" Arthur yelled. The edge of the rug burst into flame. Kelly screamed and scrambled out of the way. Flynn dived for the flames, dousing them with water that pooled across the ground. The scent of sodden fibers and charred fabric filled my nostrils, driving the burning rage to the surface of my skin.

"Could you stop trying to burn down my house!" Ryan roared. Red fur bristled from his cheeks.

"All of you, *shut up!*" Jane screamed.

My mouth snapped shut. Kelly sniffed, folding her arms across her chest. Rowan buried his face into the back of the sofa. Arthur dropped his sword back into his scabbard and stared gape-mouthed at Jane.

"Much better," Jane glared at us with a look I knew would terrify Connor once he grew up enough to finger paint on the walls. "I've got a baby asleep in the next room, so can we keep things civilized? Or else I'm going to force the person who wakes Connor to put him down again, which would serve you right. As fascinating as it is being a fly-on-the-wall for all this witch stuff, you're all acting like a bunch of children. Since I'm a representative for the ordinary, non-magical human race – one of only two in this room, I might point out – I suggest you all take a breath, stop throwing around insults and fireballs, *put away that bloody sword*, and focus on the immediate problem. Which is what happened last night. There's a dead boy who needs to be honored and buried, a police investigation going on, and a village full of people who've had their minds warped."

I sucked in a breath, trying to calm the rage that bristled in my veins. Rage was good – it was better than numbness. But Jane and Kelly were right. I wasn't thinking straight. None of us were. I was so focused on having Daigh at our mercy that I'd forgotten all about the village and Briarwood and what the humans were thinking right now. I needed to suck it up, to be a High Priestess, even though that was the last thing I wanted to be.

"At least the village doesn't hate us anymore," Blake said. "Maeve and I saw to that."

"Are we sure?" Jane asked. "A night in jail or in the hospital getting fae wounds stitched up might be enough to undo the force of your little trick. And what are they going to do now that they've seen the existence of the fae for themselves? What are the *police* going to do? How are you going to keep your secrets? These are all practical issues you need to deal with before you get all stab-friendly with the fae king. And honestly, you guys are *messed up* right now. You lost someone special. Take a step back before you do something you regret. This room is filled with people who respect and support and love you – let them deal with some of this shit."

"Jane—" My shoulders slumped. *She's right.* Of course she was right. Arthur's hand fell off his sword hilt. Rowan covered the side of his face with his hand. Flynn's features crumpled. The surface of Blake's emerald eyes shattered into shards. Our grief hung heavy in the air, fresh and wet with dew. We *were* messed up. Completely lost. We needed Corbin to hold us together, but Corbin wasn't here. "I'm sorry."

"Don't be sorry. Just… let Kelly and I help." Jane always knew how to bring an emotional situation back to practicalities. "Hell, just answer our bloody questions. Starting with this one – I want to know why the fae tried to kill Kelly. She's not even technically related to Maeve. She doesn't have any powers."

I shook my head. "I couldn't tell you. That sixth stake was supposed to be for me."

"You only thought that because Daigh told you so," Aline said. "It looks as if he knew all along who he intended for the sixth stake."

I frowned. "Why could I never see it in the dreams? If I'm a dreamwalker then I should have been able to reach that sixth stake, but I every time I got close it was like there was this invisible wall holding me back."

"Sorry, Princess," Blake said. "That was me. I've been in your dream every time. I blocked you from seeing that stake."

What? "Why?"

Blake's shattered eyes bore into mine. Even though his expression was as smooth and stony as ever, his eyes betrayed pain he'd buried deep, rising to the surface for the first time in his life. He didn't know how to handle it.

He looked away, closing his long fingers around the curled arm of the sofa. "Because I knew who was on it. And I didn't want you to see. Daigh had already hurt you enough."

"Damnit, Blake!" I yelled. "If I'd seen Kelly on that stake I would've known Daigh was lying. I would never have deactivated the charms." *Corbin might not've died.*

"You should have known that anyway," Blake shot back. His head whipped around and his eyes flared with darkness – a simmering rage that forced back the pain. "He's lied this whole time. That's what he does."

"Don't blame Maeve for this," Arthur boomed. "You're the one who's been keeping secrets. You never told the truth about who you are, and you've been double-dealing with your fae friend and sneaking around with Flynn. For all we know, you're still loyal to the fae king—"

"After all this time, you still don't trust me." Blake's lips curled back into a smirk that bore no resemblance to jocularity.

"You shouldn't have kept that from her, Blake," Flynn said.

"You mean, like all the things *you* kept from her?" Blake's fierce eyes darted between Flynn and Arthur. Arthur's hand flew to his sword, and Flynn crossed his arms across his chest, his features completely devoid of mirth. Blake's posture remained relaxed, but his nails tore the upholstery. Tension crackled between them, rising off them like a hurricane, dragging out their darkest fears and battering them against each other in a clash of wills.

This isn't what I want. I was pissed at Blake, sure. I was pissed at them all. But that was just because I loved them so much. We needed each other more than ever. If their friendships fell apart because of Corbin's death, we would lose *everything*.

"Guys, don't do this," I pleaded.

"This is his fault," Arthur growled, drawing his blade out and pointing the tip toward Blake's chest. "You should have just stayed in the fae realm. We should never have let you into the coven."

No.

I wanted to reach across and slap the words off Arthur's lips, but it was too late. He'd loosed them into the maelstrom. They whirled through the air like rotor blades and slammed into Blake's face. His head snapped back, slapping against the sofa. His chiseled features crumpled completely as his mask fell away, revealing hurt so deep and so fathomless my stomach plunged into my toes.

Right there in front of me was Blake Beckett, stripped of all the ego and fortitude that Daigh's tutelage had bestowed upon him. All that was left was the human boy, the vulnerable child who'd been taken from his parents and forced into a life where he didn't fit. The lost soul who had risked everything to join us and now had all the evidence he needed that he didn't fit here either. He didn't fit anywhere.

"Arthur, how could you?" I cried.

"Mother Mary, Arthur," Flynn breathed. "That was ratshite, mate."

Arthur's piercing glare didn't leave Blake's face. He didn't speak, and he didn't lower his sword.

Blake stood up, brushing a strand of his long black hair behind his ear. "Thanks for your honesty, Arnold."

I grabbed Blake's arm, trying to force him to look at me. He didn't react at all. His eyes fixed on some position on the wall behind me. A lump rose in my throat. "He didn't mean it, Blake. He didn't—"

"He *did*, Princess. That's his way. At least he did me the

honor of honesty, which was not something I could give you." Blake's shattered eyes darted back to Arthur, as if they hoped he might lower the sword and extend a hand instead. I glared at Arthur, but if he noticed, he didn't react.

"Old Aragorn doesn't speak for all of us," Flynn piped up. "You're my brother, mate. We've all made mistakes. Arthur's making a stupid one right now."

Blake slid his arm from mine and stepped toward the door. I grabbed him around the chest. Tears stung the corners of my eyes. I blinked them back. Once they started, I'd never get them to stop. "Don't go. Please. I can't lose another person I love. Corbin wanted you here and I... I need you."

Blake curled his long fingers around mine and pried himself from my grip. "You don't. You never did. It'll be easier if I'm not here now. It was never meant to be. Maybe I'll go back to my people," he shrugged. "I've heard they're in need of a new king."

"Do that!" Arthur growled.

Flynn threw his arms around Blake and I, mashing our bodies together and trapping Blake between us. Another heavy body fitted in behind mine, and Rowan's familiar thyme and flour scent crawled up my nostrils.

Ryan leapt at Arthur, his hand clamping on his arm and forming an enormous fox paw. Arthur yelped in surprise and relaxed his grip on the hilt enough that Ryan could knock it from his hand. The tip stuck into the wooden floor, burying the blade so it remained upright, quivering.

Arthur spun on his heel and slammed his fist into Ryan's face, sending the artist sprawling backwards. "Fuck," he growled, gripping his bleeding nose. Andrew leapt off his chair, grabbing Arthur from behind and trying to tackle him to the ground. Arthur slammed Andrew's back into the bookshelf, sending a shower of books down on top of them.

Andrew pushed Arthur's head into the carpet and Arthur raised his fist and shot a fireball over his shoulder.

"Arthur!" I yelled. Andrew jerked his head to the side just as the fireball exploded against the bookcase.

"Jesus!" Flynn shot a jet of water at the bookcase, putting out the flames and drenching the rows of books.

Ryan leapt at them, transforming mid-air into an enormous fox. Kelly screamed. I choked back my own cry and Ryan scrambled up Arthur's back and sank his teeth into his shoulder.

"Yeeeow!" Arthur swung around, sending another fireball across the room. Clara flattened herself against the rug it sailed over her head. Gwen reached up and hit it with a wall of water, extinguishing it in midair.

"Fun!" Smithers broke away from Aline's grip and darted into the fray. He pressed his hand to the floorboards, which sprouted with a series of vines that curled across the floor. Arthur kicked one of the vines, and it responded by flaring up like a snake and wrapping around his ankle. Between the two guys, the fox, and the vines, Arthur's heavy bulk crashed on the floor.

"Get off me!" he howled, struggling against his captors as he tried to reach his sword.

"Guys, please stop!" Kelly cried.

"Apologize to Blake!" Flynn yelled as he forced Arthur's shoulder into the carpet. Blood dripped from between Ryan's teeth.

"Flynn, it's fine," Blake said. "I'll go."

"You're not going anywhere. If anyone's to blame, it's that bitch over there," Flynn jabbed a finger at Isadora. *"She* was the one who gave Daigh everything he needed to feck up Maeve's life. I say we—"

"What about Corbin?" Rowan yelled.

The room fell silent.

Everyone turned to stare at Rowan, who didn't even flinch under the scrutiny. Flynn and Andrew slid off Arthur. Corbin's name floated in the air between us, dissipating Arthur's cruel words and all the chaos they had wrought. It was the exact effect Corbin would have had if he was here.

Rowan stood rigid, his face bent up and lips pressed together. He screwed his eyes tight, so he didn't even have anything to count to keep himself calm. "What about Corbin?" he said again, louder this time, his voice deeper and harder than I'd ever heard before.

"Corbin's gone, mate," Arthur said, his voice suddenly gentle. Flynn and Andrew loosened their grip on him and he crawled onto his knees, wiping a strand of dirty-blond hair off his sweat-streaked forehead. Something in Rowan's voice had released the tension in his shoulders, and his whole body slumped in defeat. "Trust me on that. The coroner has his body now. We'll get it back after they've finished their investigation and then we'll have a memorial—"

"We can't do that." Rowan's lips quivered. He gripped the back of the sofa, his knuckles pale.

"Why not?" Ryan said. He sounded tired.

Rowan sucked in a breath. His eyes flew open, deep pools of hope and longing. "Maeve had a dream this morning."

"Rowan, don't," I warned.

"Corbin spoke to her. He says he's in the underworld, and that if we work together with him we can stop Daigh forever." Rowan jerked my shoulder. "He said we could bring him back."

Bring him back.

Corbin's earnest face flashed in my vision – the dream as clear in my mind as if it was a real memory. But it wasn't. Corbin wasn't coming back, and the more Rowan wanted to believe it, the more certain I was it wasn't true.

"Maeve, why didn't you say something." Aline stood up. "If Corbin spoke to you in a vision, then—"

"It wasn't a vision. It was a *dream*," I said. "I just lost someone special to me. Of course he's going to show up in my dreams. I relived my parents' accident again and again in my dreams after they died. It doesn't mean they were trying to speak to me from the underworld."

"That you know of," Isadora said with a smirk.

"Don't speak to me," I growled at her.

"Can you tell us about this dream?" Aline said. "Entertain your mother and her belief in prophecy, just the once. Maybe there's something to it."

Spirit magic sparked against my palms. I wanted to press them to Rowan's cheeks and *show* him how painful it was to see Corbin in his dreams. The flood of anger that rose inside me and was directed at this beautiful guy I cared about so much terrified me. I stepped back and shook my head, not trusting myself to speak.

"Come on, Einstein," Flynn cooed. "Is it such a stretch to believe that he could reach you in your dreams? You *are* our resident dreamwalker."

"We don't even know what dreamwalking *means!*" I yelled. "Dreams are just our brains processing information while we sleep. I might be able to give other people my dreams and pull their own nightmares out of their heads, but that doesn't mean I can process information I'm not supposed to know yet. Magic is still a natural force – it can't break the laws of causality. If you don't believe me, then look at the evidence. The stakes and the radiated earth in my dreams didn't come to pass. Daigh had the dream first and gave it to me and then used the stakes because he knew it would scare us. Science was right – retrocausality can't work on a macroscopic level, precognition is impossible, and chaos prevails."

"Or maybe Corbin figured out how—"

"He didn't," I growled. "I *really* want to stop talking about this. Take me to Daigh."

Rowan's face fell. "But what about the dream—"

I balled my hands into fists. "This discussion is over. I'm the High Priestess, and I'm seeing Daigh. *Now.*"

8

MAEVE

his begins and ends with Daigh.

My supposed father. The King of the Unseelie. Blake's kidnapper and torturer. The murderer of my parents and Corbin. Every word out of his mouth so far had been a lie. He was right here in the same building as me, stripped of his magic and completely under my power.

And I had a motherfucking *score* to settle.

"Are you sure that's a good idea—" Clara began, but as her eyes met mine, the words died on her lips. She nodded.

"I'm going with you," Blake piped up.

Arthur opened his mouth to say something, but Flynn glared at him and he shut his mouth.

"We're coming, too." Aline squeezed Smithers' hand.

Whatever. I didn't care. I needed to get out of this room. I needed them all to stop attacking each other and talking about Corbin as if there was some possibility he was still alive. Rage had forced out the numbness, and I needed to do something with it before its fire consumed me from within. As much as I wanted to throttle every witch and human and fox in the room, this rage wasn't for them. I needed to give it to the person who *deserved* it.

Ryan glanced from me to Blake to Aline, and then back to me again. He looked like he was going to protest, but then thought better of it. He shrugged. "Fine. Follow me."

Ryan led us down another drab hall, through a thick glass and steel door into a temperature-controlled vaulted gallery filled with majestic paintings. Bright colors leered out of the walls, assailing my eyes with woodland scenes and bold abstracts that suggested the world was richer and more beautiful than I knew it to be. I balled my hands into fists, resisting the urge to tear down an image of a young girl carrying a heart-shaped balloon and smash it over Ryan's head.

Down another short hall, the walls lined with stacks of large, flat boxes I guessed contained more artwork, we came to a large metal door. Ryan rapped on the door with his knuckles, resulting in a dull thud of solid steel. "I had this safe installed a few years ago to store my art collection when I rotated the displays. It's the most secure place in the house. It's also ventilated to prevent condensation damaging the paint."

"The perfect prison," Blake said in his usual easy tone. I glanced up at him. He had his mask on again – the still expression and cocky smirk that always enchanted me. But his eyes... the darkness.

Ryan tapped a code into the keypad, and the door swung inward. I leaned in to squint at the darkness.

A shadow launched itself at the door, knocking Ryan across the hall. Daigh's fingers raked at Ryan's throat, raising red scratches. Red fur poked through Ryan's skin, and he yelped as he struggled against Daigh's attack and his uncontrollable shift.

Blake lunged forward but I got there first. "Get back," I

growled, grabbing Daigh's head and funneling all my pent up pain and grief into my palms.

Daigh's skin crackled under my touch. Flashes of memory that felt familiar but that didn't belong to me burned through my mind – blood running under a dark sky, dancing with entrails strung around my body like streamers, gorging myself on drink and food and misery, rage, pain, jealousy... and love. Love so fierce and twisted it became an ugly hate. Love that wasted the body and poisoned the mind.

Love for Aline. Love for... me.

I drew all that love to the surface and threw it back at Daigh. I poured his own twisted dreams back at him. Joy filled me as he sank to the floor, his body convulsing as he lived every dark moment of his life all at once.

This is what you deserve. You destroyed my life. You killed everyone I love.

I drove the memories hard and fast into him until they became a blur of fire and hate. Daigh crumpled into a ball, clutching his head in his hands. Inhuman wails issued from his lips, becoming one with the screams inside my head. A faint smell of roasting meat tainted the air.

"Maeve, stop!" Hands pulled me back. I cried out as my mind was torn from Daigh. The memories evaporated, replaced by Blake – his statuesque face frozen in concern.

"Why did you stop me?" I growled. "He *tortured* you, remember? He should suffer for what he's done to us."

"Oh, I enjoyed that very much, Princess. Cut his fingers off one by one and make him eat them if that's what makes you happy. It would make me happy."

"Let's go, then."

Blake's fingers gripped my shoulders. "Only if you won't regret it. Your sister may be wiser than you give her credit for. I don't want you to do anything you regret."

I glanced down at Daigh. He'd curled up into the fetal

position, his knees hugging his chest as he rocked his head in his hands. Red spiderwebs crisscrossed the skin on his face and ran down his arms. A wave of revulsion coursed through me.

I did that to him.

I cursed. Blake was right. As quickly as it came, the rage eased. A different memory flashed in front of my eyes – me as an eight-year-old crying in my room because a bully at school had stuck the fire hose through my locker and destroyed all my science books. Louise Crawford gathered me in my arms and listened to all my revenge plans and recited from Scripture about how Jesus turned the other cheek.

That was what Kelly wanted me to do, to be like Jesus. And she was right. I felt it in my bones. I had to do the right thing even though the right thing was hard and I was hurting and I wanted Daigh to suffer.

Goddammit, why couldn't I have been adopted by a Jewish family? From what I remember of the Bible, they're nuts for revenge.

I stepped back from Daigh and collapsed into Blake's arms. "What did you do to him, Princess?" Blake whistled through his teeth as we watched Daigh writhe on the floor.

"Nothing he didn't deserve," I replied, my body trembling.

A noise behind us startled me from my thoughts. I whirled around. At the far end of the hallway, Robert Smithers was on the ground, too, his head in his hands. He murmured nonsense. Aline cupped his shoulders, tears streaming down her face as she tried to coax him back to reality.

"I don't know if it's in his head or if he really feels Daigh's pain, but there's still a connection between them," she cried, her eyes pleading me.

"I'm sorry. I didn't mean to hurt Rob." I burrowed my

THE CASTLE OF SPIRIT AND SORROW

head deeper into Blake's shoulder. His sleek black hair fell over my face like a waterfall.

"Let's get him back inside," Ryan said. Blake reluctantly slid out from my grip, and he and Ryan lifted Daigh's arms and dragged him into the safe. I followed them, leaning my back against the cold wall and sucking in deep breaths.

What have I done?

I hated this man (and he was just a man now) with every fiber of my being. But when I saw the red welts across his sweat-soaked face from my magic, a sick feeling twisted in my gut. I wanted to inflict pain – as much pain as he'd given me. He was our prisoner and I wanted to torture him and take pleasure in his screams.

It was like when I'd watched Uncle Bob's house burn, his terrified expression as he realized what I truly was and that *he* was at *my* mercy. I wanted him to hurt for the hurt he'd done to Kelly. Was this the person I really was, twisted by a desire for revenge?

Was I any better than Uncle Bob? Was I any better than Daigh?

As if reading my thoughts, Daigh raised his head and stared up at me with crystalline eyes filled with pain. "I had always dreamed you would inherit my cruelty, daughter."

His words turned my stomach, but I needed him to talk, to give us something that might tell us what was coming and how we might stop this forever. I stood over him, arms folded, legs wide in the stance Arthur had taught me emanated power. "That's right. And now you're under my power, and I need you to talk. If you lie to me, Blake and I will just drag the truth from your nightmares, and you won't enjoy that. I want to know why you gave up your powers."

"Isn't it obvious?" Daigh sneered. He held the haughty expression for only a moment before his face collapsed in a painful spasm. A knife twisted in my gut.

"Obviously not," I folded my arms. "Or we wouldn't be asking."

"You wanted to reach Maeve," Aline said from the doorway. "And me."

I glanced up at her. Beside her, Smithers knelt on the ground, a trembling hand pressed to his temples as he stared at Daigh. Something about being in the same room as Daigh was hurting him. I glanced at Aline, but she shook her head. She had no idea what was going on, either.

"Robert, Robert, Rob, Rob, Rob…" he murmured, walking his shaking fingers across the floor toward Daigh. "You are not you anymore. You are darkness and death, spirit and sorrow."

Daigh slapped Smithers' hand away and grinned up at me. "You were hiding in your castle, dearest daughter. I needed to reach you, but the only way to get through the wards was to engage the use of a demon friend. He cleverly pointed out that if I was no longer a fae, the wards could no longer keep me out. I had to lose my fae powers, so I traded them."

"What did you trade them for?"

Daigh grinned. "That's my business. All you need to know is that once I understood how much those stupid humans meant to you, I decided to made this sacrifice so that we could be a family."

In a weird, twisted way, I could see how he'd come to this conclusion. It was the kind of logic that made sense to an Unseelie.

I snorted. "You used the dream you gave me to make me believe this was all part of my story, that I was destined to lose my coven. But it didn't happen like that, did it? You played this completely wrong, and you lost your powers for nothing. We're never going to be a family. Biologically, that man on the floor over there is my father. My mother stands in the doorway, and she'll never want you again now. You're not one of us, and I'm not your daughter. End of discussion."

Daigh sneered. "What did that blood test say?"

"We haven't got the results yet. But they'll confirm my conclusion, because that's how genetics *works*. And even if you *were* my father, even if you hadn't occupied Smithers' brain by force, then I would still never join you. Family is about more than blood, and you took mine from me. I might not kill you for that, but I won't forgive you for it, either."

Smithers dragged his body across the floor and wrapped his arms around Daigh. "Something's wrong with Robert. Rob will fix him up."

"Get off me, you gibbering fool." Daigh tried to push Smithers off him, but he was too weak. He sat glumly, enduring the other man's embrace. "You'll be keeping me in this metal prison, then?"

"What's our alternative? You can't be trusted."

"That's fair. But don't you think I could help you? What are you going to do about Liah? About the Slaugh?"

I let the corners of my mouth draw up into a sly smile, as if we had it all planned out, as if we knew exactly what we were doing. As if we weren't pinning all our hopes on a swelling supply of belief magic we had no idea how to control.

"None of your business," I said, as I backed out of the room.

"Wait," Daigh lunged for the door. "Maeve, I want—"

I slammed the door in his face.

9

ROWAN

*M*aeve and the other spirit witches went down to speak to Daigh. Part of me wanted to go with them. I wanted to look into the eyes of Corbin's killer. But I also knew that seeing Daigh wouldn't heal the hole in my heart or give me the answers I craved.

Besides, I knew Corbin wasn't dead, and now was the perfect time to start figuring out how he'd pulled that off.

Everyone else who hadn't gone to interrogate the fae king remained slumped in the sodden and charred drawing room, faces stupefied, not sure how to continue the conversation. There was so much that still needed to be said. Simon announced there was food in the kitchen if anyone was still hungry. Arthur got up to follow him, and I trailed after Arthur, touching his hand. He jumped at my fingers on his skin, his hand flying to his sword.

"Hey," I whispered. "You okay?"

"No," he growled. His hand didn't leave the weapon. I stepped back from him, anxiety rippling through me. The rage that dripped from his voice took me back to a time before Briarwood, before the squat, where I'd lived in fear of that kind of rage.

He's your friend. You can't think of him like that. He's not a monster. He's hurting, too.

But Arthur's hurt was becoming dangerous. He'd turned on Blake, and those fireballs... I never met Arthur when he first came to Briarwood, but Corbin had told me stories about the rage that burst out of him and incinerated several priceless tapestries. Arthur needed Corbin's calming influence to conquer his anger. But Corbin wasn't here.

We have to find a way to reach Corbin, wherever he is. We aren't complete without him.

"Arthur, can I talk to you for a moment?"

Arthur nodded. He ducked into the nearest room. It was another drawing room, this one decorated in buttercream tones. Arthur collapsed into an overstuffed sofa, resting his boots on the corner of the table and sliding his scabbard onto the cushions beside him. He didn't remove his sword belt.

"Arthur," I sat down across from him. "I need to ask about Corbin."

A storm raged in Arthur's eyes. "No."

"Please. Just tell me when you last saw him alive. That's all, I swear."

"Rowan, don't torture yourself."

"I'm not. I just need to know."

"Don't torture me, then."

"It might be important. Maeve isn't going to talk about her dream because... because she's Maeve. But I just have this feeling..."

Arthur sighed dramatically. "We were in the entrance hall. Corbin yelled at me to hold the villagers off the first floor. I guess that was so he could get you and Maeve into the priest hole. I was on the staircase throwing down some covering fire when he appeared and yelled at me to hold my breath.

He sucked all the air from the room, and we managed to get past the gasping villagers and out the door. I could see a bonfire flaring in the meadow, so we headed right for it. I was first down the path but as I passed through the gate, a phalanx of fae approached and Corbin charged past me and plunged into their ranks. Of course they pounced on him. He didn't even fight them. He just let them drag him away."

"Why did he do that?" I whispered.

"Fucked if I know!" Arthur yelled. "Probably he was trying to be a chivalrous bastard and sacrifice himself so they'd leave us alone, like he always fucking does. Well, it worked, didn't it?"

Tears pricked the corner of my eyes. Arthur's anger washed over me, the vein above his eye reminding me of my last foster father, the one who'd locked me in a closet for three days. "Why are you so angry with me? I just want—"

"Because I didn't save him!" Arthur yelled. "I was right *there* and I had a weapon and I would've cut down every last one of those bastards if only I'd been stronger and faster."

"Do you need—"

"I need everyone to leave me the fuck alone!" Arthur yelled.

I ducked as a fireball hit the wall behind me. "Shit!" Arthur yanked a throw blanket off the back of the sofa and flung himself at the wall, smothering the flames. Above our heads, the fire alarm beeped.

"What the hell's going on in here?" Ryan yelled, rushing in. Simon clattered after him, carrying a crystal pitcher of water, which he threw at the smoldering wall.

I slipped out before I got caught in the crossfire between Arthur and Ryan. Flynn came running down the hall, his palm raised in front of him. "It's Arthur, isn't it? Jesus, Mary and Joseph and all their wee carpenter friends, can we live in one grand building without burning it down?"

"The house is fine. The fire's out. Arthur's about to get a bollocking from Ryan. He's probably not so fine." I lowered my voice. "Hey, can you tell me about Corbin... the last time you saw him that night."

Darkness flashed in Flynn's eyes. "Are you trying to figure out if he's still alive? Because he looked bloody dead as a doornail to me. I know Maeve's had magical dreams before, but sometimes a dream is just a dream. You shouldn't be getting your hopes up, mate."

"I'm not." A lie. "I just... if Corbin were here, he'd make us explore all the possibilities."

"Right you are." Angry voices drowned out Flynn's words. He grabbed my arm and led me down the hallway, toward the kitchen. "So here's what I saw. After the villagers broke down the front door, I heard my scone-mix trap go off. That was satisfying. The rest of you ran down and I went back up on the roof to put out the fire in my workshop and the new one Arthur started in the entrance hall like the big eejit he is. I saw a big crowd of people surging out of the inner doors, chasing Corbin and Arthur toward the meadow. I was focused on the fire when someone snuck up behind me and marmaladed me. Next I knew I was tied up on the field."

"Corbin was still alive when you saw him?"

Flynn peered into a stainless steel cookie jar. "You need something to eat, mate?"

"I'm fine. So Corbin was still alive?"

"Yeah, yeah. I'm right foddered. I saw Simon icing a carrot cake this morning. I wonder where he's hidden it." Flynn slammed cabinet doors and peered under the sink. "It's not as nice as your chocolate whiskey cake, but it'll do the job."

I tried to ask Flynn another question, but he found the cake and busied himself hunting down a knife and plate. I wasn't going to get anything out of him. At least he was going to use a plate – back at Briarwood he would scoff handfuls of double chocolate whiskey cake straight from the cooling rack, leaving trails of crumbs over the floor that drove my anxiety wild.

The thought that I might never clean Flynn's crumbs off the kitchen floor at Briarwood again slammed into me. Would the castle survive? Could we rebuild it? If I couldn't find a way to bring Corbin back, would it even be worth it?

Dejected, I returned to our bedroom. Ryan had given us an entire wing to ourselves – a room each – but I knew I couldn't bear the idea of being separated from Maeve and the guys right now. We'd given Maeve the largest room at the far end of the hall, and that was where we'd all slept last night. I shoved open the door and was surprised to see Blake sprawled across the bed, his fingers knitted across the chest and his crystalline eyes watching a fly buzz around the ceiling.

I never spoke to Blake much. Truthfully, he unsettled me. His face only had two expressions – the statuesque one he wore now, where you had no hint of his thoughts or even that he was alive. And the one when he did something that pleased him, which was basically the same except the corners of his mouth turned up into this evil smirk.

There was a heroin addict who lived on my floor of the squat for a few months. He was a wealthy kid – I could tell by his expensive clothes and the way he didn't cling to his possessions like they were his only link to the world. He lay on his bunk for days at a time, lost in a dream world where he was an elf king or a meerkat or a water droplet. He moaned with ecstasy as the drugs painted over the world with clouds and rainbows, but there was a fragility to him that hid a demon below the surface. He spoke with a tender softness that terrified me, caressed my shoulders with a languid hand that had, he once murmured, strangled his father with his own belt. He slept next to me and I watched him through my eyelashes all night, my body rigid with fear, so certain that if I drifted off he'd stab me in my sleep.

Blake reminded me of him. So beautiful, so dangerous.

"Hello, Rowan," Blake purred.

Anxiety shot through my body. I thought about backing out of the room, but I had intended to speak to him. I just... wanted to psych myself up first. "Um... hi."

I slid along the wall, keeping a wide berth around Blake, in case he thought I agreed with Arthur, that all our troubles were Blake's fault. My hand groped for the arm of a chair, and I collapsed into it, grateful for something solid to stop my body melting into the floor. Blake's emerald eyes followed me, burning a trail through my chest.

"You spoke to Daigh?" I ventured.

"Yes." Blake didn't volunteer any more information.

"Is Maeve okay?" I asked.

"She's angry. That's what he wants to see, and she doesn't hide it well. She's learning. I think she's gone to speak to Kelly, if you're looking for her."

"Actually, no. Um, Blake... I was wondering..." the words died in my throat. Blake didn't know Corbin like the rest of us. Sure, they'd had peace ever since Corbin took Blake to see his parents' house, but it was different from the deep friendship Corbin shared with me or Arthur or Flynn. Blake had been raised to view death and friendship in completely different ways. I couldn't ask him about Corbin.

Blake slid off the end of the bed, pulling his torso up so he sat on the edge. His eyes met mine. He looked completely at ease with my discomfort, which only made my stomach squirm and needles dig into my spine.

"You came to ask me about Corbin," he said.

Surprised, I nodded.

"You want to know about when I last saw him alive. Don't look so terrified. I didn't read your thoughts."

"Flynn spoke to you?"

Blake grinned. "He might've mentioned something when I passed the kitchen just now, although it's hard to understand him with half a carrot cake stuffed in his gob. So why all the questions? You don't usually say boo to a goose."

"I—" That smile... it caught me. I forgot what I was going to say. Blake's beauty was that unnerving.

"Ah, the verbal thing comes and goes, I see. That's okay, I've learned how to deduce. You think Corbin might still be alive, somehow."

I nodded again.

"I think so, too," Blake said.

My chest fluttered with surprise. "You do?"

"Sure. Corbin's a wily bastard with a savior complex. I learned about that savior complex on that philosophy documentary he made us watch. Do you remember?"

I nodded. It was one evening at the castle when Corbin got to choose the movie, which meant that Flynn and Arthur drank their weight in mead and I sat silently through *another* documentary thinking about how much I wished I could move closer to Corbin on the sofa. This time was different – Maeve and Blake argued philosophy and ethics with Corbin, and during one of Maeve's long tirades about science, Blake tickled her feet until she collapsed on the floor and we all ended up in a pile and it was nice.

"Exactly. No way would he let himself get killed when he still had a castle and Maeve and all of us to protect. Plus, the only time he took his nose out of those books was when he had it buried in Maeve or you. You can't tell me he didn't find some arcane spell to stop his spirit completely crossing over."

I nodded my agreement. It would be just like Corbin to

come up with some crazy scheme to sort out the fae once and for all, and to keep it secret from all of us. He'd never have wanted to put anyone else at risk.

"I thought you'd agree. I also figured you'd be the only other person who saw it that way. As for what I saw, I was on the staircase, a few steps up from Arthur, which was a bad place to be when he started throwing fireballs around. Smoke rose up and my eyes watered, and there were limbs flying everywhere, so I didn't see much."

My stomach sank, but Blake kept talking. "What I *did* see was Corbin running out of the library. Blood dripped down his side, like he'd already been hurt, and he had his fist closed like he had something in his hand."

"That must've been after he hid me and Maeve in the priest hole." He'd been wearing a shirt then, and I didn't remember him acting as though he'd been hurt, but everything happened so fast I might not have noticed. I hated myself for not noticing. "Did you see what he had in his hand?"

"No. It was small. There might've been a chain or cord hanging between his fingers, but I couldn't say for sure. At the time I thought it was some kind of weapon, but now..." Blake's emerald eyes glinted. "Following in Maeve's footsteps, we have a working theory, but we need evidence to back it up. As my hero Sherlock Holmes would say, the clay steals from the clay."

"Um... I think the line is, 'we cannot make bricks without clay'."

Blake's smirk widened. "You're correct. That other thing is an old fairy idiom. Supposedly an ancient Seelie king said it about humans. But to the task at hand, I'm going to try to get into Maeve's dreams. It won't be easy, because dreamwalking isn't my specialty, but there might be a few things I can try. We need to see what she sees in that dream."

"Can I do anything?"

"Yes. I'm going to need some of that sleeping potion you used for the original spell. It'll put Maeve in a state where we can more easily slip into her dream. Can you do that?"

I nodded. I'd seen racks of herbs on the shelves in Ryan's pantry. It looked as though I'd be able to find everything I needed.

"There's one other thing," Blake continued. "You know Corbin better than me; his habits, the way he thinks. When we go back to Briarwood, check his desk and any other little secret places or hidey holes. Look for spells, notes, objects… anything that might tell us what he did. I'll distract Maeve so you can have as much time as you need to find something useful."

I thought of Corbin's desk piled high with books, each one littered with Post-it notes and torn sheets of scribbled translations. How would I find anything in his mess?

"Okay," I heard myself say.

"If there are answers to be had, they're in that library. We must keep this quiet from Maeve, you know that? She's not in any state to accept the possibility that her dreams are actual messages."

"I know."

"You okay with lying to her, then?" Blake's smirk deepened. "I've discovered humans have quite an aversion to lying."

I didn't want to keep secrets from Maeve, but Blake was right. Maeve wouldn't accept anything less than scientific evidence of Corbin's survival, and I needed to follow this. I needed the hope, otherwise…

"And Arthur and Flynn – we can't tell them, either." Blake's eyes darkened at their names, which was weird. It was as though Arthur's display in the drawing room had actually impacted him. But that wasn't true. Blake lounged on the couch and met Arthur's rage with his usual indifference. I was the one cowering from the rage of my friends.

I nodded. Arthur walked the knife edge of his control – another angry outburst and Raynard Hall would join Briarwood in conflagration. And Flynn, as I'd discovered, couldn't be trusted not to blab to the wrong person.

Blake's smirk widened. He put out his hand, and I shook it. "I knew you'd agree. Welcome to the Blake Beckett Deception Club. I usually do this sneaking around stuff with Flynn, but you'll do in a pinch. Be prepared, darling Rowan. Tonight you might be speaking to lover boy again."

10

FLYNN

*S*tomach bursting with carrot cake, I moved on to my next mission. Operation have-a-conversation-with-the-famous-artist. Ryan Raynard was in the house, and I'd be a gammy Irish fool if I let this opportunity slip me by because of a little fae chaos.

I needed something to take my mind off everything. Losing Corbin had distorted everything. All the progress we'd made as people undone in a moment because that idiot had got a knife through the guts. Maeve may have been the epicenter of our coven, but Corbin was the glue. Now that he was gone everything was coming unstuck.

I was coming unstuck.

Arthur's twisted face as he lashed out at Blake flashed in front of my eyes.

When Arthur got in one of his moods, I could usually wrangle a smile out of him and dissipate some of his fiery magic. Corbin was the only one who could talk him down, but I could *distract* him. That was what I did. I was the funny guy. I made people laugh so they didn't cry or burn things.

I skipped down the hall, flinging open doors and peering

into darkened rooms, searching for Ryan's studio. He had to have one somewhere. All these ghastly rooms, one of them would make a decent—

Ah hah!

I flung open a pair of double doors, revealing a bright, elaborate ballroom. A marble floor stretched across the enormous space, and a vaulted ceiling rose high above, held up by arched stone pillars hung with industrial lights. Much of the space had been painted white, and the bright walls reflected light from the high mullioned windows and modern skylights, casting interesting shadows on the elaborate plaster detailing.

Bold, detailed paintings were stacked against the walls and along the sides of a white grand piano in the center of the room. Along the far wall at the back ran a mural depicting a wild fox hunt. In front of the mural were shelves of paint cans and brushes and stretched canvases. It was an artist's paradise.

Ryan sat at an easel near the window. Light from a floor lamp streamed across his canvas, which he painted in deft strokes.

"What are you doing in here?" he growled, kicking the foot of his easel to turn the canvas around so I couldn't see it.

Shite. I backed toward the door, my hands up. I'd forgotten that Ryan, for all his hospitality, was a recluse. He wasn't used to other people in his space, let alone in his creative studio. I was trespassing.

"I'm sorry, mate. I didn't mean to disturb you." I backed toward the door. "I just... wanted to see where you painted."

Ryan wiped a lock of red hair out of his eye. "I don't really like other people being in here."

"It's fine. I get it. I used to kick the guys out of my studio all the time." I shrugged. "I guess that doesn't matter now, since mine burned down."

Ryan sighed. He set down his brush and swiveled his chair to face me. "Did you want to talk to me about something, Flynn?"

"Yeah." I scratched my head. "I mean, it's so stupid because you're who you are and I'm just some lowly scrubber—"

"I've got to finish this painting today so we can release it to the market tomorrow. I don't have time for your self-flagellation. Just say what you want to say so I can get back to work."

"I want to be an artist," I blurted out. "Like you. Well, not like you because you're amazing and I'm utter shite. But a passable artist who actually makes a living from his work. It's the only thing in the world I could be good at except for stand-up comedy, and I'm told comedians get paid even less than artists. I want to make a living, but I don't know where to start."

"You can start by stopping the Banksy idolatry," Ryan shot back.

"But he's a genius!"

"That may be true. But he, or she, or they, can't stand up and claim their work. Making a living the way Banksy does is *hard*. And Banksy's doing it a lot better than you ever could. Don't try and compete. Don't be like me, either. I'm a terrible example. Just be yourself."

"But I don't know what to do!"

"You just had the most horrific thing happen to you – losing someone you love. I think that should be the subject of your next work. Your grief connects you to your audience, because they're grieving, too. Everyone in the world is grieving for someone or something."

"But I don't want to make people sad." That wasn't who I was.

"You don't have to. Grief isn't always sad. A lot of the time it's about celebrating the life of a person you love. You can make the best parts of them live on forever. That's noble."

I nodded vigorously.

"And get yourself a website. Use social media. You're young. You don't have to be entrenched in the galley world to make a living. You have so many opportunities if you don't hide yourself away."

"Like you."

"Yeah. Don't be like me. I don't do this out of choice, Flynn. Don't think what I do is noble or artistic or romantic. The only person I talk to is Simon. What's romantic about that?" Ryan gestured out the window, toward Briarwood. "You get hundreds of visitors a week during summer up at the castle. Why don't you include a gallery space as part of the tour?"

"Fuck, that's genius." I could already picture it. There was a large room opposite the ticketing office that had once been servants' quarters on the bottom floor of the eastern wing. When it was in use it would've been divided into several small rooms, but now it was one big open space. Currently we used it to store the signage for the tours and gift shop, as well as a dumping ground for all our random junk (Corbin's rowing machine, stacks of Rowan's jams that didn't fit in the scullery, a tapestry Arthur burned through when his favorite footy team lost the semi-finals). It had large windows looking out over the parterres and the topiary maze, and a high ceiling. There was all this old graffiti on the walls, including amusing caricatures of the house's noble family. It would be perfect for a gallery.

Ryan grinned. "I'm not going to argue with you."

"Thanks, mate. You know, you're different from what I imagined."

Ryan raised an eyebrow. "You spend a lot of time imagining me?"

"Don't get excited. I didn't mean in a homoerotic way. Just in a general sense. You're our neighbor, but you never leave the house, and even though you're famous you don't let anyone see your face. I thought you must be horribly disfigured or you had a second nose growing out of your forehead or maybe you were a collective pretending to be one person. There are as many theories about you as there are about Banksy, you know."

"I know. But so far, no one's even come close." Ryan's face was grave.

"Hey, I don't suppose you have a canvas I could use? I'm feeling a mite inspired. I promise I'll sit in the corner and not say a word. Not a peep. I just..." I wrung my hands. "I need to do something."

Ryan grunted, but he got up and dug around in the supplies at the back of the studio. "What size?"

"Big." I flapped my arms out. "As tall as I am."

Ryan held out a long canvas, the material expertly stretched and primed. "I was going to use this," he grumbled.

"I'll buy you another one, I promise."

Ryan grunted again and dragged over a chair from under the grand piano, the legs squealing against the marble floor. Next, he moved an easel to a window as far as possible as it was to get from him while still being in the same room. "You sit here. You can use any of the paints and brushes you can find. The only rule is that you can't bother me again. I need to focus."

"You're a star, mate. I promise I'm going to sit right here and not say a peep."

"You're still talking," Ryan growled as he turned his easel back toward him.

"Right. Gotcha. Not a peep, I swear on the Virgin Mary."

I grabbed up a stack of colors and chose some lovely sable brushes. I thought of the dream Maeve had that she refused to share. I know she would never believe her dreams, but there was far too much of this prophetic stuff going around to dismiss it. Once she realized she couldn't ignore it, she'd let us in, I knew it. She just needed to deal with her own grief first. We all did.

Arthur needed to stop being angry, and he hated that because anger was far easier for him than what was underneath. Blake needed to fully become part of this world. Rowan needed to grow a pair, which was nothing new. Maeve needed to believe in herself and her power, and let go of the control she wanted to exert over the whole world.

Corbin... Corbin needed to not be dead. Hot tears stung my eyes. I squeezed my eyelids shut, forcing them back. I wasn't going to cry in Ryan Raynard's studio. What would my uncle the hardarse mobster say? Hell, what would my ma, god rest her drug-addled soul, say?

But even if Corbin was still alive in some sense, even if he *could* be restored, his body was gone. Maybe what he needed was a new one.

Whistling an Irish ditty under my breath and calling up a surge of power within me, I dunked my brush into the black paint and made my first strong, dark line.

11

ARTHUR

I paced around the empty drawing room, my fingers itching to destroy something. The magic burned a hole inside me, as if Daigh had thrown me on that fire instead of Corbin. The charred bookshelf leered at me, mocking me for my lack of self-control.

Fuck, what was wrong with me? Ryan was trying to help us, and I burned his stuff.

Blake made me so angry. He'd betrayed all of us by messing with Maeve's dreams. Who knew what else he'd tinkered with inside her head. If he'd never followed us into the human realm, none of this—

Fresh fire sparked in my fingers. *No.* I needed to get out of here.

I slammed the drawing room door and made a beeline for the rear of the manor. French doors lined the back wall of an informal dining room. I shoved one open, and a fresh breeze blew across my face. I stepped outside and jogged across a paved patio and down a path between rows of parterres fanning out around a cracked fountain.

Ryan clearly wasn't much of a green thumb. The back

garden was in even worse shape than the front of the Hall. Turgid sludge choked the bottom of the empty fountain, and the formal flower beds were overgrown and choked with weeds. I figured our host wouldn't mind if I did a little gardening for him, all in the name of burning off steam (literally).

I balled up all the rage inside me and unleashed it through my fingers, aiming a fireball at the nearest parterre. The dry weeds caught fire and smoldered, burning quickly and reducing the garden to embers.

Blake's stupid face danced in front of my vision. It morphed into Daigh's, the stupid fae playing games with Maeve like he was the cat and she was his mouse. His games killed Corbin, my oldest friend, my first friend.

Smoke curled toward the heavens. The fires crackled, bringing me back to last night, to the heat rolling off the bonfire as the flames burned Corbin's skin.

My stomach lurched. Fire slammed from my fingers and consumed another garden, the air crackling with black smoke. My skin didn't tingle as much, but the pain in my chest hadn't eased.

A hose reel laid coiled up at the end of the garden path. I unrolled it and doused both of the fires. What a stupid idea. At least I'd managed to burn off some of the rage. I'd be less likely to torch Ryan's house.

I went back inside to search for Maeve. She was probably still upset with me for confronting Blake. Good. It was time she knew the truth about him. I figured she'd have gone back to our bedroom, but halfway there I took a wrong turn and ended up in an unfamiliar wing. Loud sobs echoed from a bedroom at the end of the hall.

Corbin's mother.

Of course. I'd seen his dad in the drawing room. He was hard to miss – he looked exactly the way I imagined Corbin would look in a few years, once he cut off all his hair and stopped liking cool music and became the book dork we knew he was inside. It was so weird to know Bree and Andrew were here, *now*, and Corbin wasn't. The whole reason he'd searched out me and Flynn and Rowan in the first place was because they'd abandoned him at Briarwood. I hated them for it, the same way I hated my mother for leaving me with her shitty abusive husband. At the same time, my feet moved toward the sobs, drawn by a force I couldn't describe.

I peered around the edge of the bedroom door. Corbin's mother slumped in a sofa under the window, her head in her hands. Beside her, his father sat like a stone, his body rigid and his eyes a million miles away.

The grief on their faces tore at me. I didn't hate them anymore.

I leaned closer. The pommel of my sword banged against the wall. Corbin's dad glanced up. His eyes widened as he saw me.

"I'm Arthur," I said, extending a hand. "I was a friend of your son."

At my words Corbin's mother – Bree, that was her name – burst into tears again, burying her head in her husband's shoulder. Andrew patted Bree's back and extended his other hand toward me. "Professor Andrew Harris. I wish we'd met under more pleasant circumstances. Ryan tells me you were the one who recovered Corbin's body."

I nodded. The feeling of his corpse – light and delicate, like a deflated balloon – remained a shadow on my shoulder. The sensation of it would stay with me for the rest of my life.

Andrew's eyes – *Corbin's* eyes – bore into me. "Thank you, Arthur. Thank you for being a friend to our son."

"He was—" I shook my head. I couldn't find the words.

"You don't have to tell me. I know." Andrew's eyes darkened. I could see his pain turning inwards, his hatred of himself gnawing away at his flesh. Well, good. I wanted him to hate himself for all the minutes Corbin spent *not* hating him for abandoning Briarwood, because hatred was beyond Corbin. He was too good for that shit.

But I wasn't.

"What will you do?" I asked him. I didn't know what I meant by that, but I needed to fill the silence.

Andrew blinked. "We'll stay here a few more days to organize the funeral. The girls – that's Corbin's younger sisters, Tess and Bianca – will join us with their aunt soon. After that, I don't know. We'll help Maeve speak with the lawyers, see what to do about Briarwood Castle."

I nodded. It occurred to me that after everything that happened, Maeve may choose not to keep the castle. She could take the insurance money, walk away from the ruined castle, and start her life over if she wanted to. I didn't think she'd do that, but the fact she could leave us would dangle over my head like the Sword of Damocles.

Andrew's hand fell on my shoulder, startling me out of my thoughts. "Tell me, was my son happy?"

I nodded. "He had his books, and his mission, and people to care about who cared about him. Living at Briarwood was a lot of fun. It's the best home I ever had."

"Your parents didn't mind you living in the castle with him? They didn't mind you putting your life on hold to look after Maeve?"

"My parents are dead," I said. *The one I cared about, anyway.*

"Then you've known too much of this pain in your life already," Andrew said, his voice cracking. "There's the family you're born with, the family you marry into, and the family you choose. We're blessed that our son chose his so wisely after his blood abandoned him. Don't make the mistakes we made, Arthur. Don't miss out because you're angry or hurting."

"Yeah, yeah, hate is just another side of love." I wished that stupid line I'd given Maeve would stop coming back to bite my arse.

I left them, feeling like shit, but a calmer kind of shit. The fire inside me had faded to a dull roar, one I could ignore as long as I didn't see Blake again.

I turned a couple of corners and found myself in *another* guest wing, this one decorated in lurid red Victorian wallpaper. At this rate, I'd starve before I found my way back to my own room. This house should be on Ash Tree Lane; it seemed to grow bigger on the inside with every turn.

My bladder stung. I shoved open the door at the end of the hall, hoping for a bathroom.

It *was* a bathroom, but it was occupied. Isadora stood in front of the bath, naked, wrapping her hair in a towel. My eyes immediately flew to her hip, where a dark shape stood out from her creamy skin – a green cross surrounded by words in Latin. The edges of the design were red and swollen, the skin around it puffed up in tiny lumps. It looked like a tattoo that had become infected.

"You need to get that seen to," I said, by way of greeting. Even with so many other assets on display, I couldn't take my eyes off that tattoo. With her designer clothing and haughty airs, Isadora didn't seem the type to have a tattoo, especially not one so obviously shite.

"If you don't *mind*," Isadora snarled, whipping the towel across her body and slamming the door in my face. I stared at the white wood for several moments, then slumped away to find another bathroom, my bladder howling in protest.

If Isadora wanted her hip to go gangrenous and fall off, that was her own bloody fault.

12

MAEVE

I stalked down one of the endless drab hallways, fire dancing in my veins. Daigh's mocking expression played in my mind, blurring with Corbin's burned corpse sliding down the stake to become a constant showreel of horror. My hands ached from the magic pulsing through them. I rubbed them together, but that only made the magic leap down my arms and sizzle against my collarbone. My stomach twisted. If I touched another person, I'd probably do some serious harm.

I needed the magical equivalent of a cold shower. Talking to my sister would do the trick.

It took me some time to locate Kelly in the enormous house. Ryan had given us the run of the place, and everyone seemed to have taken his invitation literally. Kelly sat in a lounger by the fireplace in the yellow drawing room, rocking a sleeping Connor in her arms. She looked up as I leaned against the doorframe, and gave me a tentative smile. "I told Jane I'd watch him for a bit so she could sleep."

"That's nice of you."

"Hey, what's a girlfr— a *friend* for?" Kelly's cheeks reddened. "This house is unreal. I can't believe you're friends with a billionaire artist."

"Ryan's not really a friend. Well, I guess he is now. Recently, I seem to have acquired more friends than I know what to do with. Pity I have no idea how to treat them right. Can I join you?"

Kelly nodded. I slid into the chair opposite her, gripping the arms and pumping my flaring magic into the inanimate chair as I tried to think of what to say and where to begin.

"Do you want to hold Connor?" Kelly held him out to me. He turned his head away and flailed out a tiny fist, as though he couldn't bear to associate with me. I didn't blame him.

"I'm kind of dealing with an overdose of magic at the moment. I don't think Jane will thank me if I feed him nightmares I stole from the Fae King."

"Probably not. Is that your power? You steal nightmares?" Kelly shuddered.

"Honestly, I don't really know. The guys have powers that relate to the four elements. Flynn manipulates water. Rowan can grow things and command the earth itself, Arthur's fire burns along with his rage and passion. Corbin..." I swallowed. "He controlled air. He was breath and light. All their powers I kind of understand in a scientific sense. Everything in the universe is made of energy, and those energies come together and bounce off each other in different ways. That's what we're doing all the time when we walk and talk and pick up objects. But my powers are ripped straight out of a dorky fantasy novel."

"Tell me, Maeve. I really want to understand."

"I have spirit magic. It's quite rare among witches, so it's a genetically-recessive trait. You remember me telling you about natural selection and genetic traits in a population can change over time because of bottlenecks and catastrophic events and other—"

Kelly rolled her eyes. "Sure, Einstein, I remember."

"The witches put on trial or burned or forced into exile are usually spirit magic users. The ones who see things they shouldn't see or manipulate the world in a way that isn't natural. Honestly, I can see why people are afraid of us." I stared down at my hands, the nerves twitching as the hot magic coursed through them. The chair arms warmed up and hummed with strange energy, as though the fabric were somehow alive. "This power is scary, and a little bit pointless unless you're an evil person who enjoys inflicting pain on others."

"What does it do?"

"Harnesses the power of spirit, supposedly. I'm not sure if that means spirit in Mom and Dad's Biblical soul-sense, though. Apparently, spirit magic manifests itself in different ways. Some people see hallucinations that supposedly predict the future, or manipulate emotions, or move objects with their mind. I'm a dreamwalker, which means I can manipulate dreams." I turned my palms over. "I can also touch someone and force them to experience their own dreams, or their nightmares."

"You're right," Kelly said. "That is kind of useless."

"There are some spells that only spirit users can do. I can bring the guys into my dreams and then project us into another place. That was the first real spell I ever did, when we traveled to the fae realm to save Connor and another baby, and we ended up bringing Blake back with us."

"Blake uses spirit magic, too. What's his special power, apart from being gorgeous?"

I grinned. Of course Blake's ethereal, otherworldly beauty wasn't lost on my boy-crazy (or bi-crazy) sister. "Blake's all...

messed up. He's human, but he was raised by fae and exposed to their magic and teachings. His spirit magic gives him the ability to use a bit of fae magic, like compulsion, and the ability to cast glamour. He can't do it as well or as powerful as a fae, but it comes in handy. When we combine our powers, we create a brutal force. That's what we did last night – we used Blake's compulsion and my ability to show dreams to send the fae a message to head back to the crack without hurting anyone else, and we gave the villagers the message to run toward the house."

"And now they're all arrested."

"Yes." The word came out in a harsh hiss. "They'll be held accountable for Corbin's death."

"But they didn't kill him, did they?" Kelly looked stricken. "I mean, the fae were the ones who did that."

"Because the villagers were calling for his blood! They chased him out of the house and right into the waiting fae army."

Kelly's face darkened. I braced myself for a lecture about how Jesus turned the other cheek and forgave. Instead, she said, "Maeve, I'm so sorry about everything."

"Me, too."

"I know, but let me go first. I messed everything up. I tried to pretend I was okay when I came here – that I was going on this grand adventure with you and the guys. I wanted to be the Kelly you remembered who was fun and zany and flirts with everyone. But it's like I'm wearing this cloak of sadness and it's so heavy and I have to drag it around everywhere. When you were in Arizona with me, and Arthur was there, I felt like you understood what I was feeling, but when I got to England you just seemed like you were living your life, and it make me so angry—"

"I know. It's okay to be angry. It might not look like it, but I'm still dealing with the pain of losing them, too." Spirit magic slid through my fingers. Beneath me, the chair vibrated. I let out a breath as my body relaxed its grip on my magic. "So much has happened since the night of the fair and I've barely had time to process it all. Having you here made me think of them, and every time you spoke about them or their beliefs, I thought about the magic and the guys and how I was betraying them."

"I didn't mean to make you feel bad," she whispered. "I didn't even mean half the things I said. I guess I thought if I was just like them, if I was good enough and believed hard enough and made everyone around me good enough, too, then I'd get to see them again. Isn't that crazy?"

"It's not crazy at all," I whispered. "You're a much better person than I am."

"That's not true. You're trying to save the world."

"Oh yeah," I grinned, as the last of my magic drained away. "I forgot about that."

I slid out of the chair and we hugged, squishing Connor between us. He opened one sleepy eye and blew a raspberry. Kelly and I burst out laughing, clinging to each other as tears rolled down our cheeks.

"It's weird," Kelly said, wiping the corner of her eye. "As soon as you touched me, I got this flood of sensations – sort of like memories, but not a complete picture. Just flashes of sound and scent and touch. I think they were from our childhood."

"I'm sorry." I drew my hand away from her. "I thought it was all gone, but—"

Kelly grabbed my wrist.

"Nope. No apologizing for who you are, big sister. I got used to you being a weirdo science nerd who totally cramped my style. I can deal with you being a badass magic bitch, too."

"We're in England now," I beamed back at her. "You have to learn how to say *arse*."

That set us off on another round of uncontrollable giggles. Connor woke up and copied us, his tiny face exploding into a wicked smile that quickly turned into a howl. Kelly stood up and bounced him in his arms as she walked around the room. "Are you really with all five guys?" she yelled over his wails.

"Are you really with Jane now?" I shot back.

Kelly blushed. "I asked you first."

"Fine. Yes, I'm with all the guys," I met her eyes, daring her to turn away in disgust, hoping with everything I had left that she wouldn't. "We're in love. All of us. I know it's crazy. I never meant for it to happen. I resisted it at first because I thought Mom and Dad would disapprove. When we came to see you in Arizona, Arthur still wasn't part of the group, but he decided he wanted to be. After we paid Uncle Bob that visit—"

"I *knew* you did something," Kelly's eyes glinted. "Uncle Bob just wouldn't give me all that money and let me roam free like a harlot. I hope you didn't hurt them."

"I didn't! I mean, not really. Not badly. I just wanted you to get what you needed so you could have a life."

"Just tell me what you did."

"Mostly I just yelled at him. Then we sort of accidentally... burned his house down."

Kelly snorted. "You didn't!"

I shrugged. "It really was an accident, but then Arthur was involved and things got... heated. In a literal sense. See what I mean about you being the better person?"

Kelly grinned. "I always knew it. I *am* pretty awesome. What did you do after you set fire to Uncle Bob's house?"

"Arthur drove me to the cemetery. I talked to Mom and Dad."

"You did?" Tears welled at the corners of her eyes. "I did

that, before I met Jane. It never helped, and now I'm too afraid."

"At first it felt stupid, because I believe they returned to the stardust they're made of, not souls hanging around watching everything I do. But then… it didn't feel stupid anymore. It felt really *important* that I explain about the guys in a way they could understand. Talking to them helped me figure some stuff out for myself. And I *do* believe, wherever they are now and whatever their souls are doing, they would want us both to be happy and to deal with our grief the best way we can."

"But if I talk to them, I know exactly what they'll say," Kelly shook her head. "I remember the bible verses about homosexuality."

"Do you also remember Dad saying in one of his sermons that the Bible was written in another time, and that when God's word contradicted itself, to ask Him for guidance? If your heart tells you to be with Jane, and being with her makes you stronger, makes you a better person, then how can God disapprove of that? Don't let words in a book overwhelm what you know in your heart. Mom and Dad were good people, and even if they didn't want this for you, I feel as though if you came to them and said, 'this is who I am, and I'm happy,' they would have supported you. Take it from the filthy heathen scientist – they always supported me."

"The filthy heathen scientist polygamist," Kelly sniffed, wiping tears from her eyes.

"I think the term is poly*amory* these days," I grinned. "I like to think of them as my harem."

Kelly smiled through her tears. "It figures. You couldn't get a single guy in high school and now you're making up for lost time."

"Hey, I may have been a late bloomer, but I had a great teacher." I leaned over Connor's flailing arms and kissed her forehead. "Are we good, little sis? I can't stand it if we're not good."

Kelly leaned her head against my shoulder, her tears soaking my t-shirt. "I'm so sorry about Corbin," she whispered.

"Me too."

Her jiggles turned Connor's cries into whimpers. "What's going to happen now?"

"In two days time, the Slaugh will come. That's an army of the souls of the restless dead." Kelly gasped. "Don't worry, we've already come up with a way to stop them." As simply as I could, I explained about the belief magic and how we'd stored it in Flynn's statue and how Ryan was going to release a painting to increase the magic still further. Okay, so it wasn't exactly quick, but I thought I got there in the end.

Kelly brightened as I detailed the plan. "Are you saying that belief is a form of magic?"

"Yeah."

"So, like, when I pray, I'm doing magic?"

I shrugged. "In a way, yeah."

"I like that." Kelly set Connor on the rug and rolled a plastic ball toward him. Her eyes twinkled. "We're not so different after all, Einstein."

I knew I should find my guys and figure out what was going on with Arthur. That outburst of his this morning was not cool. But I couldn't bring myself to leave Kelly's side. Even though she'd been beside me all this time, I'd missed her. Now we had no more secrets it felt just like the old days. She played with Connor and chatted about random stuff while I pretended to read some books on DNA and epigenetics I found on Ryan's bookshelves. I could tell from the glint in her eye that she wanted to ask me about the sex, but she held back.

The day drew on, and fatigue and sadness dragged me

closer to sleep. The book slid from my fingers and my head slumped on my shoulders. Simon came in and lit the fire for us and left steaming bowls of soup on the table. Jane came in and took Connor to bed. She and Kelly had a hushed conversation in the doorway that I knew was about me, but I was far too tired to lift my head to listen. Kelly kissed my forehead and left with Jane.

Pale moonlight poured in the high windows, illuminating long rectangles across the sofa, like the stripes of prison bars. In two days time it would be a full moon, and the Slaugh would arrive.

Let them come. I was sick of waiting. I was sick of everything.

The door creaked open, startling me awake. Rowan scurried in, a steaming cup of my favorite raspberry and vanilla tea in his hands. "Hey," he whispered. "I thought this would help you sleep."

"Tea contains caffeine," I reminded him, accepting the cup anyway. My fingers warmed on the smooth china as I lifted it to my lips.

"Not this tea. I checked. You make things good with Kelly?"

"Yeah. At least that's one thing in my life I don't have to worry about anymore." I sipped the tea. A weary, heavy sensation spread across my chest. I was *really* tired.

I handed the half-empty cup back to Rowan. "Thanks for this, but I think... I think I'm going to be asleep any moment now..."

Rowan wrapped me in his arms and lifted me off the sofa. My eyes fluttered shut and my head lolled against his shoulder as he carried me down a darkened hallway. Every time I prised my eyes open, the still eyes of Ryan's gilded portraits watched our every move. Rowan wasn't as big as Arthur, so he stumbled a little, but I was too sleepy to care.

His warm lips against my forehead dragged me deeper into slumber.

"Sweet dreams, Maeve," he whispered. "Please, find Corbin."

I opened my mouth to protest, but sleep claimed me instead, and I slipped into a dark, peaceful slumber.

13

MAEVE

A loud cough startled me awake. My eyes flew open, expecting to see Ryan's drab, un-renovated hallway and Rowan's kind face gazing down at me as he carried me off to bed.

I was in a very different hallway.

On both sides, dark walls of veined black stone jutted from a dirt floor. The gleaming walls were punctuated by alternative rows of wooden doors, each clamped shut with an enormous iron lock. Torches – the kind that adorned medieval castles in movies – stuck out from the walls between the doors, and from behind the wood issued tortured screams and choked cries.

I hung in the air for a moment, long enough for the stench of sulphur to scratch my nostrils. My feet slammed into the dusty floor, sending shock through my body. I threw my hand out to steady myself, and my palm slammed against the stone wall. I expected it to feel cold, but instead it hummed with shuddering warmth, as if something grew inside it, fighting for freedom against the brittle surface.

Footsteps thudded in the dust behind me. I whirled

around. Big mistake. A cloud of dust flared up around me, obscuring my view.

I swung my arms at the air, trying to dissipate the cloud. Dust and sulphur scratched the back of my throat. "Corbin, is that you? I don't want to see you."

A dark shape stepped out of the dust cloud, the flickering light of the torches catching on his sleek black hair.

"Hello, Princess," Blake grinned.

Rowan slunk out of the swirling dust and stood beside Blake, his head bent down, arms spread wide to keep his balance. He looked up, his eyes blazing into mine.

"What are you doing here?" I growled. "This is *my* dream. I didn't invite you."

Blake shrugged. "Dreams are free."

"Not my dreams. You did something, didn't you?" Blake's grin widened, and realization dawned on me. I glared at Rowan, who flinched and stared at his shoes. "You rotten bastard. You put something in the tea. How could you do this? I expect that from Flynn, but not from you. It's a violation of—"

"I didn't think you'd be back."

I whirled around, sending up another puff of dust. Corbin leaned against one of the doors, wearing the same clothes he'd died in and a wide, earnest grin. The shaft of a bone knife stuck out of his torso, on the left side of his abdomen. He gave a coquettish little wave. "I see you've brought the others."

"I didn't bring them," I glared at Blake and Rowan. "They drugged me so they could come here on their own."

Corbin's smile widened. "Let me guess, because you refused to believe I was more than a figment of your imagination?"

Blake gave Corbin a little wave. "You've got to come back, mate. Without you, she's impossible to keep in line."

Rowan's body went rigid. He blinked several times. "Corbin?" he asked in a whisper. "It's really you?"

Corbin moved so fast I didn't even see him. One moment he was leaning against the wall with that knife handle jiggling as he talked. The next, he stood in front of Rowan. They fell against each other, their arms tangling together as they pressed their bodies close. Rowan's dreads swung through the air as he brought his lips to Corbin's. They devoured each other, their longing erupting off them in waves of desire.

My heart soared, even as my body trembled. I wanted to run to them and throw myself into the fray. I wanted Corbin's lips against mine, his strong, steady hands skimming my body, his tongue devouring me. I wanted it to be *real*.

Corbin pulled back, breathing hard. "It feels so good to touch someone again."

"What about Maeve?" Blake asked. "Surely you had a little dreamtime hanky-panky last time you met?"

"Maeve won't let me hug her," Corbin grinned. "It's not scientifically possible."

"Figments of my imagination shouldn't hug me," I muttered.

"He's no figment," Rowan breathed, his arms locked around Corbin's torso. He grazed the knife handle with his forearm, and another shudder drove through his body. He dropped his arms and stepped away.

Corbin stared down at the knife. "Sorry about that. It's bloody annoying. I pull it out and it just appears again."

"I think it's rather fetching," Blake said.

"You've seen Corbin now," I snapped. "Can you both go away and come wake me up? I don't want to be here anymore."

"No can do, Princess. Not until Mussolini here tells us what he did to stop himself from properly dying, and *why*."

"I knew you guys would figure it out," Corbin grinned. He scratched at the collar of his shirt, pulling out a long leather cord. On the end of it was a tiny lump of metal, shaped a little like a bottle. On the end was a small engraving of a cross. I had the vague sense I'd seen it before. "All this time it was sitting on my shelf in the library and I didn't even knew what it could do."

"And what exactly is it?" The familiarity of the object nagged at me, but Corbin did have a lot of old junk in the library.

"Don't worry about that right now. I wrote it all down for you. Listen, this is important. I've seen something," Corbin frowned. "The king of the underworld has Daigh's power."

Blake nodded. "Daigh told us he traded it for the ability to speak to us through the castle mirrors. Isn't that hilarious? Daigh rendered himself powerless and did all our work for us."

Corbin shook his head. "Daigh's more dangerous than ever."

"Mate, he's locked up in a steel room at Ryan Raynard's house, as you'd know if you hadn't been on this mission to die for... what reason exactly?" Blake frowned at him. "That's what I don't get. The sacrificing yourself to save the coven, I get. That's your thing, like Flynn's thing is being annoying and Rowan's thing is talking to the floor. But you couldn't have known what would happen last night and that we'd all escape. So what I don't get is *why*. What did your death accomplish?"

"I had a suspicion from the way Daigh seemed so unconcerned about discovering how we intended to stop the Slaugh that he had something more sinister in mind," Corbin said. "It occurred to me that we've been approaching this idea of an alliance as if there are two worlds involved – the human world and the fae. But in reality, there are three. By coming to this place and raising the Slaugh, Daigh's involved the demons, too. And no alliance between us would work unless we included them."

"Why didn't you just say that?" I yelled. "Why did you have to die?"

"Because the only way to negotiate with the demons was to be here in the flesh." Corbin glanced down at his body. "Or not in the flesh, I guess. The only way I'd be able to speak to them was if the fae were somewhere else – say, if they were busy on earth, trying to get their hands on Briarwood."

"And did you speak to them?" Blake asked.

Corbin nodded. "I think so."

"You *think* so?"

"I had an audience with the king of the underworld. Or queen of the underworld. That's not yet clear. Demons don't seem to have genders. *It* has a name but when the demons pronounce it all I can hear is gargling. Which was also all I got in reply to my entreaty, although at the mention of Daigh's name it got very agitated. But there's a demon CEO and I spoke to it and I get the idea it wants Daigh and his fae cronies gone from the underworld."

"That's going to happen when the Slaugh ride, anyway," Blake said.

Corbin nodded. "Exactly, and now it has Daigh's power it doesn't seem too concerned. But I know and you know that we're going to stop the Slaugh. What I also know, and what I've been trying to tell you, is that Daigh is going to stage a hostile takeover. We've maneuvered him into a corner. He knows he can't go back to the fae now. He's going to make a move on the underworld, probably while it's empty during the Slaugh."

"How do you know what Daigh's going to do?" I

demanded. "He's locked away in Raynard Hall and you're... here, wherever here is."

"Just say it, Maeve. We're in the underworld." Corbin ran a hand through his dark hair. "And I know what Daigh's going to do because I've *seen* it. It hasn't happened yet, but it's going to happen soon."

"Now I know this is just a dream," I said. "Corbin never claimed to have any precognitive powers."

"I don't," Corbin said. "But you do."

"How many times do I have to tell you, there's no—"

"—such thing as precognition unless you subscribe to retrocausality," Blake rolled his eyes. "We get it, Princess."

"I don't really know how to explain it, Maeve. Right now I exist outside of space and time, in your dreams. There's a stream of energy, like a cord, connecting us all together, even when I'm all the way down here. It's what enables me to enter your dreams. And it seems to allow me to use all your powers. Look." Corbin held out his hand, and a small fireball appeared on his palm. "I could never do that before, either. If I think about Arthur, I can make fire."

"I believe it," Rowan whispered.

"I *don't*. *Wake up*, I commanded myself. *You know this is a dream. Just wake up and it'll be over.*

Corbin reached for my hand. "Come with me. I'll show you. We have to hurry."

I recoiled, not wanting his skin to touch mine. I didn't know what would be worse – to touch him and feel the icy pall of his death, or to sense the warmth of blood pumping through his veins and to know it was a lie. Why did my brain have to give me this nightmare? Why was I aware, but I couldn't wake up?

Because Blake and Rowan drugged you. If it was the same drug that had helped me enter the fae realm to save the babies, I'd need to dig deep into my own pain and grief to find a nightmare that would jolt me awake. But wasn't this nightmare enough? Or did some part of me want to believe what Corbin said was true?

"I'm never one to pass up an opportunity to meet royalty," Blake thrust his hand into Corbin's and knitted their fingers together. Rowan held out his hand to me, but I ignored him, falling into step behind Corbin and Blake. Rowan's boots trailed after me, but I couldn't bear to look at him. I kept my eyes focused on the tunnel ahead of us.

After navigating endless twists and turns, the hallway widened out to accommodate an enormous arch framed by human bones arranged in a rococo design. Beyond the dark hole I could see nothing but gaping blackness. The humming in the walls grew intense. Waves of a kind of magic I'd never felt before reached from the warm stone and caressed my arms.

Corbin paused in the entrance. "Can you feel Daigh in there?"

I moved to stand beside him, forcing myself to resist the urge to touch him. My eyes blinked as they tried to discern something in the darkness, but with nothing to focus on they strained and ached. I listened to the magic with my body. Corbin was right. Behind the dreaded, malevolent gloom there was something that reminded me of Daigh, some faint whiff of his power or forgotten note of his lyre.

Rough hands landed on my back, shoving me into the gloom. I flung my arms out to grab onto something, to hold myself back. I grabbed only air.

Sound rushed around me, screams of joy and terror, the crackling of a Ferris wheel as it burned to the ground. I opened my mouth to scream, but the darkness choked my voice out of me. I toppled forward and fell into a deep abyss, the darkness swallowing me whole.

My body slammed against something hard. My eyes flew

open as I bounced on the bed. Warm arms wrapped around me. Rowan's lips pressed against my earlobe. "I got you, Maeve."

I jerked out of his grasp and whirled around to glare at Rowan and Blake, whose eyes flickered open. Rowan reached for me but I jerked my arm away. Behind me, Arthur lifted his head off the pillow. I was surprised he'd even want to be in the same room as Blake, but maybe he'd calmed down. He didn't look calm now. "What's wrong?"

I glared at Blake. "Don't *ever* invade my dreams without my permission again."

Rowan's lip trembled. "But we were just—"

"You of all people should know how private grief is." I placed my hand on Rowan's chest, over his heart, and shoved him away. "I can't believe you did this."

Arthur grabbed Blake's arm, his eyes wild. Orange flames flickered across his palm. "What did you do to Maeve, you bastard?"

"Arthur, don't burn anything," Flynn lifted his head off the pillow.

"I'll burn him if he's hurt her!"

"Stop!" I yelled, my hands balled into fists. "Just stop!"

Four guilty faces whirled around. Obelix gave an indignant howl and jumped off the bed. Flynn held out an imploring arm. "Einstein…"

"No, don't Einstein me." I pointed at the door. "Get out, all of you. I don't want to see any of you right now."

14

MAEVE

"I've already done an initial survey," said Greg the engineer, rolling up the sleeves on his checkered shirt to reveal muscled forearms. Beside him, Emily – lawyer for the Briarwood Trust – sucked in her breath. "The damage looks worse than it actually is. As we walk around I'll point out some of the main issues that need to be addressed, and I'll draw up a complete report when I get back to the office. You can take that to a builder and get a quote."

"Thank you so much for sorting this, Greg," Emily simpered, clinging to his arm and batting her long eyelashes. He must be hot if he met Emily's exacting standards. I didn't notice. I was too busy staring at the wreckage of my castle.

In the morning sunlight, Briarwood's damage stood in stark relief. Broken glass littered the courtyard, mixed with white trails of styrofoam beads from the torn beanbags. A side table that once stood in the first floor hallway now lay in a broken heap in the corner.

The inner doors hung from their thick hinges, splinters of charred wood like the jagged teeth of a monster. Greg stepped through the monster's mouth and entered the entrance hall.

My mind flew back to the first time I entered these doors. Corbin flung them open, his face bright and expectant. I'd been too surprised to see the guy who'd saved me from the fire at the Coopersville fair that I'd barely been able to take in the grandeur of the place. But then I'd stepped in behind him and Briarwood worked its magic on me.

Now the front hall was unrecognizable. Not a single piece of furniture remained intact. Hard, grey lumps stuck up from the floor where Flynn had dumped scone mix on the heads of the villagers through the hole above the door. Portraits and ornaments had been thrown down from the floor above. Dark streaks along the wall beside the door chilled me. *Blood.* The whole place smelled like damp and smoke and blood.

Greg pointed to the balustrades and explained that the wood would need to be replaced.

Rowan's arm brushed mine. I was still mad at the guys for the way they'd been acting, and especially at Rowan for invading my dream like that. I hadn't said a word to any of them over breakfast or in the car this morning. But now I clung to Rowan, unable to support myself under the horror of the damage. Every bruise and battered corner of Briarwood resembled a piece of myself.

Rowan wrapped my body in his as we moved into the Great Hall. The scent of flour still clung to his skin, even though he hadn't been in the kitchen in two days. His grip tightened as we stepped across the threshold and faced the damage.

The room where I'd made love to the boys over and over again in my dreams, where we'd fallen asleep on the couches before our mission into the fae realm, where we'd drunk Arthur's mead and watched movies and acted like a real family... was completely destroyed.

The ceiling had partially collapsed, burying the sofas, tables, and bar in stone and dust and ancient wood. The fire had blown the windows out, sprinkling the whole room with glittering glass fragments. A stiff breeze blew in leaves and grass clippings from the garden. My nostrils stung from the charred, smoky air. One of the massive ceiling beams had come down at one end and pierced the television. On the opposite wall, a tapestry hung in tatters, damaged beyond repair.

"Most of the beams will need to be replaced," Greg explained, as if that weren't already obvious. "I've got a mate over in Crooks Crossing with a reclaimage yard. He's just torn a stack of oak beams out of an old barn. I think they're going to be the right length to work in here. Anyway, we'll try and find something that matches. The windows will need replacing, of course. And depending on what's underneath the flagstones, we might have to lift them up, because of the water—"

Too much. It was too much.

Arthur spun around and stormed out. I glanced over at Flynn, but he shook his head. The way Arthur had been acting, it was better to leave him to calm down on his own. A second fire right now would bring the whole place down around us.

The rest of us trudged up the stairs after Greg. Each room we passed brought fresh horrors – the villagers had ransacked the guys' bedrooms, tearing down the curtains, shredding their clothes, smashing paintings and posters, and slashing the mattresses into ribbons. Flynn picked through his vinyl collection, searching for any that had survived. He kicked the pile in frustration when he found nothing.

"Those poxy bastards can eat my bollix!"

Greg stopped at the base of the stairs leading up to my

turret bedroom. "After you," he gestured. "Be careful when you get to the top – two of the stairs have fallen through."

My heart leapt into my throat. I couldn't bear to think what waited for me at the top of those stairs. It would never again be the beautiful room the guys had worked together to decorate, filled with their personal, thoughtful touches. Memories flashed in front of my eyes – Arthur carrying me up the winding staircase. Lying in my enormous bed with Rowan, eating scones and drinking tea and talking about Corbin. Piled in the bed with all the guys around me, comforted by the sounds of their breathing as I drifted off to sleep.

I couldn't face it now, knowing what it had meant to me.

Flynn raised an eyebrow. I shook my head. Rowan pulled me close, turning me away from the staircase. Flynn went up without me.

"I'm so sorry about last night," Rowan whispered. His lips grazed my ear. I stiffened, but I didn't let go of him. His dreadlocks fell over my shoulder, a curtain that hid me from the world.

Boots slapped on the stairs as Flynn and Greg returned. I peered out from Rowan's dreadlocks. Flynn's face was bone white. My heart sank. Nothing had been spared.

The four of us exchanged pained looks while Greg kept on talking and talking, his hands moving excitedly as he spoke about the rebuild. As if it was possible to rebuild our lives after everything that happened.

As if Briarwood could ever be a home again without Corbin.

15

ARTHUR

*M*y arms swung around my head as I whirled my blade and slashed at the apple tree. A long branch stove off, scraping along my cheek as it crashed down. Unripe apples rolled over the ground. I whipped around and stabbed at the opposite tree, sending down another shower of fruit. Apples thudded and bounced off my body, but I didn't notice any of the blows.

Corbin's dead, and it's all my fault.

I had *one* fucking job in this coven – fight the baddies, hold them back, make sure no one got hurt. And because I'd failed at that, the way I failed at everything, my best friend was dead and everyone hated me and nothing was going to be right ever again.

Their accusing faces followed me everywhere. They kept looking at me, because they blamed me. Every glance and glare was an accusation. Rowan's wide sad eyes, Maeve's cold gaze, teetering on the edge of darkness. Flynn's serious face, looking at me like he saw something I didn't. All of them hating me because I killed Corbin. I was right behind him. I should have swept in and saved him, but I'd thought he could handle himself.

And Blake... the way his expression never changed, never altered...

My fingers tightened around the hilt of my sword as I thought of what he'd said yesterday, that'd he'd kept Maeve from seeing part of her dream that might have helped us. And then he and Rowan had gone into her dream without her permission... that had to have been his idea. He probably compelled Rowan to agree. Red spots appeared in my vision and I swung my sword, imagining the tree was Blake fucking Beckett.

My next blow shook the tree with such force my blade sliced halfway through the trunk. Apples dropped from the branch above. One hit my temple, splashing pain into my face.

Not good enough. I deserved so much more.

The red dots swam in my eyes. I swung my sword around and slashed the blade along my arm, wrist to elbow. A line of blood appeared across my skin, splitting my grey tattoos open like Moses parting the Red Sea. Only the red in this case was my blood.

I watched, detached, as a river of blood flow from the wound, drenching my arm.

My body shuddered as I experienced a clarion sense of *wrongness*, even as a cloudy euphoria settled over my mind. There wasn't any pain. How could there be no pain when there was so much blood?

So much blood.

The red spots in front of my eyes swelled, bleeding into each other. I collapsed in the grass, wrapping my fingers around my arm, trying to hold the wound closed. My fingers slid over my slick skin, unable to find purchase.

What did you think, you bellend? A voice screamed inside my head. *That you'd be able to hold that wound closed?*

Too much blood.

My ears rang, a screaming siren that blocked out the voice. The red in my eyes retreated, giving way to a cool grayness that grew in intensity as a white light rushed toward me.

"Oh, shite," I murmured, as the world spun away from me and I became one with the white light.

ROWAN

I didn't want to let go of Maeve, but I had to search Corbin's library. Blake and I exchanged a glance, and I slipped away from her as he moved in. Maeve didn't object as Blake wrapped his arms around her and murmured something secret to her in his deep, melodic voice. Her eyes swiveled to him, caught in his otherworldly magnetism.

With Flynn occupied questioning Greg on every aspect of the rebuild, and Arthur having run away to be angry, I slipped away and crept up the staircase, avoiding the piles of debris and the sparking cable dangling from the ceiling. My stomach churned. I swirled my gaze up to the chandelier to count the wrought-iron leaves, but the chandelier had been torn down. And if I looked down I was going to be sick.

Stop it. I tried to force the anxiety back. *You've got to do this.*

But anxiety never listened to reason, especially not when I stood in the middle of the ruin of my life. Soot clung to every surface. The carpets squelched under my feet. Several of the paintings had been torn from the walls. I paused at the library door. My gaze flicked to the shelf on the right – the one I always counted before I entered the room. Someone had flung all the books on the floor.

If you can't count, you can't enter, my body screamed.

My stomach tightened. A sharp pain stabbed between my shoulder blades. I gripped the edge of the doorframe, trying to force my feet forward.

A tremor shook my whole body as the familiar scents slammed into me. Parchment and old leather furniture. The whiff of whiskey from the bottles stored in the globe bar. Dust and old things. And beneath it all, Corbin's unique scent.

"Give me strength," I whispered. Corbin believed I could do anything. I needed that belief magic now.

I wrote it all down for you.

If Corbin really was somehow still... alive, still able to be brought back, then the answers were in this room. I lifted a shaking foot and placed it on the rug in front of me. My body howled in protest. My mind rebelled, certain that entering the room without finishing my ritual would result in some horrible consequence.

What could be more horrible than losing Corbin?

I dragged my other foot across the rug, my eyes flicking over the shelves. Apart from the books strewn across the floor and the priest hole door swinging free on its hinges, the library had remained remarkably intact.

The desk. Get to the desk.

Another step. Another stab in my heart. My vision wobbled. Every nerve in my body screamed at me to go back.

I balled up my courage and surged forward, grabbing the edge of the desk. I was there! I did it! A swell of triumph momentarily beat back the anxiety, and I held that triumph against my heart, hoping it would last as long as I needed.

I slid into Corbin's chair, drawing strength from his lingering scent and the familiar shape his body had scooped out of the cushion. As usual, he left his laptop off to one side and piled a wall of books around him, the same way I yanked my hair in front of my face when I didn't want to face the world.

I pulled the first book on the stack toward me. It was the grimoire Clara brought us, the one that once belonged to the Soho coven. She didn't seem to be as big a fan of Post-it notes and scribbled margins as Corbin, which meant that the five colored bits of paper sticking out of the leaves had been placed there by my lover in the last couple of days.

I wrote it all down for you.

I flipped the book to the first Post-it note, expecting to see a personal message. I skimmed over the scrawling diary entry from the book's original owner. On his note, Corbin's jagged writing noted some features of the belief magic story Clara told us. Nothing about bringing him back from the dead. I flipped to the next note. This marked an alchemical diagram – probably the arrangement of a ritual – that Corbin had redrawn with different letters at the cardinal points. I snapped a picture of the page on my phone and stuffed the note into my pocket, in case it was important.

On the third page, a towering pile of skulls grinned back at me. A demon danced on top of the pile, tossing a skull in the air like some fairground amusement. A crown of bones and horns circled his head.

The spell beneath was in Latin, but Corbin had translated it across three Post-its.

A spell for entering the world of the dead.

My heart hammered against my chest. *This is it. This is what he did.*

Corbin, you sneaky, lying, glorious, beautiful bastard.

I grabbed the Post-it notes, snapped a picture of the page, and slammed the book shut. The full weight of my discovery soared in my veins. If we could figure out the spell Corbin had performed, we could reverse it and bring him back, the way Maeve brought Aline back from the between-world in the painting.

I swiveled in the chair to look out the window behind the desk. Corbin had a sweet view from here over the grounds, from the topiary maze across to where Flynn's workshop used to stand, right down the sloping lawn into the orchard. I jumped as a figure moved between the apple trees, spinning and lunging at an invisible foe.

Arthur. His sword caught the light as he moved through his wards. I couldn't make out his face, but the set of his shoulders and ferocity of his movements betrayed his fury. I glanced away, feeling ashamed to be watching him, like I was intruding on something private.

Corbin could see down into the kitchen gardens. A delicious shiver ran up my spine as I looked down into my walled garden, which miraculously had survived the attack on the castle intact. Corbin could have watched me gardening from up here. If he wanted to see what was going on elsewhere in the castle, he had a tall window on the other side of the library looking into the courtyard.

My eye caught a weird movement in the orchard. I searched the trees for Arthur. At first I couldn't see him, but then I spotted him lying on the ground, his face to the sky. His sword lay a couple of feet from his body.

Cold fingers clenched my heart.

Even from this distance, I could see the blood pooling from his arm, spreading in a dark puddle across his shirt.

Not Arthur. Not him too.

I rose to my feet, my legs trembling. I used the edge of the desk to support me as I stumbled from the library and lurched toward the staircase. "Maeve? Flynn? Call an ambulance," I gasped against the rising panic. "Arthur's in the orchard and he's bleeding real bad."

*M*y heart hammered against my chest. Rowan pressed a vial into my hand and sank against Flynn, who was on the phone with the ambulance. My fingers closed around the vial and I tore out of the castle, Blake hot on my heels.

No, no, no. I can't lose another one.

I slammed into the orchard gate, the wood splintering as it crashed against the post. I tore down the row to the spot where the apples trees were spaced wide enough apart for swinging a two-handed sword in a complete circle. Here, Arthur and I had practiced sword-fighting and spilled our secrets to each other. Here, he kissed me for the first time.

At first I didn't see him, because he towered so tall and large in my mind that I wasn't looking down, down in the dirt. He slumped across the roots of an apple tree, his head flopped against his shoulder and his arm crossing his chest. Blood saturated the front of his shirt and darkened the grass beneath him.

So much blood.

A long, even cut sliced down the center of Arthur's arm.

Blood flowed freely from the wound, pouring out of him like water from a faucet. Bile rose in my throat, and my body surged with this tremendous sense that something was incorrect, inexact – a feeling usually reserved for looking over Kelly's physics homework.

All that blood should be inside him. He can't have much left.

Blake crouched over Arthur's limp body, slapping his cheeks so his head bounced against the tree. "Hey, Arnold, are you awake in there? Can you hear me?"

More blood poured from the cut. I cupped my hands over my mouth, trying to hold my stomach inside me.

Blake shook my arm. "Quick, Maeve. The medicine."

My eyes watering, I fumbled in my pocket for the small vial Rowan had given me. He must've grabbed it from the kitchen on his way to us. My fingers slipped on the lid, and it slid from my fingers into the grass.

"Here." Blake snatched it up and tipped out the paste onto his hand. Arthur's skin was so slippery with blood it took Blake a couple of tries to hold up his arm and rub the paste around the wound. That done, Blake tore off his shirt, ripped it in half down the middle and wrapped the material around Arthur's arm to hold the wound together. When he stepped back, his arms and chest were covered with dark blood.

The metallic smell invaded my nostrils. My legs gave way and I collapsed in the grass. I picked up Arthur's other hand and held it in mine. His fingers hung limp, lifeless. Were we too late? Had my warrior gone where I couldn't follow?

Footsteps pounded down the hill. Paramedics sat a stretcher down in the grass beside Arthur, and started calling out instructions to each other in medical speak. Blake pulled me back so they could work. "We'll take good care of him, luv." A paramedic gave me a reassuring smile.

Panic and sorrow welled up inside me. *It's not your job. It was my job to take care of him, and I failed him. And now he's done this to himself and it's all my fault.*

~

"*P*lease, please wake up," I sobbed into Arthur's shoulder. The nurses had laid his body out on his back, his hands at his sides and his lids closed over his glassy eyes. He was so big and tall that his feet hung off the end of the hospital bed. Under the fluorescent lights he was all hard corners and pale skin. Behind him, machines beeped and thumped as they breathed for him and pushed fresh blood through his empty veins.

Nothing about him seemed alive at all.

First my parents, then Corbin, now Arthur. How many people will I lose?

A warm arm fell around my shoulder, tugging me back from the bed. "He'll wake up," Flynn cooed in my ear, mashing his body against mine. "He's strong."

"He did this to get away from me," I sobbed. "Because of what I did."

"Maeve, you didn't *do* anything."

"I did! I let the fae into the castle. I trusted Daigh and got Corbin killed and Arthur hates me because—"

"He doesn't hate you and you're not responsible. He doesn't hate Blake, either."

"Well, then he's a bloody good actor," Blake piped up from the back of the room.

"We're all blaming ourselves for Corbin's death. He was the one who looked after all of us. He made himself into our protector, all because of his own guilt over Keegan." Flynn patted Arthur's bandaged arm. "Arthur did this to *himself* because he blamed himself for Corbin's death. Don't you see?

All that time he was yelling at Blake, he was really talking to himself."

"He might've just *said* that," Blake said.

"That's exactly it," Flynn's voice cracked. "This guilt's tearing us apart – it's seeping in all the cracks and poisoning everything good our coven stands for. We all need to do a little less blaming and a little more forgiveness."

I shook my head. "I'm the High Priestess. This *is* my fault."

"Maeve, I—" Rowan's face crumpled with pain.

I held up a hand. "You can't take the responsibility for this away from me. I'm in charge and if I say I'm responsible, then I'm damn well responsible."

"Maeve," Rowan's voice rang high and clear, startling the words out of my mouth. "I only saw Arthur because I... I went upstairs to look at the books in the library. In the dream, Corbin said, 'I wrote it all down for you,' and I had this idea that what he wrote down was how we could bring him back from the dead."

"Don't start on this again," I warned. "I'm not—"

"Listen, *please*. I found this." Rowan dug in his pocket and pulled out some bright colored paper. Five Post-it notes, scrawled with Corbin's spiky handwriting.

My heart thudded to see that familiar scrawl. "What are those?"

"I don't know, but they come from the book Clara stole from the Soho coven. Corbin was making notes on these spells." Rowan dug his phone out of his pocket. "I got photos of all the pages because the police said we shouldn't remove anything from the house. Look," he flicked through photo after photo of demons and skulls and Latin text.

"Rowan, come on—"

Rowan waved his screen in my face. "Just *look*. He even changed the letters on this alchemical diagram." He held up one of the notes. Behind him, Blake twisted his head to the side. "All these spells are about resurrection and something called the Mysteries of Lazarus—"

Seeing that writing snapped something in my chest. Rage bubbled up inside me – that Corbin was gone and Rowan wouldn't accept it. Because when he did finally accept it, his heart would shatter, and my own heart would break all over again watching him go through that.

"I don't want to hear it!" I yelled.

"Maeve, you've got to—"

"*No.* This isn't like Aline, who was trapped in what I can only gather is an extra dimension within the painting. Corbin is DEAD. We all saw his body. He was burned and had a stake pushed through his chest. All the wishing on a fucking star isn't going to bring him back."

Rowan's features froze. He slunk out of the room. Instantly, I regretted my anger. I stood up, but Blake stepped in front of me. "Let me talk to him."

"Don't put ideas in his head," I growled. "The sooner he stops denying the truth, the better off we'll all be."

Blake's eyes bore into mine, and the corner of his mouth curled up into his trademark smirk. He spun on his heel and sauntered after Rowan. It didn't escape my notice that he hadn't agreed to what I'd asked of him.

I flopped back down into the hard plastic chair beside Arthur's bed, burying my face in my hands. "This is a nightmare."

"Have you considered they might have a point," Flynn said, his voice soft.

"Of course I have, but it's impossible." The things Corbin said to me in the dream flashed through my head. I opened my mouth to tell Flynn about them, but something bit my tongue. I didn't want to give him false hope, either. Rowan was carrying around enough for all of us.

"I know you need a logical explanation for everything,"

Flynn said. "But maybe this is new scientific ground. Maybe it's never happened before, and that's why it can't be explained. You've already released Aline from her prison. You could be a pioneer in resurrecting the dead."

"Aline didn't leave behind a body, because her body went to the other dimension with her. Corbin left behind a body, and it's gone. Even if he is stuck in the underworld and we could somehow bring him back, he doesn't have a body to go back *to*."

Flynn's face wobbled. Shit. He was close to losing it. I wrapped my arms around him. Something crackled in the pocket of his hoodie. "What's that?" I asked, feeling a thick envelope inside.

"Oh, that thing." Flynn pulled out a crumpled envelope and handed it to me. "This was in the mailbox at Briarwood. I was gonna give it to you back at Ryan's place. It's from some laboratory in London."

My DNA results. I glanced down at the envelope without much interest. What did it matter any more?

"Open it. I want to see." Flynn hopped from foot to foot. "Of course, I'm a wee bit dim, so you'll have to explain all the squiggly graphs."

A smile played over my lips. There was something about Flynn's very presence that made every scary situation bearable. And there was something about him that was different right now. Over the last few days he'd been a real support. Instead of his usual ill-conceived humor, I remembered how he'd tried to hold Arthur back and talk him down when he'd attacked Blake. Now we were in Arthur's hospital room and Flynn was making speeches about not feeling guilty to try and hold us all together. It might not be working, but he was trying harder than anyone.

I didn't care about the DNA results, but maybe Flynn needed the distraction.

I flipped the envelope over and slid my finger along the seal. My mind flashed back to the last time I opened a letter – standing in the library at Briarwood, sliding Corbin's sword-shaped letter opener under the wax seal of my mother's letter, a letter he'd saved and guarded for me since he took over the castle from his parents.

Ten sheets of A4 paper fell out into my hands. I scanned the first page. I expected to read a form letter about decoding my history and unlocking the secrets of the past, but instead I had a personal letter from the laboratory's director, inviting me in person for further study. "Inconclusive results... never seen anything like it before... almost appears as if you have two fathers, which is of course completely impossible... please contact the lab immediately..."

My hands trembled. The letter slipped from my fingers and fluttered to the ground.

"Maeve?" Flynn waved his hand in front of my eyes.

My head spun. In my lap, graphs fanned out, dotted with anomalies marked in vivid red ink, as red as Arthur's blood.

It was irrefutable scientific proof – I had two fathers.

I was part fae. I carried inside of me some of Daigh's magic.

18

ROWAN

"*R*owan… Rowan!"

Blake's voice followed me down the echoing hallway. I stopped next to a vending machine, supporting my body against its snack-filled belly, and waited for him to catch up.

"She won't believe me," I whispered, staring at the Post-it notes in my hand. I felt so sure I held the key to saving Corbin, but Maeve didn't want to see it. If everything he'd said in her dream was true, then with every minute we were moving closer to the Slaugh and Daigh's attempt to usurp the throne of the underworld. Although how he'd do that locked up in Raynard Hall without his powers, I couldn't guess.

"I *did* tell you," Blake grinned. "We're on our own for this, darling Rowan."

"Did you want something?" I needed to be alone right now, get my thudding heart back under control.

"Only to show you this." Blake grabbed a Post-it note out of my hand and held it up. It was the alchemical diagram, with symbols and arrows pointing in every direction.

"I've *seen* it," I said, exasperated. "I don't know what it means—"

Blake flipped the note over.

Cold crept down my spine, and my chest clamped so tight I struggled for breath. There was writing on the back. Corbin's spiky handwriting spelled out an address, and above it, the words, *Rowan, I'm sorry.*

I hadn't even *thought* to look on the backs of the Post-its. I missed this personal message from Corbin.

I wrote it all down for you.

I knew without looking it up who lived that that address. My grandparents, Lord and Lady Pembroke, who disowned my mother after she married a black witch. The grandparents who knew I existed and that I was an orphan but instead of taking me in, allowed me to enter the foster care system and cycle through abusive homes until I'd broken and went to live on the street.

"I take it from your expression that this address means something to you," Blake said.

I nodded.

Blake snapped his fingers. "Let's go, then."

"Huh?"

"Corbin left you this note. He obviously wants us to go there. Maybe it's a clue."

"Blake, I don't think—"

But Blake was already heading to the entrance, his fingers swiping across the screen of his phone, calling up a rideshare. Numb with fear at what I'd discover at that house, I trailed after him.

~

*T*he heavy knocker fell on the door, hammering in my chest like an earthquake.

Pembroke Hall towered over me, a Georgian facade of

gleaming white columns and high, narrow windows. Although it was only a stone's throw from the castle, I'd never seen this part of Crookshollow before. I never had much cause to leave the house. This place looked like the kind of house filled with chairs you couldn't sit on and golden toilets you weren't allowed to piss in.

It looked like the kind of house filled with secrets and ghosts.

My teeth rattled in my mouth. *What are you doing here? Go back to Briarwood. You're dealing with enough right now between Corbin's death and Arthur's hospitalization, without adding this to the mix. Maeve needs you, even if she is being a stubborn science nerd. Go back to her.*

I turned away from the door. Behind me, Blake's mouth curled up into a smirk. He reached around me and battered his fist against the door.

My heart stopped. My legs froze in place. I stared at the door, willing it to open and at the same time hoping it would remain closed forever. When no one came I turned away, relief surging through me. *No one's home. I'll come back tomorrow, or maybe next week, after the Slaugh. That's a good idea—*

The door jerked open, startling me. In the entrance stood a stern-faced woman with silver-streaked dark hair pulled back into a severe bun. Her hip cocked haughtily, in a similar way Maeve did when she wanted one of us to listen to her. "What do you want?" she frowned at me.

"Ah…" The careful speech I'd composed flew out of my head. I fumbled for my pocket where I'd stashed the paper. "Um… you see, I…"

"Didn't you read the notice on the gate?" the woman snapped. "No solicitors." She tried to shut the door, but Blake shoved his foot into the gap. She slammed the door against his foot, but all he did was whistle between his teeth.

Thank the gods for Blake.

147

"My name's Rowan." I muttered, staring down at my shoe as she battered the door against Blake's boot. "I'm Dana's son."

The door flew open as the woman stumbled back, her hands on her mouth. Her eyes – deep and dark and green, a mirror image of my own – widened, shot with fear.

"You're not supposed to contact us," she gasped. "I gave very strict instructions."

"He never got your *instructions*," Blake said easily. "He grew up in the street."

"I'm not here to hurt you," I said. "I know you've got your life here. I don't want money, and I'm sorry about my friend putting his foot in the door. I just want to talk… *please?*"

She glared at me, but she did hold the door open. "Fine. Only you. Your friend waits outside."

"Fine by me," Blake lifted his boot and grinned. "I think I'll go for a walk."

"I've got a panic button under the table, and the police will be here in a moment if you try anything."

"Noted. Thank you for your hospitality." I slipped my boots off and padded across the foyer after her. She led me through an opulent Georgian hall decorated in shades of white, and into a pale yellow drawing room. The house was silent, save for the ticking of an antique clock over the mantelpiece. Shelves on either side of the fireplace housed gold and crystal objects.

No wonder she never wanted a child in this house. This was no house for a nervous kid. I'd have spent my entire childhood sitting on my hands, so terrified I'd break something that my magic would've rebelled and built into a localized earthquake that would've broken everything anyway.

The woman – my *grandmother*, Lady Pembroke – sat in a high-backed chair in front of the fireplace and rang a bell. A moment later, a short, stocky woman in a black dress and sensible shoes appeared by the door. Her skin matched mine – a dark smudge against this white house and its white furnishings. I wondered if she ever accidentally tried to scrub herself away.

"Some tea for me and my guest," Lady Pembroke barked without looking at the maid.

"Yes, Mrs. Pembroke." The maid ducked away. I stared at my knees, too terrified to speak.

My grandmother didn't speak either, and after an eternity punctuated by the ticking clock and a white cat slinking into the room and curling up at my feet, the maid returned with a tray of tea. She placed the silver tea service on the table next to my grandmother. Lady Pembroke poured the tea with meticulous attention to old fashioned service, and proffered me a cup and saucer.

I took the cup, just to have something to do with my hands. As I moved the saucer to my knee, my shaking hand splashed hot tea on my lap. I set the cup down and picked up a shortbread instead.

I took a bite of shortbread. Big mistake. It was a terrible recipe – too sugary and dry. It stuck in my throat and crumbled all over my jeans. Across from me, Mrs. Pembroke frowned as she observed my atrocious table manners, no doubt second-guessing her invitation. I wondered if right this moment the maid stood outside the door, her finger poised over the panic button, waiting for a signal to turn me in.

"Let us get straight to the point," Lady Pembroke said. "If you are Dana's child – which I refuse to believe until I see your paperwork – you'll get no money from us. We made it very clear that we were not to be involved in your life in any way."

"I already told you, I don't want money." Blood roared in my ears. The yellow walls swelled and buckled in front of me. Opposite the fireplace was a white bookshelf containing rows of books with matching white and gold spines. I counted them. *One, two, three...*

"If that is so, you have until the bottom of this teacup to tell me what you want, or I'm calling the police."

"My best friend just died," I said.

"I'm sorry to hear that." She sipped her tea, not sounding sorry at all.

"He took me in when I was on the streets, gave me the first real home I ever knew. I was in foster care before that. I ran away. I couldn't take the abuse. It was the bravest thing I ever did, but also pointless. I lived on the streets, and the abuse never stopped. I'm easy to hurt."

The words caught on my tongue, arriving stilted and out of order. I'd never said this many words to a stranger in my entire life, at least not without drugs coursing through my system. "I didn't come for you then. Corbin came for me instead. I was lucky enough to have a family. I live at Briarwood Castle. It's just over the hill. It burned down the other night."

"I saw that in the newspaper. Unfortunate business. I've visited the castle for the historical tour. You have an admirable topiary maze and some fine antiques, although your guest amenities could use some work. Why are you *here?*"

Seven, eight, nine...

"I see that you and Lord Pembroke never had any other children, and I thought... I wondered... could we get to know each other? Could you tell me about my mum?" The word was so foreign on my tongue. It had been years since I allowed myself to think of my parents are real people. "I never knew her and I see now that... that it's important to keep alive the memories of people who meant something to us."

Lady Pembroke glared at me from across the table, her teacup hovering in midair. I braced myself for her dismissal. I thought I heard the stomping of standard issue police constable boots clattering down the hall, coming to arrest me for daring to approach a woman of her status. Instead, she set down her cup and rose to her feet. "Follow me."

I trailed after her up the staircase, not daring to touch the gleaming mahogany bannister or the textured white wallpaper. The first floor was decorated in the same grand Georgian style as the rest of the house, all in shades of white and cream that made my dark skin seem even more out of place.

Lady Pembroke threw open a door at the end of the hall. "I've left it exactly as she did."

I stepped into a bedroom about the size of the Great Hall. An enormous four-poster bed dominated the space, hung with white lace curtains and made up with cream silk pillows. A white dresser stood under the window, the mirrors angled inwards. White, white, white. The starkness of it stifled me. The girl in this room had no place in her life for a messy, dreadlocked black baby.

It reminded me of the room at Corbin's parents house, the one that captured a moment in time that had never really existed. A memorial to the two sons they'd lost. A place to remember, and to forget.

A vase at the windowsill held a bunch of cream roses, their petals browning at the edges. I touched my hand to the flowers, sending a thread of magic through my palm. When I withdrew my hand, the roses bounced back to life, and their fresh scent wafted across my nostrils.

Mrs. Pembroke gripped the door jamb with white-knuckled hands. "Earth magic," she whispered.

"I'm sorry," I whispered back.

She shook her head. "It's been many years since I have seen it."

"You don't use yours...?"

"Heavens, no." She scoffed. "I've worked a long time to restore my reputation. I won't sully it by associating with sorcery."

I walked around the room, taking in details, trying to piece together my mother from these ancient remnants of her life. Details leapt out, the kind of details that were only obvious to someone like me. Objects on her dresser lined up so all the edges were parallel. The toes of her shoes perfectly even. The tops of the candles shaved off so they were at the exact same height. Posters hung at exact right angles to each other. And everything in even sets – two pillows on the chair, two paintings above the bed, two scarves on each hook. Two candlesticks on the mantelpiece when three would look more aesthetically pleasing.

A weird look crossed over Lady Pembroke's face as she saw me looking at the candles. "Dana was always doing that – lining up objects in her strange way. She was obsessive about it. We'd go to cocktails with our neighbors and she'd be rearranging their mantelpieces. Lady Shetland once accused her of stealing a Wedgwood plate. She made a huge fuss in the middle of a ball and all Dana had done was move it to another shelf so it was in a pair."

Bookshelves lined either side of the fireplace. I touched the edges of the volumes. Dana – my mother – had even arranged them in size order. "Did she ever... have panic attacks?"

"Only every other week. We took her to all sorts of specialists abroad. She was having cognitive behavior therapy down in London, and she was getting better, until she met *that man*." She spat out the words like she'd swallowed something foul.

Her words rocked through my body. *My mother was in therapy. My mother heard the voices, too. She was just like me.*

There was a photo album on top of the bookshelf. The picture on the front was of a lovely white girl with the same dark hair as her mother, only hers was long and free, encircled with a chainmail headdress. Beside her was a tall black man with a wide, genuine smile.

My parents. I never got to know either of them, but I felt like I understood my mother now. We had a connection – we were both messed up in the head.

Lady Pembroke took the photo album from my hand and placed it back on the shelf, so the photo faced down. "Your friend who died…"

"Corbin."

"Was he the boy killed in the fire at the castle?"

I nodded.

"Nasty business. I hope you're making someone pay for it." She held the door open, sniffing at the air as though it gave her allergies. "Well, you have seen what you wanted."

"Thank you."

"If you want to come again for tea, that would be fine." She frowned at me. "Don't bring your friend next time."

"I won't. Thank you, Lady Pembroke."

"Yes." She nodded. Downstairs, she held open the door while I shoved my feet into my sneakers. Outside, Blake stood on the steps. He flashed her with his unnerving smile. She slammed the door.

"What a warm, kind-hearted soul," Blake mused as we walked back through the manicured front garden.

I nodded, my mind a million miles away, back in my mother's room, in her perfectly symmetrical candlesticks and her arms around my father.

Corbin had kept this information from me to protect me. But it had given me something to cling to. If only Corbin was alive to see how well I was doing.

I was determined that he would be.

19

FLYNN

"You'll love this one, mate. An Irish priest is driving down the M1, and he gets stopped for speeding. The constable smells alcohol on the priest's breath and then sees an empty wine bottle on the floor of the car. He asks the priest if he's been drinking. 'Just water,' says the priest. 'Then why do I smell wine?' asks the constable. The priest looks down at the bottle and gives a start, 'Good Lord! He's done it again!'"

It was weird telling jokes to an audience that didn't react. Arthur's face should have been crumpling with resignation, not pointing flaccidly at the ceiling. Even Maeve couldn't muster a reaction. From across the bed, her eyes stared right through me.

After Blake and Rowan went off, I'd stayed with Maeve and Arthur, racking my brain for every shite joke I knew to fill the gaping silence of the room. At least my voice drowned out the beeping machines, and there was always the chance Arthur would wake up and marmalade me.

I'd never looked forward to a beating so much in my life.

Someone knocked at the door. Maeve didn't move, her

eyes never leaving Arthur's face. I opened it as Aline, Clara, and Smithers bustled in, declaring they'd come to relieve us and we should go back to the hall. Maeve refused to leave, as I knew she would, but I couldn't pass up the opportunity to witness the moment when Ryan's finished painting would be revealed to the world.

"Go, Flynn." Maeve kissed my cheek. "I'll be fine. I'll call you if anything changes."

When I entered the studio ballroom, Ryan and Simon had the finished painting mounted between two stone pillars on a bare white wall, surrounded by lights and filters. My breath hitched as I got the first glimpse at Ryan's masterpiece.

He'd painted a woman who might've been a storybook witch, complete with black cloak and hood and pointed black shoes with buckles. She sat on a fallen log in a forest of twisted trees – a signature detail of Ryan's work – tossing scraps of food to animals that scurried around her. Foxes, rabbits, and other critters leapt and scrabbled at her feet while bright-colored birds perched on her shoulders. The scene would be idyllic, if not for the witch's stance. She paid no heed to the animals. Her body twisted as she peered over her shoulder to gaze longingly at a group of women walking through the trees behind her. They were dressed in bright, modern clothes, and their heads bent together, their hands over their mouths as though they were whispering secrets or stifling cruel laughter. The canvas dripped with loneliness and isolation – the witch who did good deeds but had to hide in the forest, her desire to be part of a community showing in the hunch of her shoulders. The gossiping girls who had no concept of the damage they did. In the trees, a pair of gleaming emerald eyes surveyed the scene. A fae hiding in the shadows, waiting to strike. Ryan had titled it, *The Witch's Lament*.

It wasn't the picture I'd expected to see – it was a gazillion times better. After everything the villagers had faced on the meadow, and how Maeve and Blake had planted the idea that witches were on their side, this poignant scene would remind them that they played a part in turning witches into the bad guys.

Simon snapped pictures from all angles, then spoke into Ryan's phone as he made a quick YouTube video, zeroing in on details of the witch's face and the playful animals. It was weird that even though Ryan was the artist, the face of his social media was the laconic old butler. Ryan told me that Simon even had his own Facebook fanpage, where he posted videos about etiquette and traditional British baking.

"It's exquisite," I breathed, unable to contain my excitement.

Simon frowned and dropped his phone. "Please refrain from speaking. Now I have to start the video again."

"If you want to stay in the studio, go over there," Ryan jabbed a finger at the easel he'd set up for me under the window. "And be quiet. We're on a deadline. If I hear so much as a brush scratching the canvas from over here, you're out."

I mimed zipping my lips shut and settled into my stool. My painting looked like shite compared to Ryan's master-piece. I hadn't lied when I told Candice that I was rubbish at two dimensions. My portrait of Corbin looked like a kid's fingerpainting. But after hours hunched in that hard hospital chair, trying to fight back the darkness that threatened to consume our coven, my fingers itched to finish it. There was something calming about painting that sculpture lacked. My thoughts rolled off in a million directions, and I found I could think of Corbin without wanting to punch the sky. All I needed was a glass of whiskey to make it almost fun. If I believed in fruity woo-woo shite, I might've called it a meditation.

I'd used streaks of black and purple to form Corbin's hair spilling across the canvas and right over the edge, as though the square wasn't enough to contain him. Inside his tresses I painted galaxies and constellations, pulling up star charts on my phone to copy the patterns exactly. Just for a giggle, I added all our star signs. Maeve would say they were all wrong because of the earth's wobbling shenanigans, and her nose would wrinkle and her voice would get that school-teacher tone that was so fecking sexy—

"I like it," a voice said behind me, startling me out of my thoughts.

I whipped my head around. Ryan leaned over my shoulder, staring at my canvas with a furrowed brow.

How could Ryan Raynard like it?

I squinted at my painting, trying to see it through his eyes. All I saw was a mess. Ryan's paintings always looked like stuff. If you wanted to know his mind, you just had to study the different elements of the image. Mine didn't even *look* like Corbin. Instead, it contained all the things that made him who he was – dark brown rectangles representing his books, splashes of color for his quick mind and dry humor and his love of drinking mead and talking shite with the rest of us. The runes he translated for Arthur followed the wavy lines of his hair, and a shaft of light that was meant to represent Maeve and the coven pierced through the center of the canvas. It was supposed to be a patchwork of Corbinness, but like all my paintings it looked so much better in my head.

Now Ryan fecking Raynard was standing in front of it and saying he *liked* it, like he considered me some kind of equal.

"You don't have to pretend." I rested the palette on my knee and raised the brush to add another layer of brown to the book rectangles. "I know it's shite."

Ryan snorted. "I'm not in the habit of giving out unearned

praise, Flynn. You're competent. With more discipline, you could be good. No," he pushed my hand down. "Don't tweak any more. You'll overthink it and ruin the rawness. It's time to let it rest. When you come back to it, you'll see if it needs anything else. We're going to release my painting now, if you want to see."

Did I want to see one of the most famous artists in the world release a painting to the world? You bet your Irish whiskey I did. I threw down the palette and practically skipped down the hall after Ryan and Simon. Ryan unlocked a door to a room I hadn't seen before, and ushered me into an airy office.

I thought there'd be some kind of ceremony, with press and and a grand unveiling with the painting behind a velvet curtain. But I forgot momentarily that Ryan was a recluse. He seemed so *normal* – not like artist savants in films who couldn't hold a normal conversation. He didn't even have any of Rowan's weird ticks. Apart from the whole being a fox shapeshifter thing, Ryan just didn't seem to care what anyone else thought of him, which was why it was so weird he made all this effort to avoid being seen in public.

I liked that he didn't give a shit. I wished I could be like that. But I cared a whole fecking lot what other people thought.

Simon had the auction house in London on speaker, and as soon as a clock on his desk counted down, he pushed PUBLISH on an image of the painting on Ryan's website. There were gasps on the end of the line as the collectors got their first glimpse of Ryan's genius.

My stomach fluttered with nervous energy as the bids rolled in. *Eighty-five thousand... a hundred-and-five thousand... Two-hundred twenty thousand...*

I reeled at the numbers. How in the world did *anyone* have two-hundred and twenty thousand pounds to spend on a *painting?* Ryan leaned against the wall, completely stone-faced, as if the money was of no consequence to him. Probably it wasn't. I bet he blew his nose with hundred-quid notes.

After much fanfare, we reached a final number – £331,000. Simon switched to a private call to arrange payment and delivery with the buyer. I threw my arms around Ryan. "Congrats, mate. You're richer than Croesus. Who is Croesus, anyway? You should bust him up and steal his money, too."

A weird fluttery feeling arced across my chest. *Corbin would know all about Croesus.*

Ryan shoved me off. "Save the caresses for your girlfriend."

I backed away, not wanting to annoy him. "What are you going to do with all the money? Indoor-climbing wall? Fill a swimming pool with one-pound notes? Lifetime supply of saffron and caviar-flavored ice cream?"

"I have some ideas, but I'm not rushing into anything." Ryan gave me a laconic smile. "After all, if the world ends tomorrow, I'm not really going to get much use out of an indoor climbing wall."

Ryan took over the computer while Simon fielded phone call after phone call from press and gallery directors. I watched in fascination as Ryan's social media pages lit up with talk about the painting and the sale. Email notifications popped up so fast they blurred the corner of the screen.

"The crew will arrive within the hour," Simon called to Ryan. A local gallery was going to display the painting for three days before it went to its new owner. This would draw an incredible amount of attention to Crookshollow and its witchy, haunted history – all fuel to stoke our belief magic stores.

"Flynn," Ryan gestured for me to follow him. "Come help me move the painting down to the entrance hall. We need—"

A buzzer sounded on the wall. Ryan pulled up a computer screen with a camera trained on the main gate. I was shocked to see hundreds of people clamoring around the gates. Vans and other vehicles had blocked traffic on the avenue. The press had arrived. How had they got here so quickly?

"Ryan Raynard?" A voice crackled through the intercom. "Is this—"

"No comment," Ryan barked into the speaker.

A police badge slammed against the camera. "This is a police matter. I want to speak to the tenants of Briarwood. Let me in or I'll come back with a warrant."

The badge pulled back, and Detective Wallace's chin came into view. From over his shoulder I made out the round face of Officer Judge, which didn't make any sense. After Wallace caught her participating in the lynch mob that attacked Briarwood, surely he'd have suspended her. *What's she doing here?*

Ryan sighed. "I'm guessing they're here for you," he said.

"Tell them I've gone to the pub."

"We can hear you, Mr O'Hagan," Inspector Wallace said.

"Fine. You can come in. But don't let any of those blood-sucking journalists follow you."

Ryan buzzed them in, slamming the gates shut behind them to keep the surging press out. Reluctantly, I left Simon's office and went down to the entrance hall to speak to them. Ryan came with me because I couldn't remember where the entrance hall was, but he darted away before the coppers could get a look at him. I wished I could do the same.

Wallace and Judge stood on the stoop, looking all staunch and officious. Judge stared up at the ornately-carved ceiling, her mouth dropping open in awe. I shoved my hands in my pockets and grinned up at them, hoping to unnerve them.

Growing up with my uncle in Dublin had given me an ingrained distrust of the police. We usually dealt with them in the Irish way – by being complete gobshites. "What can I do for you, officers?"

"Is Maeve Crawford here? What about your other friends who live at Briarwood?"

"Just me. Arthur had a wee accident, and the others are at the hospital with him." I didn't know where Blake and Rowan had gone after they'd had that fight with Maeve, but Inspector Wallace didn't need to know that.

"That's fine. We have to speak to you all at some point, but you can fill in the others when they return. Is there somewhere we can talk?"

I led them into the blue drawing room – the only room with sofas with a location I could remember. "I'd offer you coffee," I shrugged. "But I don't know where the kitchen is, and I haven't got the magical superpower that allows me to conjure the butler at will."

"That's fine." Inspector Wallace sat down. Judge stood behind him, pacing the length of the couch as she inspected the singed bookshelf and stacks of damp books Simon had piled up ready for recycling. I flopped down on the sofa opposite, placing my boots on the table, all casual-like.

"What happened here?" Judge pointed to the charred edge of the bookshelf.

I ignored her, because she was partly responsible for Corbin's death and I didn't owe her an explanation. "What's she doing here?" I asked Wallace, indicating Judge. "Why does she still have a badge after what she did?"

"*She* has a name," Judge shot back.

"Sonia was working undercover for us," he said. "We believed the villagers would be more likely to accept her presence since she'd been at the church."

"But you yelled at her?"

"She'd taken too long to alert us about the danger. If we'd had an alert sooner we might've prevented the fire from spreading. I didn't realize at the time she had a concussion."

"A concussion?" I raised my eyebrow at Judge. More like a bout of fundamentalism.

"Someone knocked me over when the crowd surged into the castle. I think I hit my head. I was woozy, felt like my thoughts weren't my own," she said, her eyes boring into mine. My stomach squirmed. She remembered hearing the conflicting voices in her head. It was going to be hard to explain that away.

"You're not in any trouble. We're here to keep you updated on the case." Inspector Wallace leaned forward and knitting his fingers together. "We've taken statements from several of the people at Briarwood last night. There's a lot of chatter about you in the village, Flynn. Especially concerning a controversial piece of art that appeared overnight in the town square."

"I don't know anything about that," I said.

"That incident at the pub suggests otherwise. That statue is an impressive piece of work. What'd you use to attach it to the plinth?" Wallace narrowed his eyes at me. "I saw Bill Riley out there the other day with his jackhammer and he didn't even make a dent in the base."

"The only thing that could hold it in place is magic," I wiggled my fingers at him, grinning. It *was* the truth. My Ma always said you should tell coppers the truth.

"Fine," Wallace sighed. "We're still conducting investigations, you understand. But from what Officer Judge has told us, this statue of yours—"

"Not mine," I grinned. "Although I bet the fella who did it was rakishly handsome."

"—along with that scuffle in the pub inflamed some old tensions within the village. That, combined with a ludicrous rumor that a dead woman has been spotted at your castle, seemed to be the motivation behind this attack. Apparently this dead woman – one Aline Moore – used to live at the castle, and she had a reputation as a bit of a cult leader. She filled Briarwood with all sorts of derelicts and runaways and flower children. People thought they were up at the castle having orgies, taking drugs, conducting satanic rituals. Parents feared for their children. And then she disappeared."

"Seems like a load of bollocks to me," I uncrossed and crossed my legs.

"I thought so, too. But then I dug around in the council records and discovered that an Aline Moore was the last owner of Briarwood House, and that she had indeed disappeared in mysterious circumstances, as reported in the *Crookshollow Courier*, and that this very year the ownership of the castle would pass to her only surviving relative – her daughter, Maeve."

"Aye. Maeve is the daughter of Aline. What of it? They look alike, but it takes a special kind of eejit to see Maeve through a window and assume she was a ghostie."

"I believe all these events – the arrival of Maeve, the five of you – all good friends – all holed up here at the castle instead of participating in village life, the tragic geological event at the church, the appearance of the statue – has ignited some long-held superstitions about Briarwood and her inhabitants."

"Motives are all fine and dandy, officer, but I want to know what's been done about the crimes that were committed."

"We've identified five of the main instigators, and will be pressing charges within the next few days. The others have been allowed their freedom, under the condition they stay off the Briarwood property and don't bother you or your friends. Given the level of remorse about the act and the death of Corbin Harris, I have no reason to suspect they'll be a further problem."

I nodded. It was a good thing Arthur wasn't here. He'd be raving about how jail wasn't good enough, how they should be strung up by their bollix with rusty fishing wire for what they'd done.

Then I remembered Arthur's lifeless body in that hospital bed, and I hated myself for thinking it. I'd rather have that big guy storming around setting fire to shit any day.

Wallace seemed to have Arthur on his mind, too. "I need to warn you, members of the public saw your friend Arthur swinging a sword around. Under normal circumstances I'd have to haul him in and confiscate the weapon. Since no one was hurt beyond a few minor burns and cuts and some hallucinations, and your home was burned down, I'm going to be lenient. But don't let me hear about him doing that again."

"I promise you won't," I said darkly. If Arthur survived the wound he'd given himself, Maeve and I were going to make sure we took every last sword and dagger out of the castle and throw them back to the Lady of the Lake. "What of Corbin Harris? Will anyone be charged with his murder?"

"It's early days yet, mate. We haven't even got the pathologist's report from the coroner yet." Wallace scratched his head. "Eyewitness accounts say they saw a guy in a strange black outfit stab Harris. Two men in green threw him on the fire and then slid him onto the spike. Any ideas who they might be?"

"Someone in the village, I presume. Isn't that your job, sir?"

"No one we questioned that night matched their descriptions, but we're still looking. It doesn't help that all our eyewitnesses seem to be affected by the hallucinogenic vapors in the black cloud. We've been told all sorts of wild stories, let me tell you. I've got the geologists taking samples at the meadow and comparing them to those at the church. I'm convinced the two events are related."

"If you say so, sir." I jiggled my leg against the table, trying to keep my voice even. I didn't want Judge to see how much the idea of Corbin's body lying on a slab being dissected was getting to me. "When will you do the autopsy?"

"Within the next day or so. We'll contact you when we're finished, and you can arrange with your funeral home to collect his remains. In the meantime, if you have any problems with people in the village, let me know. We'll be keeping you updated as the case progresses, and you may be asked to testify." He glanced at the window toward the gates. Cameras flashed at the house, and people waved their arms through the bars in the gate, like the flesh-eating zombies in my favorite video game. I supposed, in a way, they were out for flesh. "In the meantime, keep a low profile. That means *exactly* the opposite of hanging out with Ryan Raynard after he releases a new painting that features witches as the subject matter and brings a media circus to Crookshollow."

"Gotcha," I snapped my fingers at him.

Wallace stood. "I suppose we should go out and move the media along. No chance of speaking with Mr. Raynard himself? I've heard some stories about this house, let me tell you—"

"I need to use the bathroom," Judge announced, her eyes boring into mine.

"When we're back at the station," Wallace said.

"It's urgent, sir."

A pained expression crossed Wallace's face, as if he knew this conversation all-too-well. I wondered if he had daughters.

"I'll show you where it is." I got to my feet and led Judge down the hall, in what I hoped was the direction of a bathroom.

As soon as we turned the corner, Judge grabbed my collar. "What's going on?" she demanded. "Am I going crazy?"

I shrugged. "Are you?"

"Don't pull that bullshit with me, O'Hagan. I've seen way too much weird stuff over the last couple of weeks. First those babies go missing and found on your property, then twenty-two people are swallowed by a weird black fog after fighting with three-foot-tall furry monsters with knives made of bones. *Then* a statue of a witch appears in the village and gets everyone scared and desperate."

"Bit of a shite week, aye? I could do with a whiskey—"

She continued as if I hadn't spoken. "I stood in the Briarwood courtyard while a battle raged in my mind – one voice in my head screaming at me to kill the witches, the other telling me to go home and crawl into bed with a cup of tea. Next thing I'm crouched in a field trying to call for backup on a phone that won't work while creatures that weren't human burned a guy and shoved him on a *stake*. Your friend Maeve touched my face and I saw my own worst fears as reality flashing before my eyes. It wasn't a hallucination – for that moment it was *real*. I lived in my nightmares. People had thoughts planted inside their heads that weren't their own. This can't continue, you hear that? I need to know what's going on and I don't want any more fibbing or nonsense about geology."

"What's the point? You won't believe me."

Judge jabbed a finger in the direction of the drawing room. "*He* won't believe you. His brain ain't set up that way. But I'm no idiot. I've lived in Crookshollow my entire life. This village is superstitious with good reason. It *is* the most haunted village in England. My grandma's house has a resident ghost, and if you'd seen some of the weird shit that went on down at the precinct... Point is, I've got an open mind and

I *know* what I've seen can't be explained by science. I'm right, aren't I?"

I nodded. "I'm guessing we don't have time for a long explanation. So here's the Twitter version: Those guys you saw in the green and black, with the bows and arrows, the ones that killed Corbin? They're fae. Fairyfolk."

Judge's eyes widened. "They didn't have no wings."

"There are lots of different types of fae. Some of them have wings. Some have claws. Some are three-foot tall and covered with fur. Those ones were court fae – think Tolkien elves, only more evil."

"And these fae, what've they got against you and your friends? Why'd they kill Corbin Harris?"

"Hundreds of years ago they were banished from the human world into a separate realm. It's like another dimension only it's really, really tiny. Understandably, they're still pissed at us for banishing them, and they want the earth for themselves. There's a doorway to their realm behind the castle. It's our job to guard it, to stop them coming into our world. We're witches, as you've probably figured out. This one fae, Daigh, he found a way to get here without going through the portal."

"Don't tell me," Judge smirked. "He made a deal with the devil on a crossroads at midnight."

"Pretty much exactly that. Only it turns out he's also Maeve's father, and he wants her to rule the world with him. He's the one who killed Corbin. We've got him with us, locked in a secret room so he can't hurt anyone else. But he lost all his powers, so he's not important now. As part of the deal these fae made with the underworld, in less than two days a host of restless souls called The Slaugh will ride across earth, killing everyone they encounter until there's no human left to oppose the fae. That's why Ryan—"

"I don't know what you're all playing at," Judge hissed.

"The whole village is a circus. People are pouring in from all over the country to see this painting before it goes into some private collection. Is this really a good idea with those bloody fae and restless souls around?"

"It's how we're going to stop them. There's a kind of magic that's created when people believe in something. Like how everyone in the village now believes in magic and witches, and that belief is spreading because of Ryan's painting and the story of the statue appearing in the town square. We've figured out how to use objects like artwork to store that magic and then unleash it at the right time. It's going to overwhelm the Slaugh before they do any damage."

Judge glanced at her watch. "I've got to get back. I can't believe I'm saying this, but if you need help with anything, you know where to find me."

"Why?" I wasn't used to people believing me so readily or jumping to my aid. Eloquent speeches that stirred hearts and changed minds were Corbin's department.

"Corbin helped us out on a case a couple of years back," Judge said. "It was the first dead body I'd ever seen. A professor committed suicide up at one of the old houses on Holly Avenue. He wrote the note in Latin. One of the other officers used to be in a medieval reenactment club with Arthur, and apparently he used to bitch about his brainiac housemate who knew all these old languages, so I called in at the castle to get Corbin to look at the note. He translated it in three minutes flat and discovered one of the verbs had been conjugated incorrectly. His evidence eventually convicted the professor's brother of his murder. Corbin's one smart kid, and he dropped everything to help us without demanding a reward. People always ask what's in it for them, but Corbin Harris never did. I don't want any other people to die on my watch."

I vaguely remembered Corbin mentioning he'd helped

the police out while I was over in Arizona. It sounded exactly like him, to do something just for the sheer joy of the intellectual challenge.

Officer Judge released my collar, and we walked back to the drawing room. Inspector Wallace bent over the singed bookshelf, running his fingers across the ruined surface. He straightened up when we entered. "All done, then?"

Judge nodded. "Ready to brave the crowds again, sir."

"Thank you for your time, Mr O'Hagan. We'll keep you updated. No more guerrilla art in my village, right?" He tipped his head at me.

"You got it, sir." I winked at Judge. She nodded.

20

MAEVE

*line's arms draped over my shoulders. "Sweetie, you should go back to Raynard Hall. You need sleep."

My eyelids sprung open. The edges of a dream pressed against my temples, like a locked door with a misplaced key. Corbin had been there, and he'd been shouting something about a crown, and his hand was clasped around that metal lump he wore on a chain, then I'd fallen into the darkness. There were other details, but when I grasped at them, they faded away. I rubbed my eyes, but that did nothing to halt the weariness spreading up my spine. "I'm fine. I'm staying right here."

"You'll do no good for him sapping your strength like this. He'll wake up when he's good and ready."

Arthur's lifeless face stared up at the ceiling. I'd never seen him so still for so long. Arthur was a fireball of energy and passion. Now even his beard looked as though it was made of stone – a statue of a Viking warrior at peace with his gods.

No, I raged against the notion. *He's not at peace. Inside that thick skull of his, he's fighting for us, for me.* I had to believe that.

I grabbed his good arm – the one he hadn't mutilated – and shook it. "Arthur, you bastard. *Wake up.*"

"Sssssh, honey bee." Aline placed her hand over mine and drew me away. A warm, calming feeling shot up my arm. I glared at her. *Don't use magic on me. I need to feel this. I need to feel all of it. It's the only way I'll be strong enough.*

Hatred isn't strength, Aline answered inside my head, but the warm feeling disappeared.

"Maeve, you've been here long enough. Why don't you call Rowan or Blake? They can sit with Arthur for a while." I started at the sound of Clara's voice. I'd forgotten she was there as well. "Someone will be here when he wakes up."

"Robert is waking up," Smithers cooed. "Robert is greeting the birds."

Aline hushed him.

I picked up Arthur's hand. My stomach clenched as his limp fingers slid through mine and flopped back on the sheet. "Rowan and Blake aren't talking to me. We had a fight."

"What about?"

"They inserted themselves into my dream last night so they could talk to Corbin." A shudder of disgust wracked my body. The betrayal of it still smarted.

"They shouldn't have done that," Aline said gently. "Did you see Corbin in your dreams again?"

"Of course I did. I'll never stop thinking about him or wishing he was with us. But they think Corbin is speaking to me through my dreams. They think he deliberately got himself stuck in the underworld and we can bring him back," I whipped up my head to narrow my eyes at her. "And don't say you believe them."

"My question is, why are you so determined *not* to believe them?"

"Because it's impossible. Dreams have no precognitive

powers, and they're not microphones into other dimensions—"

Aline held up her hand. "Ah, I believe I've heard this lecture before. As I recall, scientists know very little about the true nature of dreams, so I think one theory is just as relevant as the others."

"You'd be wrong," I snapped.

Aline ignored my rude comment. "Very well. Then if what you say about dreams is true, and they are your subconscious mind interpreting signals from your brain to process important information, then Corbin's appearance might be your subconscious alerting you to facts or discoveries your waking mind hasn't put together yet. Did Corbin speak to you in this dream? Maybe he told you something strange or coincidental?"

I frowned. Aline was right. My brain was such a pile of mush right now, I wasn't thinking as clearly or logically as I usually did. My brain might be using my dreams to sort through all this confusing magic stuff and create some kind of logical framework. I thought back to Corbin's words in my dreams. "He said he died to stop the villagers from killing us, and also because he figured out that any agreement we made with the fae would be useless unless it included the demons, too."

Clara's eyes danced. "He's bright, that lad. None of us even thought about the demons."

"It's not Corbin! It's just my subconscious. But yes, I guess that makes sense. Daigh dragged the demons into this so if we strike a deal with Liah after we defeat the Slaugh we'll have to include them, too." I didn't bother telling them about Corbin trying to speak to the demon ruler, because that was obviously my dreamstate inventing details.

"Did he say anything else?" Aline leaned forward.

"He said that that Daigh traded his powers with the king

of the demons, which we already guessed. And that Daigh's planning something that will be disastrous for humans and fae alike." I wiped one of my fallen tears off Arthur's cheek, hating the way my fingers pressed into his waxy skin. "It's all so stupid. Daigh's locked away in Raynard Hall. He has no powers. He's not a threat anymore. Oh, and Corbin also said he'd done this in secret on purpose because I never would have let him try it if I'd known, but that he had a way to get himself back to the land of the living. It's just wistful thinking by my subconscious."

He also kissed Rowan. That kiss ached in my heart because I wished it had been real, and that I could feel Corbin's warm lips on mine one last time.

"What did he – I mean, your subconscious mind – say about coming back?" Clara leaned against the door, tightening her black shawl around her shoulders.

"He said, 'I wrote it all down for you,' and Rowan found some Post-it notes on one of his spellbooks. I think it was the one you brought from the Soho coven. It was something about the Mysteries of Lazarus." I waved my hand. "I didn't look at the notes. Corbin wrote a lot of Post-its. They were stuck all over his books. It doesn't mean he had a plan. That's why I fought with Rowan, and Blake stepped in on Rowan's side which is fucking ridiculous. I don't know where they are now, and I…"

Weariness swept over me, and I found myself unable to recall the words I wanted to use. I sagged against the bed, watching Arthur's lifeless features and begging the warrior inside to wake up and fight again for me.

"Maybe all you need to bring Corbin back is to *believe*," Aline cooed.

"Belief is nonsense," I murmured as sleep overcame me. "It's an opiate for the masses without scientific justification…"

Aline's hand rubbed circles on my back. Clara and Aline talked together, but their words blurred into a dull roar. I leaned my head against Arthur's chest, timing my own breath with the steady rise and fall of his chest as the machines kept air circulating through his body.

Arthur, if you're still in there, come back to me. We need you.

My eyes fluttered shut, and I drifted into sleep.

~

I stood in the dark hallway again, listening to the piercing screams from behind the doors. Corbin faced me, his hands in his pockets, a sad expression in his kind eyes. That weird lump of ancient metal still hung from a chain around his neck, and the handle of the bone knife bobbed in his side.

"I don't know how to convince you I'm real," he said, his voice resigned.

"Come back to me," I shot back. "Appear in the hospital as flesh and blood. That's the only way."

"I can't. You're going to have to bring me back, Maeve. And the only way to do that is to believe."

"That's the hokiest thing you've ever said," I folded my arms. "You sound like my mother, who I was just talking to before I fell asleep, so that explains why you're parroting her. You're not even a very convincing illusion."

Corbin shrugged. "If you won't listen to me, maybe I've found someone else you'll trust."

He swung his hands around, trailing the dust from the ends of his fingers so it formed strange shapes, almost like runes in the air. I gasped as the dust settled in the air, floating still and forming a faint outline of a body. A body with impossibly broad shoulders and a big, bushy Viking beard.

Arthur.

175

My mouth dried up. My heart shriveled into a raisin as the grief hit me in a wave. It rocked through my body, shattering the thin veneer of control I'd managed to exert over my emotions. I gasped as pain tightened my chest. *Don't let me lose him, too.*

"He can't speak," Corbin said, placing a hand on Arthur's dusty shoulder. Arthur inclined his head toward Corbin's hand, as if agreeing with him. "He's halfway between this world and yours. I nearly had a heart attack when I found him. What's going on up there, Maeve? Why does Arthur have one foot in his grave?"

As if answering Corbin's question, Arthur raised his arm. Even though he was only dust and air, I could make out a long dent in his skin where he'd cut himself. Corbin sucked in his breath when he saw it.

"Shite," he said.

Arthur nodded.

"You're an idiot."

Arthur nodded again.

"Okay." Corbin touched the knife in his abdomen. "This makes what happens next even more important. Maeve, I know you think I'm just a dream. That's fine. But dreams tell us things about ourselves, sometimes even about things we don't *think* we understand but actually do, deep inside. I think deep down you know I'm real in some way, otherwise you wouldn't keep coming back here. I need to you stop resisting me. Stop thinking of me as Corbin if that will help, and start listening to yourself. Can you do that?"

I nodded.

Corbin's shoulders sagged as he let out a breath. "Okay, then. Our first order of business. Allow me to introduce the person who's going to help us stop Daigh."

A figure stepped out of the swirling dust, dragging an

injured leg. Green clothing hung in tatters from her body, and one arm ended in a stump.

Liah.

"What's she doing here?" I hissed.

"Greetings to you, too, witch," Liah hissed back.

"I saved her," Corbin said. "Daigh had her tied up in one of the torture chambers. He didn't want the fae to run to her in case they found out about his little bargain. She wants to help us."

I folded my arms. "Nope. This isn't going to work, because subconscious me is an idiot. Liah is *against* us. She always was. That's why she tried to kill me in the church and that's why she was the one compelling the villagers to attack the castle. Blake *felt* her mind as she did that evil."

"He did," Liah said. "Because Daigh forced me to do it. Didn't you wonder why I wasn't on the field of battle, gloating over my victory? I was here, tied up, being poked by demons until I bent my mind to Daigh's will. You'll learn soon enough that even without his power he is no enemy to be trifled with."

I threw up my hands. "Fine. I give up!" I jabbed a finger at them each in turn. "You're Corbin, back from the dead to talk to me. Arthur's a weird dust ghost. Liah's a totally kind and trustworthy fae who's really on our side and never tried to kill me. What's all this in aid of? What do you *want?*"

"Daigh's going to try and take his power back," Corbin said. "He'll escape from his prison. He'll wait until the Slaugh ride, and then he'll make his move—"

BANG BANG.

A loud rapping noise echoed through the tunnel. The floor shook beneath my feet. Dust toppled from the ceiling high above, pouring over my body and sending me crashing to the ground. My knees hit the hard stone floor and pain shot up my spine.

BANG BANG BANG.

The floor jerked again. Corbin looked up at the roof, just as another shower of dust rained down on his head. "Looks like you've got a wake-up call."

"Corbin, wait—"

"Remember, Maeve, the clay steals the clay!" Corbin shouted at me as his body faded into the darkness.

I reached out to grab him, but he retreated into the shadows as more dust toppled from the roof. My body pitched forward, and the dust swallowed me.

"*M*aeve?"

I rapped my fist against the door to the bedroom. Nothing. I'd already tried the door handle and it wouldn't turn. Maeve must've woken up after Aline brought her sleeping body in from the car and locked it. I knew I should leave her to sleep, but I couldn't stand her not talking to me and thinking badly of me. I wanted to tell her about my visit with Lady Pembroke. I wanted to lift this heaviness in my heart with her presence, just for a moment.

I rapped again, harder, the urgency rising in my throat. "It's Rowan. Please talk to me."

No sound. Panic shot through my body. *First Corbin, then Arthur, what if Maeve...*

I jiggled the handle between shaking fingers, but it was just as locked as before. I stepped back and threw my body at the door. My shoulder slammed into the wood, but it didn't give a millimeter. Frustrated, I leaned back and kicked out with my foot, the way I'd seen Arthur do in his drills a million times.

"Ow," I moaned as pain shot up my leg. How'd Arthur

make that look so easy? Wood was *hard*. Clearly, there was some trick to this. I swung my throbbing foot back and kicked at the door again.

Just as my foot skimmed the surface of the wood, Maeve flung open the door. I flailed my arms to regain my balance, but it was too late – I sailed straight into the room, toppled over the dressing table, and landed in a heap on the rug at the foot of the bed. Pain shot up my side.

"Rowan, are you okay?" Maeve fell to my side, her voice tight with concern.

"Fine," I gasped, pulling myself into a kneeling position. I grazed her cheek with my fingers. Her eyes were ringed with red. "Maeve, please, talk to me. I can't stand it if you don't talk to me."

She leaned back against the bed and ran her fingers through her short, lank hair. "Why were you kicking the door?"

"Because you locked it and I thought…" I gasped. "I thought you…"

"It wasn't locked." Maeve stood up and turned the handle. "Look, there isn't even a lock on this door."

Relief washed over my body. I leaned against the end of the bed, hugging my feet to my chest and resting my head on top. I studied the deep-pile rug, running my fingers through the fibers. The urge to count them crept up my spine, but I was able to push it back. "I must've been so scared that I couldn't turn it properly."

"Oh, Rowan." Maeve's warm arms circled my neck. She pressed her face into my shoulder, and despite everything, my heart soared. "I'm sorry for scaring you, and I'm sorry for yelling at you before. What you said at the hospital—"

"About the Post-it notes?"

"Seeing his handwriting killed me." Maeve sniffed, snuggling her face deeper, muffling her voice in my dreads. "I can't hope. Do you understand? I'm hanging on by a thread here. If I hope, and it turns out I'm wrong and I have to mourn his death all over again, then…" she sucked in a shuddering breath. "I'm not strong enough to deal with that, okay?"

"Okay," I said. I wasn't strong enough to deal with that, either. I *had* to cling to this belief that Corbin was still alive.

"Why did he have to die, Rowan?"

I bent my head to hers, planting my lips on her crown. Corbin was everything to both of us. I thought it was Maeve that bound us all together – and she did – but without Corbin, the Briarwood coven wouldn't even exist. I'd still be living on the streets in London, if my sickness hadn't claimed me already. Flynn would be a low-level mobster in Dublin, his artistic talent limited to illegal graffiti. Arthur would be an arsonist. Blake… well, we never would've met Blake and we never would've accepted him. Corbin was the one who took broken people and made them whole again.

Maeve turned her body toward me and I fell into her arms, burying myself in her soft, short hair. We rolled on the rug, wrapping ourselves up in each other. Our lips met for the first time since Corbin's death, and we drank the sorrow from each other through warm, tender kisses.

Tears streaked Maeve's face, mingling with my own. The salty droplets puddled over our lips as we drew up our memories of Corbin into a hopeless, lonely, beautiful kiss.

"I miss him," I whispered.

"I know," she whispered back. "I fucking know."

We sank into each other, drowning in our sorrow, wishing for something that couldn't be true. My hands snaked under her rumpled t-shirt, my palms pressing into warm, living skin. My earth magic pattered against my palms like rain droplets on the garden path. She moaned against my lips, pressing her body into mine.

Maeve and I, we were alive, we were flesh and meat and bleeding hearts. As our kiss heated up, our grief transformed and became hunger, a need for skin against skin and a human connection that would drive out the pain. We tore at each other in our haste. Seams ripped. Sleeves caught on wrists. We tossed and tumbled on an ocean of grief, our bodies driftwood crashing together in the storm.

Her tongue seared against mine. My hands cupped her breasts, searching her chest for the thunder of her beating heart. Blood rushed to my ears as she wrapped her fingers around my shaft and dragged a dark pleasure through every vein and sinew of my body.

I only pulled myself from the moment to remember to grab a condom, the last one I had in my pocket from what felt like a lifetime ago. Maeve rolled it on for me and pulled me against her.

As I entered her, fresh tears streamed down her face. Maeve's body curled around me, her heat welcome solace against the cold grief washing over my heart. We moved together, riding that ocean of grief, becoming one with the battering waves.

Pressure built inside me. I collapsed against her, a mess of shuddering pleasure and wrenching pain. Maeve clung to me, her body rocking with silent sobs. I wrapped my arms around her, conscious of how fragile she was, how precious.

Footsteps bounded along the hallway, approaching our room. My heart clenched as though someone held it in their fist and squeezed. I scrambled off Maeve and managed to pull my trousers back on just as Flynn burst into the room.

"Get your arses up right now," he yelled, flailing his arms. "Daigh's missing!"

I tore myself from Rowan's arms and bolted for the door, grabbing Rowan's hoodie off the floor as I ran past. *How can Daigh be missing? There's no way he could've escaped from that room—*

It was completely impossible, and yet...

The vision of Corbin's face from my dream burned behind my eyes. *He said this would happen.*

It's a coincidence. Corbin is just your subconscious. He's not telling you what will happen in the future.

For the first time, doubt flickered across my mind. I'd seen the room where we kept Daigh. I knew how secure it was. I knew he had no powers. Not even my subconscious – which was every bit as logical as my conscious mind – would have assumed he'd escape. And the idea had been planted in my head by Corbin just moments before it really happened...

"Maeve, your trousers!"

I whirled around. Flynn tossed my jeans into my arms. I shoved my feet inside – no time for socks or panties – and scrambled into the hall. Flynn and Rowan thudded after me.

I sprinted down the grand staircase, pulling Rowan's

hoodie over my naked chest. Footsteps pounded behind me. "Einstein, wait for us."

I didn't wait. I plunged into the labyrinthine hallways, some sort of instinct directing me to the correct room. The others had already gathered in Ryan's gallery room, surveying the damage. And what damage there was.

The short hallway leading to the safe no longer existed. In its place was an enormous charred hole. Bits of drywall and shards of the steel door littered the hardwood floor where the wood hadn't burned to a crisp or curled up.

Flynn picked up a piece of metal between his fingers. "It's been shattered," he whispered. "Like it's bloody glass."

"That's twelve-inch bulletproof steel," Ryan picked through a pile of debris. He held up a tangle of cords and metal teeth – what remained of the keypad and lock. "It's supposed to be able to withstand nuclear fallout."

"Apparently it's not demon-proof," I growled. *It made perfect sense.* "A fae couldn't have done this, not with their allergy to metal. This is what Daigh traded for his powers – an escape route. He knew we'd keep him alive and try to hold him."

"He might've left my art intact," Ryan picked up the corner of a gilded frame that had fallen from the wall beside the hallway. Tatters of canvas hung from the wood. "This was a *Cezanne.*"

"We've got to find him."

"Why?" Ryan kicked debris across the floor. "He's history. He can't go back to the fae – not now they know he doesn't have any powers."

"We can't just leave him wandering around the village!" I yelled. "He could hurt people."

"He can't do anything now he's human," Flynn pointed out.

"I don't think so. A human couldn't have done this. If Daigh traded his powers, he must've done it with a demon."

"Maeve." Flynn grabbed my shoulder, shaking me hard enough to clatter my teeth together. "What's wrong? You've gone as pale as a wee goth kid."

"I had another dream," I sobbed. "I think... I can't explain it, but I just have this feeling..."

Flynn's fingers dug into my shoulders, his eyes a perfect storm of emotion. "Tell us everything you saw, Einstein."

"Corbin was there, and Arthur." Behind Flynn, Rowan flinched, his eyes filling with pain. I kept talking. "But Arthur was just this nearly invisible shape. He couldn't speak. Corbin said he had one foot in both worlds. And then he pulled Liah out of the darkness and—"

"Liah?" Blake appeared by my side, his face stony.

I sniffed. "She said Daigh was torturing her so she'd compel the villagers to attack the castle. I guess... he could have used her to hide his lack of power from the other fae. She said she was on our side this whole time."

"Fae lie," Blake whispered.

"But she didn't kill you! Back at the church, she had the chance to get to me through you, and she didn't take it. She may bear me no kind feelings, but when it came down to it she wouldn't hurt you."

"Are you saying this is a real dream?" Ryan demanded, straightening up and letting a scrap of canvas flutter to the ground.

"Yes. No. I think so." I threw up my hands. "I don't know!"

"If it is real..." Flynn whistled. "Then Corbin was right. Daigh's making a move on the crown of Hell."

"And he'll do it soon, while the Slaugh are riding and we're all distracted." I glanced up at Clara, who hovered in the doorway with Aline, Smithers, and Jane. "When will they come?"

"Tonight, at the stroke of midnight," she said.

"I'll call Officer Judge," Flynn pulled out his phone. "She'll organize a search of the village. If he can't act until then, he might be hiding out somewhere." I raised an eyebrow at the idea of calling the officer who'd been part of the mob, and Flynn filled us in on the conversation he'd had with Wallace and Judge after he returned to Briarwood. I hoped he was right, that we could trust her.

With the press at the gates, we couldn't go out to look for Daigh ourselves. Aline and Clara both tried a scrying spell to search for him, but because he didn't have his fae power any longer, they came up with nothing. I sent out my spirit magic to Flynn's statue and Ryan's painting, and found them humming with belief. We were ready. The only thing we could do was wait.

Simon laid food out for us in the kitchen. We all sat around the island, staring at the platters of cold meat and cheese and fresh bread, unable to eat a morsel. The only sound was the clatter of camera shutters and excited hum of the media circus wafting in through the open window. Finally, I pushed my chair back.

"Get some sleep," Ryan said. "Even with the belief magic, the battle tonight will be fierce."

As if I needed reminding. I trudged down the hallway toward the guest wing. Footsteps clattered after me. Flynn fell in step beside me. He ran his hand down my arm, leaving behind a trail of heat. "Your skin's sizzling with magic, Einstein," he grinned.

"Rowan might've had something to do with that." On the other side of me, Rowan stiffened.

"I guess you don't need an extra magical boost?" Flynn lifted an eyebrow suggestively. Blake appeared behind him, flashing me his trademark smirk.

"I didn't say that," I replied, my stomach fluttering with heat.

I turned a corner in the hall. Blake grabbed my hand and spun my body around, so I ended up with my back against the wall, his chest pressed against mine. His fingers grazed over my breast, bringing my nipple to attention through the thin fabric of my t-shirt.

I still hadn't forgiven him for invading my dream and running off with Rowan, but his emerald eyes smoldered with my own reflected desire. My body arched against him. I needed to lose myself in him.

Blake's lips caught mine, blazing fire through my body. All thoughts of resting and demons and the Slaugh flew from my mind as his kiss broke down all my barriers. I was wide open, and he poured his desire into me.

I hooked my legs behind Blake's. He shoved me into the wall, grinding his hard cock against my sex until my body begged for release. His hands shoved up my shirt and bra and pinched my nipples. I whimpered against his lips as the pain only heightened the burning heat inside me.

I adjusted my leg, accidentally kicking a side table and knocking over an ugly ceramic vase. Flynn dived and caught it before it smashed on the marble floor.

"We should probably take this back to our bedroom," Flynn whispered, setting the vase right. Reluctantly, Blake slid off me, and he and Flynn both took my hands. "We wouldn't want to destroy any more of Ryan's house."

My body was so fired up that right then I didn't care who saw us. I wanted the whole world to know how much I loved these boys, how they completed me in a way I never thought possible.

We ran to our bedroom. Blake sat on the edge of the bed, pulling me down so I straddled him. His cock ground against me through his black jeans. Flynn climbed up behind us, tugging off my shirt and bra and stroking my breasts until I moaned against Blake's relentless tongue.

As Blake's kisses stoked the fires of my need, Flynn kissed along my collarbone, drawing a moan of desire from deep inside me. Rowan's soft hands skimmed my sides and circled my breasts, his touch liquid fire against my skin.

"On your back, Princess," Blake grinned, throwing me on the bed. "Let all of us get a go at you."

I obeyed, clambering back and laying my body across the sheets. Blake's mouth closed over my nipple, sucking it hard. My back arched with pleasure. My hands flew to his head, winding my fingers through his hair, encouraging him to suck harder. He nipped at the tip and stars danced in my eyes.

"Oh, we want a bit of pain today, do we?" Blake's eyes glinted. He grabbed my wrists in both hands and held them above my head. "As always, Princess, I am but a humble servant."

His teeth grazed the edge of my nipple as his fingers dug into my wrists. Someone moved between my legs as a second pair of lips closed over my other nipple, catching it between teeth and tongue. Rowan's dreadlocks fanned over my thighs as he kissed a trail up my legs, his tongue darting inside me, teasing the ache in my belly to the breaking point before closing his lips over my clit.

Rowan stroked his tongue over me, soft and languid, a direct contrast to the hardness of Blake and Flynn. The ache inside me filled with a growing well of magic. My legs jerked as Rowan flicked his tongue against me, and my body shuddered with an intense orgasm.

I'd barely recovered when Flynn batted Rowan out of the way. "You've already had your turn today, mate."

"Hey," I protested, my voice tight with mounting pleasure. "There's plenty of Maeve to go around..."

My protests faded into groans of ecstasy as Flynn attacked my clit with his tongue while Blake devoured my mouth, biting my lip and pinching my nipples until another wild orgasm tore through me. I was still crying out when Blake grabbed my ankles, jerking my body across the bed and piercing me on his cock.

We crashed into each other, two opposing forces meeting in an inferno of chemical reactions. Blake drove himself into me with a power and fury I'd never known before, and I bucked my hips to meet every stroke with my own power.

Blake's smirk wavered as his muscles tightened and the lip of his cock jerked inside me. My fingers tightened around his shoulders, relishing as his orgasm claimed him, and for a moment I got a precious glimpse beyond his facade to the lonely boy raised by the fae who was learning what it was to love a family and to lose them.

Blake slunk back and Flynn climbed up beside me. I wrapped my body around his, my spirit magic crackling against his skin. Flynn, the joker who had been my rock ever since Corbin and Arthur left us, who thought he contributed nothing but was actually the glue that held our coven together. I needed to show him how much he was loved and needed. I needed him to free himself.

I rolled onto my stomach, bending my knees and thrusting my ass in the air. Flynn grabbed my thighs and thrust inside me, his cock twitching as I took in his whole length with a gasp.

Flynn bucked against me, his strokes frantic, without rhythm or sense. He had so much baggage, so much insecurity about himself and his place in the world. If I could heal him through my body, then that was the greatest gift I could give him.

Rowan came around the front of me, and I took his cock in my mouth, licking as far down his enormous shaft as I could reach. Rowan's eyelids fluttered shut as my tongue slid down his length. Every thrust of Flynn's drove him deeper into my throat. So full of two of my guys, so willing to give myself over completely to their bodies and their souls.

Flynn was the first to come, his cock driving deep as he buried his pain inside me. My moans vibrated around Rowan's cock, and it must've been more than he could take because he withdrew and shot his load across my shoulder, his body collapsing with a sigh.

We cleaned up in the bathroom, washing away our sweat and saliva with hot water and fancy soaps, then collapsed in bed together – our coven reduced to four broken people. My body pulsed with magic from the sharing of our bodies and hearts, ready to hook into the well of belief we'd stored in the artworks and unleash it on our enemies. Bring on the Slaugh.

They would come for us here, drawn to our coven – the first souls they needed to devour in order to be truly free. But we were ready.

Outside, lights flashed through the gate as the media settled in for the night. Flynn pulled up some of the news stories on his phone. "There's a queue all the way down the high street to get into the gallery to view Ryan's painting," he said, showing us the picture.

"Brits will queue for anything," Rowan grinned. I beamed at him. It was so nice to hear him telling a joke, even at a time like this.

Flynn frowned. "Watch it, mate. Unlike the opening of a Wimpy Bar, Ryan Raynard is worth queuing for."

"I'd queue for curry," Blake added.

"No you wouldn't," I said. "You'd flirt with the woman behind the counter and she'd let you in ahead of everyone else."

"True. That is what I'd do."

We huddled together, watching the minutes tick down on Flynn's phone screen. We didn't speak much, just enjoyed the presence of each other. The absence of Arthur and Corbin passed, unsaid but felt, between us.

"Do you know what Corbin said to me, the night before the attack?" I rested my head on Rowan's shoulder. "He was thinking about going to college. We talked about applying for Oxford together, and he would study useless languages and I'd study physics and we'd take the train back to Briarwood on weekends to see all of you. We joked that you could send us care packages of scones and eccles cakes."

"I would do that," Rowan said, his long lashes fluttering over sad eyes.

"Corbin said he had to let go of his need to look after everyone. I remember his words exactly. 'It might just be possible to be a Briarwood witch and have a life.'" I snorted. "I guess he's proven us wrong—Holy shit, I've got it."

"What?"

"It's an ampulla!" The magic buzzed around my head. I turned to Blake and Rowan. "Do you remember in the dream, Corbin was wearing this lump of metal on a chain around his neck? I've seen it on him in all the dreams. He never used to wear anything like that, but it seemed really familiar for some reason. I've just remembered where I've seen it before. He was telling me about it in the library when we talked about Oxford."

"I remember it now," Rowan whispered. His fingers dug into my thigh. "It was one of the objects on his shelf."

"It's called an ampulla. It's a vessel for storing holy water from a pilgrimage. Corbin said this one included a cross of Saint Lazarus, the dude Jesus raised from the dead after four days." My heart raced. "After *four days*. That's nearly how long Corbin's been gone."

"The spells Corbin were looking at in the Soho coven's

grimoire mentioned the gospels of John and something called the Mysteries of Lazarus," Rowan said, his voice catching.

Holy holy holy shit.

I knew the story of Lazarus from my parents. It was one of their favorite tales about the miraculous abilities of Jesus, and it was important because it was the last miracle Jesus performed before the crucifixion. It foreshadowed his own rise from the dead.

Corbin could have figured out how to raise the dead back to life, like Jesus raised Lazarus. He could have been telling the truth all this time.

I wrote it all down for you.

I tried to force down the hope welling up inside me, but once it had taken root in my heart, it sprouted wings and soared too high for me to rein in.

"Rowan, where are those Post-it notes?" My words came out in a breathless gush. "We've got a day to figure out how to reverse whatever spell Corbin cast. It's going to be tough if Arthur doesn't wake up, but maybe we can convince Isadora to participate. She's a fire witch, and—"

"Uh, guys," Flynn said, his body stiffening. "While I agree that hearing Einstein admit she might've been wrong about her dream is the most delightful sound, you might want to have a look out the window."

I whirled around. Black clouds rolled across the previously clear sky, blocking out the moon and plunging the garden into darkness.

The walls groaned as the earth itself rumbled. I clung to Flynn as the movement jolted us off the bed.

The ride of the Slaugh had begun.

23

MAEVE

*R*aynard Hall trembled on her foundations. We grabbed the swords and daggers Ryan had left for us, shoving weapons into our belts as we scrambled through the winding hallways. The earth tossed us into the walls and flung furniture against us, but we ducked and dived and stumbled our way to the entrance hall. Flynn reached the front door first and flung it open.

Cameras flashed at us as we staggered across the overgrown gardens, illuminating the ground in pulses of light. When the press realized Ryan wasn't with us they backed off a little. Unease rippled through the crowd behind the gate as they craned their necks up at the cloud.

My eyes scanned the cloud, hoping it was just a freak storm rolling in but knowing in my heart it was not. Flynn had his phone's flashlight trained at the sky, but the beam barely illuminated more than a halo around his red hair. At the edges of the beam, dark tendrils flitted in and out of view, like leather whips flicking through the air.

The earth rumbled – thunder rolling in beneath our feet

and above our heads. The sound came from everywhere, from nowhere.

"That's no storm!" a reporter cried.

"Excellent deduction, Sherlock!" Blake yelled back. His hand clamped over mine. Rowan moved to my other side. We crouched on the ground as the thunder rolled over us.

The rumble crushed me, invading my body and breaking apart, becoming not one sound but a great many – a thousand hooves clapping and clattering together. Churning legs shod in spiked shoes poked out from the bottom of the clouds, and dark shapes pressed against the edges, ready to burst.

"Run!" I yelled at the reporters, my hand flying to the sword at my side.

Of course they didn't. They trained their cameras to the cloud and *snap snap snap* they recorded the hooves descending toward them, not knowing they were staring at the riders of the dead.

We were all that stood between the world and total destruction. Flynn tore my hand from the sword hilt, his palm already slick with water. Blake grabbed my other hand and he and Blake linked hands with Rowan, bracing ourselves against each other. The four of us formed a circle with our shoulders touching, trying to force out the horror so we could focus on the ritual. It was going to be tougher than we thought because we were missing two witches, but we had the belief magic to draw from. That would be enough.

It *had* to be enough.

There was no looking away as the cloud burst like a balloon. Horses made of the night rolled down from the darkness, their riders tall and proud upon their steeds. Dark hoods flew back to reveal grinning faces, and I got my my first look at the army of the dead.

Toothy grins leered at me from bare skulls – not white like in museum displays, but various shades of black and brown and grey. Skin hung in patches from their emaciated bodies. Many of them bore the marks of grisly deaths – ones had an axe-handle sticking out of its back, another had one half of its skull caved in, still another had a bullet hole punched through its forehead. Diseased patches of sickly green skin tore away from one's cheeks as it flew toward us. *Just like the knife sticking out of Corbin's side.* It seemed the restless dead wore their demise like a badge of honor.

They crashed onto the overgrown lawn, the horses bending so low their bellies scraped the ground. Leather saddles creaked and swords clattered as riders bore up, half of them turning toward the iron gates while the rest faced my coven.

Now the reporters reacted. Screams echoed across the lawn as they staggered back down the road toward the village, crashing into each other in their haste to get away from the front lines. Lights swiveled at mad angles as crews abandoned their equipment and shuttered themselves in their vans. Hooves churned up the dirt as the Slaugh raced for the gates. The horses bore down, their bodies traveling right through the iron bars as though they weren't there at all.

How do they go right through the gates but leave hoofprints in the dirt? The physics of it doesn't make any sense—

"Maeve!" Flynn's voice snapped me back to reality. He yelled something else, but I could barely make out the words over the snapping and screaming and clattering as the Slaugh tore through the reporters. I couldn't see through their ranks if anyone was hurt. "You ready?"

Ice-cold wind whipped my bangs across my face. My breath caught in my throat. If I stopped to think about what was bearing down on us, I was going to lose it.

We've got this.

"Ready." I closed my eyes, shutting away the advancing army, the clattering of hooves, the creaking of leather saddles as their ghoulish riders adjusted their seat. I leaned into the guys, allowing the steadiness of their bodies, the strength of their shoulders and the tug of their magic to ground me. I sunk into myself, calling up the pillar that had been stoked by their touch. I drove it higher, pushing our magic toward the village.

The pillar burst out of my chest, rising in the center of our circle in a great cone of power. It shot high in the air and radiated out. As it moved across the horizon, it plucked magic from the screaming reporters and Flynn's statue and *The Witch's Lament* and the millions of people around the world reading about the strange goings-on in Crookshollow, England. With each morsel of magic it collected, it grew stronger and more cohesive, until it burst from its cage and spread across the heavens like a giant net made of filaments of glittering magic.

A horse reared up, the rider reaching a skeletal hand down to Blake. The light swelled, flaring out from the net to shove the horse back. Black tendrils tangled between its strands, trapping the horse in the light of belief. As I watched in awe, the light glowed brighter until it completely enveloped horse and rider. With a terrified neigh and an inhuman scream, they were swallowed up.

My heart surged. *It works!* I dug deep inside myself, touching the roots of my power, drawing up the magic in every cell of my body, the power that lurked in my DNA, and I *pushed*, and I *wished*, and I *believed* that we could win this.

The net spread wider, curling over the riders, tangling their weapons and tightening around their bodies. Horses went down in a clash of limbs and hooves, bringing down others who were moving too fast to avoid a collision. The momentum of the Slaugh slipped away as the flanks collapsed in on themselves. Horses turned around in fright, crashing into the ranks behind them in their haste to escape the advancing light.

Magic hummed through my hands as the guys fed me their power. The net tightened, tightened, pressing the beasts together, trapping them against each other so they couldn't advance. Their power surged against the light, but I held strong. I believed.

Almost done. Almost—

Blake dropped my hand.

My magic dipped as his power was torn from me. Two horses escaped from the net and bolted for the castle gates. Behind me, the line buckled as horses bore down on me, their riders spurring them on as they threw themselves at the net again and again.

"Blake?" I cried.

Blake didn't hear me. His body stiffened and his face froze in his familiar smirk. Two riders stood facing him, their horses snorting black fog as the riders cut the filaments that bound them with glowing blades of fire. The first rider lifted its hand to wave in greeting, and they both shrugged off their hoods.

Skin still clung to their faces, peeling back in places to reveal dark, charred bone, but their faces still carried the features of their human lives – their kind eyes and high cheekbones and wicked, hauntingly-beautiful grins.

My stomach churned as I recognized those features. They were decaying versions of Blake's perfect face.

I was looking at the shades of Blake's parents.

24

BLAKE

My parents.

They towered over me, resplendent in flowing black cloaks. Their horses' midnight manes streamed behind them, gold thread braided into the dark hair. And those faces…

Even though I'd only been a babe when Daigh stole me from their home and killed them to hide his crime, my body remembered their warm embrace, their gentle rocking and their soft coos. My arms itched to reach up and embrace their bony shoulders, to have their skeletal fingers encircle my wrists and pull me up onto a horse beside them.

Something tore inside me as I stared down everything that had been taken from me, at the life I could have had.

"Our Blake," the woman's teeth clattered together. "We've waited so long to see you again."

"Join us, son." My father outstretched his hand.

Any human would've crumpled under the weight of the shock and grief. But I'd been schooled in the classroom of Daigh. Nothing shocked me. Not even this.

I drew the sword from my belt, twining the blade through

the stream of magic until filaments of light darted along the blade.

I swung with everything I had and vaporized them to dust.

"Fuck you." I spat in the circle of scorched earth. I was Blake Beckett, born to humans, raised by the fae, lover of the greatest witch alive. I didn't need the ghoulish embrace of a couple of shades.

I had more love than I ever could've hoped for. And I would fight until I died for that love and for my new family.

I turned back to Maeve, shoving the sword back into my belt and throwing out my hand. She clasped her fingers in mine, and pressed her lips against me. Spirit magic surged between us, feeding into the great net of light that held back the Slaugh.

My eyes fluttered shut and I lost myself in the kiss, in the love that flowed between us and become the most powerful force on earth. Because I believed in her, and in myself.

A roar rushed over my body – a cold ice that was beaten back by a burst of brilliant warmth, like sunlight penetrating a dark pool.

I opened my eyes.

Light streaked across the sky as the net tightened and closed, trapping the riders and their mounts, tugging them back through the tear in the cosmos from whence they came. Magic crackled through the sky as the filaments tangled with black tendrils of darkness, grappling for a hold on the earth. The light won. The shadows retreated, taking the dead back to their own kingdom.

With a final surge of heat, the light exploded. A great wind knocked me to the ground. I scrambled onto my hands and knees in time to see the light fade into a single brilliant star that dominated a crisp, clear sky. A few scattered shades loped around the lawn, their horses whinnying as they searched for their mates. One skeleton had to leap down from its horse as the creature spied flowers in one of the parterres and decided to have a snack.

"Be still my wee Irish heart." Flynn pointed at the rider trying to shove his horse away from the geraniums. "Isn't that Albert Einstein?"

Rowan burst out laughing. I didn't know what the famous scientist looked like, but the shade had a head of frizzy white hair sticking up in all angles and a pained expression on his face. He dug his heels into the dirt, but his horse didn't budge.

"That's Maeve's expression after trying to make us do the dishes. Maeve, did you see—" Flynn turned around, his words dying on his lips. My blood turned cold as I stared at the spot where Maeve should have been standing.

She wasn't there. She wasn't anywhere on the field.

Maeve had disappeared.

25

MAEVE

*M*y breath burned in my throat as I pounded down the hill after the shades. Their faces flickered across my vision. I'd only seen them for a fraction of a second, just as the belief magic swept through the Slaugh ranks and bore them back into the dark cloud and away from earth forever. But that second was enough. I couldn't let the darkness take them, not again.

I broke from our protective circle and chased after them, waving my arms to shoo their horses away from the edges of the net of light. Their hooves tangled in the web, and I flung the filaments aside so the creatures could escape the snare. They galloped off around the side of Raynard Hall, and I raced after them.

My chest burned as I careened down the slope. They reached the edge of the forest that bordered Ryan's property – the same wood that met up with Briarwood. There they stopped, as if waiting for me to catch up. The largest horse snorted at me, impatient to be on its way.

I landed at the bottom of the hill, doubling over and gasping for air.

"You..." I gasped, struggling to regain my strength. Performing the spell had taken every ounce of my energy. I was in no state to be running around after shades.

But these shades...

As one, the two riders turned to face me. Without the black cloud in the way, the clear moon lit up their faces, showing every feature in brilliant detail.

From atop their midnight steeds, Matthew and Louise Crawford smiled down at me.

26

MAEVE

or the newly dead, they fared pretty well. Their discolored skin had sunken around their eyes, and Matthew's cheekbones were visible through torn flesh on his cheeks. Below the collar of his black cloak, I could see the ugly striped t-shirt Kelly and I bought him for his birthday, the shirt he was wearing the night of the fair. The collar charred around the edges, as did the hem of Louise's favorite floral maxi dress.

"Maeve, we miss you." Matthew's jaw jerked open and shut.

"Come join us." Louise's skeletal hand stretched from her dark robe. Cold fingers brushed my cheek, shooting needles of ice into my skin. My body froze, torn between two actions – wrapping my arms around them and accepting their embrace, or running as fast as I could in the opposite direction.

My jaw moved, but I could form no sound. A flicker of magic passed over my palm, and with it a fury, so raw and hard it frightened me. *I shouldn't have to face them like this. I should never have to say goodbye a second time.*

"We just want to be a family again," Matthew cracked, his jaw jerking like a ventriloquist dummy. "You, me, your mother, Kelly—"

"You stay away from Kelly!" I yelled, throwing a blast of spirit magic at him. He reeled for a moment, then urged his horse forward. The animal took another step toward me. Matthew's hand extended down, the fingers outstretched, tender, ready to scoop up his little girl and make everything okay again.

Matthew froze. His hands flew to his chest.

A green-tipped arrow stuck out of his robes, right where his heart would have been.

Matthew's mouth hung open in silent terror. The glow in his eyes flickered out and he toppled off his mount. His cloak flapped around his body. Louise screamed as he hit the ground and shattered into a pile of bone and dust.

Her scream cut off as a second arrow punched through her forehead, bending her head back and sending her toppling over the arse of her horse. Louise sprawled across the grass, her dress balled up against her knees. She opened her mouth in a silent cry as her body collapsed to dust.

The two black beasts bolted, heedless to their lost riders. They cantered down the slope, their hooves fading into the woods as they disappeared between the trees, becoming just another secret of the ancient Crookshollow Forest.

I whirled around, searching for the source of the arrows. My heart hammered in my chest as I scanned the trees sheltering the garden. At any moment I expected to feel a barb pierce my chest.

"We meet again, *witch*," a cold voice rasped in my ear.

I spun back around so fast I lost my balance and toppled into the statuesque figure standing uncomfortably close to me. A pair of brilliant emerald eyes regarded mine with the wry amusement typical of the fae. She clasped a bow in her good hand, while with the other she unwound the rope that formed her makeshift firing device.

Liah.

"They were my parents," I said, not certain if I should be hurting her or thanking her.

"Not anymore." Liah slid the bow up on her back. "I assume you know why I'm here."

"I wouldn't know."

Liah peered at me with a quizzical expression. "I thought you were the clever one. It's obvious."

"Nothing about this situation is obvious."

Liah sighed. "Corbin explained it all in your dream. I've come to help you defeat Daigh."

"That's no good. Daigh escaped. I assume a demon helped him, because the door to Ryan's safe was blown to pieces. I'd like to have that kind of power."

Liah rolled her eyes. "It's hardly impressive. It's just the right kind of energy applied at a specific pressure point, exactly as you have just done to banish the Slaugh. Even your human metals have their weaknesses."

A laugh escaped my throat. "You sound like me."

"Your lover has said as much on many occasions these past days," Liah said. "It's not a compliment."

I laughed again. "It's hard to believe that all this time, you were on our side. It would've been easier if you'd just said something."

"I was never on your side. I was only ever on the side of the trees." Liah's gaze traveled to the forest, where a crisp breeze shook the branches. For the first time ever, warmth flickered in her eyes. She held out her stump to me. "Will you come with me?"

Trust another fae? Not bloody likely.

I slipped my fingers around Liah's forearm. Thick scars crisscrossed her skin, forming a magical symbol that hummed with residual power as I traced its lines. It reminded me of the deep cut along Arthur's arm, and I squirmed. Beneath my fingers, the scars split open and black tendrils curled out, creeping up her arm and encircling both of us. They felt like ice where they licked my skin.

Liah brought up her other arm. The moonlight glinted off a bone knife clenched in her fist. In slow motion, I watched her swing her arm around and jam the blade into my chest.

I stared down at the handle protruding from between my ribs. Cold crept through my body, radiating out from the blade. I expected there to be pain, but there was none. Just a pleasant, humming numbness.

I tried to cry out, but I couldn't work my jaw. I tried to free my hand from Liah's arm, but found it quite impossible. Messages from my brain didn't seem to be reaching my body. A dull roar quaked in my ears, like the rumble of the Slaugh approaching, but from inside my head. My own doom marching toward me.

The thought occurred to me that Corbin and now I had a similar appendage. *It's like we're twins.* I burst out laughing. Blood bubbled up in my throat and splattered down my t-shirt as I gasped and chortled at the ludicrous situation.

"Good luck," Liah said. She placed her hand against my chest and pushed. I toppled backward, and darkness claimed me before my body hit the ground.

2 7

MAEVE

I woke up coughing, my mouth filled with dust. My stomach lurched and I doubled over, hacking up my lungs.

I rubbed at my stinging eyes, struggling to see through the gloom. For a moment I imagined myself to be back at Briarwood, and the villagers had returned to raze the place to the ground with me inside. Clouds of dust swirled around me, punctuated by flickering lights, like the campfires Andrew and I used to make out in the desert during our astronomy monitoring sessions.

A dark figure moved through the dust, obscuring the light so it was a silhouette in the gloom. A strong hand reached down and hauled me to my feet.

"Maeve?" Corbin's velvet voice caressed my ears. His hand on mine was warm, living flesh.

"Corbin… I… you…"

He stifled my words with his mouth, claiming me in a deep kiss. I clung to him and drank in the warmth of his embrace, the softness of his tongue against mine, the scent of old leather and parchment rolling off him. Everything about him was exactly as he always was. *Alive. But how—*

Something tugged against my abdomen, causing a bolt of pain to shoot through me. Corbin's eyes widened. He pulled away, his mouth dropping open in horror. His hand flew to the knife handle sticking out of his side.

I looked down, shocked to see a similar handle poking out of my own chest. The memories flooded back to me, along with a dull pain in my chest, as though I'd run into the corner of a piece of furniture. I remembered the black tendrils crawled from Liah's wound and encircling my arm. I remembered Liah holding my hand and thrusting the knife between my ribs.

Corbin's jaw set. He strode forward and yanked the handle. A knife blade slid out of my chest with a gurgling noise, like water going down the sink. I closed my eyes, expecting blood to gush from the wound and the pain to finally hit, but the dull ache of the wound never changed. I barely felt a thing.

I blinked, staring down at my chest. The knife was back inside me.

"It wasn't supposed to go like this! You weren't supposed to die to come after me!" Corbin yelled, shaking my shoulders so hard my head jerked back. "Bloody hell, Maeve, why do you have to be so stubborn? Why couldn't you have just accepted the dreams?"

"Liah brought me here," I whispered. "You mean the dreams were…"

"You're a dreamwalker, Maeve. You should know by now you don't have an ordinary subconscious." Corbin crushed me against his chest, his knife handle scraping my side while mine bent out to the side. "If I didn't love you so much I swear I would kill you myself, but it looks like Liah's done that for me. I told her to help you find me, but I meant in your *dreams*. She could have put you to sleep and—"

"Well, I'm here now." My fingers clasped around the metal object around his neck. "The guys and I have just figured out about the ampulla and the mysteries of Lazarus. They're putting the pieces together. We defeated the Slaugh, and now they'll bring us back."

"They'd better act quickly," Corbin gestured down the dark hallway, like a guide about to give a tour. "Because if what I've seen comes to pass, we could end up stuck here, and the Slaugh are going to be the least of our worries."

FLYNN

"*M*aeve!" I gazed frantically around, hoping to see her crouched behind one of the gardens or resting against one of the tall oaks lining the drive. Nothing. She was nowhere in sight. *But how could we lose her so quickly, unless...*

"Where are you?" Rowan's voice rose with fear.

"Maeve? This isn't funny."

The three of us spread out, searching across the lawn. A riderless horse cantered past my head as I bent to check behind a row of parterres. Nothing. No Maeve.

Rowan came running over, his chest heaving as he struggled against his anxiety. "I've got Ryan and Simon searching the house," he said, his hand over his heart like he was gonna catch it before it flew away. "Aline and Kelly are around the back. You don't think Daigh got to her somehow? That he—"

"Let's not assume the worst. Come on, I think I saw a couple of riders head around the side of the house." I tore off across the overgrown lawn, descending the slope of the hill toward the edge of the forest. Hoofprints pocked the ground.

Yep, horses had definitely been here. A crumpled shape lay on the grass at the foot of the slope.

"Shite, Maeve!"

My stomach lodged in my throat. Not even when a new whiskey distillery offered free tastings had I moved so fast. I scrambled down the slope and slid next to the lump. It was Maeve all right, splayed out on her back, her pink bangs plastered to her pale face, her chest and arms streaked with blood.

A bone-handled knife stuck out of her chest. The blade had gone in between her ribs, directly into her heart.

The world stopped.

Maeve, no no no no.

I grabbed her shoulders and shook her, calling her name again and again. Her head flopped to the side, limp and lifeless. Blake dropped down beside me, pressing his hand to her wound and uttering a string of nonsense. Rowan howled.

"She's gone," a cold voice said.

I jerked my head up just as a tall fae stepped out of the forest. Hair like white silk streamed down her back in two braids, each one woven with silver strands and vines that had wilted and blackened into black streaks. She wore the livery of a Seelie fae, although her clothing was torn and stained with dark patches. A bow and quiver of arrows were slung across her back, and her expression was one of calculated indifference.

"Liah, what are you doing here?" Blake's eyes narrowed.

"Maeve needed to reach your friend in the underworld," the fae said, tossing a braid over her shoulder. "I helped her."

"You *killed* her," I growled, raising my hand to point my palm at Liah, calling up the scrappy remnants of my magic, drawing what little I had left in me into a big enough blast of water and hoping when I sent it flying that it would drown her where she stood. My veins boiled. My jaw clenched.

If this was how Arthur felt all the time, it was little wonder he hadn't razed the world.

"Flynn, no." Blake shoved my hand down just as I loosed a blast. Water shot out of my palm and scoured out a thick channel in the hillside, crashing against the trunk of a thin oak and splitting the wood.

"Why'd you stop me?" I growled at him, my muscles spasming in protest. I was empty. Now I'd need to wait to call up more magic.

"She's trying to help us," Blake said, turning to Liah, his expression unreadable. "I think."

"I have no interest in helping you to send the fae back to their realm," Liah hissed. "But Daigh cannot be allowed to take up the underworld crown. Your friend also wished to assure that would not happen. He needed help, so I sent she who was most well-placed to help him. In that way, yes, I am helping."

"Helping doesn't mean you stab someone in the fecking chest!" I roared.

"If we want Daigh stopped forever," Liah said, raising her arm to show the stump of her dismemberment and the scar of a sigil that bled darkness over her pale skin, "this is the only way. As soon as he wears that crown, he'll hold all the demons power over life and death, and he could raise the Slaugh at any time, along with other long-buried horrors that could terrorise earth."

Blake's hand tightened around my wrist. I didn't care. She stabbed Maeve. My heart ached, as if I'd been the one she stabbed.

"You've been to the underworld," Blake said, his voice impossibly calm and even. "Can Maeve come back once she's stopped Daigh going full demon?"

Liah shrugged her shoulders. "Your friend believes so. I've

heard rumors of it done before. I was not concerned about their return – only about stopping Daigh."

"Corbin," Rowan said, his voice so soft I thought I imagined it. "If there's a chance to bring him back, and Maeve, too… then I want to do it."

"If we're right about the Lazarus thing, we've got a day to figure out how to bring them back. But now there are only three of us and I don't—"

Blake's phone buzzed in his pocket. To my surprise he drew it out and answered the call. His face brightened as he listened to the voice on the other end.

"As Flynn loves to say, Praise be Jesus, Mary, Joseph and all their carpenter friends." Blake hung up the call and dropped his phone into his pocket. "We'd better get to the hospital. Arthur's awake."

*C*orbin gripped my hand so tight that he'd have cut off circulation if I actually still had circulating blood, which I doubted. As he dragged me down the endless, dust-swept black hallway, the knife handle bobbed on my chest. I barely noticed the familiar wooden doors or the humming stone walls – it fascinated me so much to see this foreign object sticking out of me.

I should be able to feel it inside me, but instead my whole chest is numb, like my mouth after the dentist gives me a shot.

Corbin kept looking over his shoulder at me, as if he expected me to disappear. His fingers tightened around mine, crushing me with his fear. Our feet scuffed at a fine layer of sulphur dust and red-stained sand coating the floor. The humming buzzed in my ears, and it took me a few moments to realize that I couldn't hear any shrieks of pain from behind any of the doors, like in my dreams. The whole place was eerily quiet.

"Where is everyone?" I asked.

"At the Slaugh. Or rather, wherever you sent them when you destroyed the Slaugh. The shades ride the horses, but they need all the demons and fae at the rear to poke them with pitchforks or something." Corbin shrugged. "From what little my books said about the Slaugh, I think when you destroyed them what you actually did was allow those shades to pass over to the next stage of their journey, and you probably took all the demons with them. That might be a good thing, if the tortures I've been witness to these past three days are any indication."

"I saw my parents," I said. "They were begging me to come with them."

Corbin shuddered. "I'm sorry," he said, his voice wavering. "That's part of the Slaugh's power. They use your loved ones to tempt you into death. Your soul is so much sweeter that way."

"Liah shot them with her arrows and they disintegrated to dust." I closed my eyes. "That's the second time I had to watch them die in front of me."

"If it's any consolation, I think they're now finally at peace."

"What about the demons? Are they trapped on this other plane with the shades?" I hated the idea of my parents and Blake's parents being tortured somewhere I couldn't help them.

"The demons will eventually find their way back here. Natural order will have to be restored. It just takes some time. All I know is, this place is ours for the moment, but we're got to move quickly. It'll start filling up with recently deceased souls soon, and the demons and fae will return. After how you defeated them so thoroughly, it's best if we're not here when they do."

"Where are we going?"

"To stop Daigh. Quickly. We're close now."

As we rounded another corner, the ground rolled out from under me. Dust cascaded from the ceiling as an earthquake shook the hallway. I pitched forward. Corbin caught my arm before I smashed into the floor.

"What's that?" I cried, steadying myself against the humming stone wall.

"Hopefully, it's the only remaining demon kicking Daigh's arse before he gets his hands on that crown."

Corbin gripped my arm and flew down the hall twice as fast as before. My feet slipped and buckled beneath me as I struggled to keep up with him on the uneven ground. Somehow, he pulled me along and I avoided face-planting. Rocks and debris tumbled down around us. My throat closed up with fear.

Would those stone walls hold? This place had the oppressive weight of being deep underground. If the tunnel collapsed, would we be trapped without air? Did we even need air?

Are we even breathing right now?

A huge smoldering rock crashed from the ceiling, blocking our way. A lattice of cracks spiderwebbed out from its base. Black tendrils snaked from the cracks, reaching up toward my ankles. Corbin yanked me around the edge of the stone. On the other side, we faced the wide hallway and the arch made of bones leading into the gloomy chamber beyond.

My mouth dried as I remembered my dream, how I'd peered into that blackness and felt the oppressive presence of pure malevolence trained on me. Of the hand on my back, shoving me inside, and how I fell into eternity before landing in my own bed.

Only this time, I was pretty sure this wasn't a dream. As we neared the black void, the knife in my chest stung. The pain intensified.

Corbin squeezed my hands. "It's a veil, Maeve. It's designed to keep out enemies and shades. Here," he took a small stone container from his pocket and tipped it onto his hand. A thick, black mucus poured out of it. "Demon blood," Corbin said, holding up his hand. Before I could protest, he'd smeared the blood over my face, rubbing it into my cheeks. Globs hung off my eyelashes and clung to the hairs in my nose. It smelled *delicious*, like rotting meat and burning plastic.

"This is disgusting," I mumbled, not wanting to part my lips in case I accidentally swallowed a glob of it.

"You're telling me." Corbin rubbed his hands over his own face, smearing on the blood like war paint. From the black sludge, his eyes shone like bright crystals.

"How did you acquire a container of demon blood?"

"With great bravery and daring-do," Corbin grinned, snapping the box shut and replacing it in his pocket. He held out his blood-soaked hand. "But that's a story for another time. Shall we?"

I peered at the door. *Is it just my eyes adjusting to the gloom, or does the darkness not seem quite as dark as before?* Corbin slid his slimy, blood-covered hand in mine and pulled me into the gloom.

We stood at the entrance of an enormous cavern, the vaulted ceiling reaching so far above our heads its apex was hidden in darkness. The space was carved of the same dark-veined stone as the hallway, but here the veins stuck out in high relief, twisting up the walls and pulsing as though they were actual veins pumping blood through a living body.

"Shite," Corbin swore. "We're too late."

I followed his gaze and gasped. In the center of the room was a tall dais, accessed across a chasm of fire by a narrow stone bridge. The dais held a high throne made of bones – femurs fanning out into elaborate arches, piles of bones forming steep steps that led to the seat of the king of hell.

At the foot of the steps, a giant shape made of smoke and

nightmares writhed on the ground, its power fading as it wilted into nothingness. Daigh stood on its back, his bone blade raised above his head. He looked over at us and winked, then brought the blade down, burying it deep within the creature's shadow flesh.

The creature bucked and writhed, and a wave of heat shattered the air, knocking me off my feet. Corbin dragged me back as tendrils shot out of the demon's body and slammed against the walls, sending bones and rocks raining down. The fire in the pit flared, showering spikes across the narrow bridge.

With a final heave, the creature shrunk against the ground, collapsing in on itself like a star becoming a black hole, leaving behind only a smudge of black soot on the ground and a large crown fashioned from skull and bones.

Daigh tore off his crown of wilted vines and horns, and tossed it into the fire. He raised the demon's crown above his head and settled it on his dark hair. Dark tendrils snaked from between the bones, pouring through Daigh's ears, into his mouth, through his nostrils and eyes. He turned to me, and grinned.

"Hello, daughter." Even in the intense heat, Daigh's cold voice chilled me to my bones. "It's fortuitous to find you here. Now, if you'll indulge me by getting on your knees. It's polite to prostrate before the new king of the underworld."

30

ARTHUR

J opened one eye. Mistake. Bright light shot through my skull, like a laser irradiating my eyeballs. My head throbbed.

"Praise Mother Mary, he's awake." A familiar Irish voice drawled, each word a sword stabbing at my eyes.

"Flynn?" I croaked. "Why is the sun in my eyes?"

"It's not the sun, you eejit. It's the light. I'll turn it off if you like."

I heard shuffling and a click. I tried my eyes again. The room was still bright, but it wasn't killing me. I blinked again. Blobby shapes started to materialize, becoming bodies and limbs and faces. Familiar faces, all looking weirdly solemn. Behind Flynn was a huge contraption, like something from the medical bay on the *USS Enterprise*, all flashing lights and intermittent beeps.

I tried to sit up, but it was like my whole body was underwater. "Where am I? What happened?"

"You're in the hospital, mate." Flynn squeezed my arm. His fingers on my skin shot more knives through my body. "You've been here for the last three days."

"Three days, but…" Something nagged at me, some important thing that I had to do, that I couldn't miss. I searched my foggy memory. "What about the Slaugh?"

"The Slaugh are toast. Goneburger. Finito. We defeated them like *that*." Flynn snapped his fingers. "It turns out belief magic and my amazing artistic talents are a killer combination."

"Ryan Raynard's painting stunt helped a little," Blake pointed out.

I slumped back against the pillows. I'd missed the Slaugh. I was the warrior. My arm rubbed against the thin sheets, sending shivers through my skin. I looked down at it and noticed it was wrapped tightly in layers of gauze.

If I missed the Slaugh, then how did I get injured? Why was I in the hospital?

"What happened to me?"

"Don't you remember?" Flynn scratched his head. "They said you might not remember much. You cut yourself with your sword, mate. You hit a main artery and lost almost sixty percent of your blood. We were fecking lucky Rowan saw you and Blake called an ambulance and gave you some herbs to quell the bleeding a bit. If it wasn't for him, you'd have joined Corbin and Maeve."

Flynn's words took a few moments to fully register. I'd done this to myself. I'd lost all that blood…

And Blake… Blake had saved my life.

The door flung open, banging against the wall. The sound mashed against my skull like a mallet. Jane, Connor, and Kelly crashed into the room and surrounded my bedside.

Kelly wrapped her arms around my neck, squeezing so hard I was afraid my head would roll off my shoulders. "I'm so glad you're okay."

Everyone was here to see me. Flynn, Rowan, Blake,

Kelly... I glanced around for Corbin before the memory of his death bounced off my skull like a rock.

Corbin. That was why I cut myself. Because he was dead.

The rest of Flynn's words sunk in. *Or you'd have joined Corbin and Maeve.* I searched the room for her face, but she wasn't there. "Where's Maeve?"

Kelly leaned back. The guys exchanged a telling glance. My chest tightened. Behind me, a machine beeped at double-speed.

"Flynn," I demanded.

Flynn cleared his throat. "Right, there's something we have to tell you, and you're not going to like it. But we need you to stay calm and don't burn down the hospital until we've finished talking, okay?"

"Bloody hell, just tell me!"

"Maeve's gone," Blake said, his voice hard and cold. "She's gone to the underworld to stop Daigh becoming the fully-fledged demon king."

3 1

ROWAN

*I*t took a lot of convincing, and some low-level compulsion from Blake, to get Arthur discharged. As soon as we were piled into Ryan's car and Simon had started the engine, I explained what I'd found in the library. I pulled my phone out of my pocket and showed them the pictures of the book, as well as Corbin's Post-it notes. "Corbin was reading about these Mysteries of Lazarus before the attack on Briarwood. I think he might've figured out how to protect himself in the underworld."

"That wanker," Arthur breathed, holding one of the Post-it notes up to the window. "Why didn't he just tell us? Surely he doesn't expect us to learn Latin or bloody Elvish so we can bring him back."

"He must not've got that far," I stared at the Post-it notes. They still made no more sense now than they had before.

"Or the answer was so obvious he knew we didn't need the books to figure it out," Blake piped up.

I whirled around to face him. The corner of his mouth twitched up.

"You might've said something!" I yelped.

"I wasn't sure," Blake grinned. "I'm still not sure, in fact. I'm just trying to think like Corbin. Maeve said there was an object around Corbin's neck that usually sat on the library shelf – an ampulla."

"What's that?" Flynn asked.

"It's a medieval vial for holding holy water," Arthur said.

"How do you know that?"

Arthur gave a small smile. "I picked it up once and Corbin gave me a boring lecture."

My chest pinched. I could just imagine Corbin launching into a long-winded description of how the pilgrims used the ampulla.

"What's the plan here, gents? Are we going after Corbin and Maeve?"

"I think that ship has sailed," Arthur looked up at the pale moon, where the last traces of the Slaugh riders had disappeared. "Unless we're all planning a suicide."

Flynn frowned. "Jeez, mate, ease off."

Arthur glanced at Flynn, then stared at his hands. "Sorry, bruv. I forgot."

"I don't think Corbin intended us to follow him," Flynn said. "I think there's something we're supposed to do on our end to bring him back. And of course now we've got to get Maeve back, too."

"Do we need another ampulla?" I asked

"I don't know!" Flynn threw up his hands. "I'm not the expert in all this magicking shite. I don't think an ancient pilgrim hip flask is the kind of thing you can buy from Sainsburys."

"Whenever we've needed to reverse a spell, we've performed it backwards," I pointed out.

"But we don't know what spell Corbin did," Arthur said,

holding out the Post-its. "We've got these diagrams, but no idea what they mean."

"No," I said, reaching for my mobile phone. "But there's one way we can find out."

3 2

MAEVE

*S*hadows slithered from the glinting eyes in Daigh's crown, flickering across his skin and darting through the crevices of his clothes. I winced as they burrowed under his fingernails and drilled into his ears. When he opened his mouth to speak, black tendrils whipped across his lips.

"You do not prostrate yourself before a new king?" he asked mockingly. "I thought you would wish for an accord between our worlds, in the same way you asked for a treaty between fae and humans. Surely, you would begin negotiations with deference to my position."

"What position?" I scoffed. "You can't just call yourself the king of the underworld. You have to actually *have* a kingdom. In case you haven't noticed, yours emptied out to go and fuck up the world, and when they get back they won't be happy to learn you've killed their ruler. You're the king of empty halls and useless torture chambers."

"You did me a favor, dear daughter. You occupied the demons for time enough that I could come here and dispatch the one who stood in my way," he laughed. "And now here you are, delivered to me as my gift from the traitor Liah. It is too perfect. You will be my heir, my princess. Your friend can be our grand vizier. What a beautiful court of chaos we'll have."

"I'd rather die," I shot back.

"You're dead already."

He had a point.

Daigh descended one step, his boot crunching against the skulls. He waved a hand in front of his face. Black tendrils shot from his fingers. I screamed and flinched away, covering my face as the tendrils circled me, sliding across my skin like blades before returning him. "Freshly dead, I see, but like your friend here, you're not on an official stay. Your presence here upsets the balance of things. You both still retain your souls. The boy has an amulet that allows resurrection, and with that blood on your face you bear the three essences that allow you to return also, but without a soul offered in exchange, you will never leave my court. So you may as well make yourselves comfortable."

Daigh swept his arm in a graceful arc. Something butted against my legs. I turned around, and saw two stools made from bones, each with a cushion of crushed purple velvet, waiting for me and Corbin.

I yelled and kicked the stool. Mistake. It would appear that even thought I was technically dead, I could still stub my toe.

"Since I know you so love facts, daughter," Daigh drawled, fluttering his hand and making the stools slide after us as we backed away. "I will give you one before I take your souls so you will remain by my side. I did not kill the demon king, for there is no king to kill." He patted the crown on his head and smiled his cold, dark smile, and a rage such as I'd never felt before surged through my core.

I wanted Daigh to *burn*. I didn't just want him to die, I

wanted to watch his face as he realized he was about to die, and I wanted to twist the knife into his skull myself and feel his life draining from his body. I wanted him to *suffer,* as he had caused everyone I loved to suffer.

Daigh tossed his head back, his laugh booming through the cavernous space. He spread his arms wide, like a corruption of Christ's passion. "If you want to kill me, daughter, come. I accept your punishment."

I broke into a run, my boots clattering across the bridge. My hatred bubbled up inside me, flaring through my body with a magic that was stronger and sharper and more real than any power I'd felt before. My veins lit up, my teeth clattered, my eyes burned with rage and lust. My whole body flared with white hot power. I had Daigh in my sights and I *believed* I would have my vengeance.

Hatred is just another side of love.

Arthur's words echoed through my head, followed by Kelly's sickened face as she begged me not to kill Daigh. Bile rose in my throat. I tried to push the sensation back down, but my stomach lurched, causing my magic to flicker.

No. I will not feel guilty for doing what is right. For everything I've lost, and for everything he's taken from the people I love. I will finish him.

I slammed into Daigh, knocking him back against the steps. He raised his hands and flung his dark tendrils around me. They tightened against my skin, burning and flaying my flesh. But the pain only fueled my fire.

I pressed my hand to his temple, and I loosed everything I had.

ROWAN

"Ah, yes." Clara leaned forward in Corbin's chair and ran her fingers over the cover of the book. "Trust Corbin to bring to light what has long remained in darkness."

Flynn leaned over her shoulder and nodded his head, rubbing his stubbly chin as if he could read archaic Latin and had discerned Clara's cryptic comment. The others crowded into every corner of Briarwood's library. All except me. I waited in the hall, my anxiety flaring up my spine like needles, stopping me from crossing the threshold into that space that smelled of Corbin. The books from my counting shelf were still scattered across the floor. I couldn't cross without counting them, not when I was this fired up.

I gritted my teeth as Clara continued to pore over the book. We only had a day left to bring Corbin and Maeve back. Every minute counted, and we'd already lost a precious few waiting for Clara and the others to meet us at the castle. The reporters had returned to camp out outside Ryan's gates, and they'd been joined by more of their ilk from London and Dublin and Glasgow and Europe. Grainy photos of the demonic riders were blowing up the internet, although the rumor was that it was a publicity stunt from Ryan Raynard.

Aline grinned as she told us how they eventually bested the press by sending Simon out the front gates in Ryan's car with a bunch of his clothes stuffed under a black hoodie in the passenger seat. The reporters chased the Jaguar into the village, and Aline snuck out behind them in Simon's own car with the whole crew jammed in the back and Smithers singing 'Spirit in the Sky' at the top of his lungs.

I would've laughed at the image if not for the fact that the retelling of it took yet more precious minutes.

"*What* has remained in darkness?" Arthur growled. He was already losing patience. I didn't blame him. Inside my head, a clock ticked down the seconds until our fourth day was up and we lost our window to save Corbin and Maeve.

"Rumors have circulated over the centuries that if you wore the blood of all three magical creatures – fae, demons, and witches – and knew the proper incantation, you would be able to walk through the worlds unbidden."

"In non-magical gobbledygook, that means you could be raised back to life from the dead," Aline said from the her spot beside the globe bar. She tapped her fingernails on the lid in a steady rhythm, as if she too was counting down the seconds.

"You're not suggesting that we might be able to recover our son and Maeve from the underworld?" Andrew Harris asked, his arms around his wife. His voice was stern, but the lilt at the end of his sentence betrayed his hope.

"That's what Corbin has led us to believe." Clara flipped to the page in the book with the picture of the alchemical diagram. "Here, the writer recounts a famous Orthodox tale about Lazarus' life after he returned from the dead. Apparently he was forced to flee Judea for Cyprus, where he became the first Bishop of Kition. He never smiled in the thirty remaining years of his life, as he was haunted by the visions of the unredeemed souls he'd seen during his four days in the underworld. The only exception was one time when he caught a thief stealing a pot from the market, and he remarked, 'the clay steals the clay'."

"Corbin said that," I whispered, gripping the doorjamb. I tried to force my leg over the threshold, but it wouldn't budge. "In Maeve's dream."

"Some witchcraft scholars believe – and the writer of this page agrees with them – that Lazarus' comment carried a double meaning. He referred in the first instance to the transience of man, and of life. That in the grand scheme, the thief's life was no as dirt between the fingers. He was part of a greater whole, a building block of the world, crafted by God for his own divine purpose. The other meaning refers to the mysteries of Lazarus, to the spell that brought Lazarus his eternal life. For as clay is a raw material that must be moulded by a creator, so too is blood in ancient medicine the raw material, the carrier of life. And who was it that granted him this everlasting life? Jesus, the blood of God, who would wash away the sins of the world. The son of God was the clay who stole the clay." Clara pounded the book with her tiny fist. "Don't you *see?*"

I didn't see anything, except a ticking clock. Arthur frowned. Flynn stroked his beard. Neither of them had a clue, either.

Corbin would've got this immediately. It would've been so obvious to him, that's why he said he'd written the spell down for us, even though he clearly gave us nothing but—

"I've got it," I said. "It's the spell. The clay steals the clay. It's the incantation to bring them back to life."

"It's been right here in this book all this time," Clara breathed. "And I never saw it. But your Corbin did. He's a truly gifted witch."

"He is the most gifted witch of his generation," beamed Andrew.

"He's a bloody book nerd—" Arthur leaned over the book, his beard twitching. He jabbed a finger at the page. "What's this cross here?"

"That's the cross of Lazarus," Clara explained. "It was the symbol of a particular chivalric order. The knights tended the sick, and some witches believed they were beings of power themselves, who guarded a store of demon blood they could use to bring worthy souls back to life. At that time, of course, the fae were of this world, so their blood could be easily acquired. But demons do not come to our world, nor ours to theirs, unless something has broken in the universe. Only the fae could travel into the underworld and collect demon blood, and they did so at great sacrifice—"

"I've seen this cross before," Arthur interrupted, his gaze flicking around the room. He bolted across the room and stormed through the door, nearly knocking me over as he stomped down the hallway.

"I wish he'd stop doing that," Flynn sighed. Everyone filed out of the library and followed Arthur as he slammed doors and peered into closets. "Isadora," he bellowed. "Get your bony arse out here right now!"

"Such language." Isadora appeared at the doorway of the kitchen. She didn't even glance up from her phone screen, which she tapped with her red talons.

"Show them your tattoo," Arthur growled.

"I'd be glad to, as soon as your friends pay my fee." She waved her phone at him. "Will that be cash or credit card?"

"She has a tattoo of that Lazarus cross on her arse," Arthur muttered, folding his arms.

"How did you see that?" Flynn grinned at him.

"I walked in on her in the bath. It looked all grody and diseased. Where did you get it?"

Isadora slid her mobile down her impressive cleavage. "I hardly see how that's any of your business."

"It's our business because we've got less than a day to bring back Maeve and Corbin." Venom flashed in Arthur's eyes. His hands balled into fists. I noticed that he couldn't quite pull his fingers together on his injured arm. "It was Daigh, wasn't it? This is something to do with your bargain with him. What secret of yours was Daigh carrying?"

"Isadora, please," Andrew implored her. "That's our son down here. We might have a chance to save him and give him a normal life. You have to help us. *Please.*"

Isadora's face remained impassive, but her bottom lip quivered. She slumped into a chair at the kitchen table. "I'll tell you, but you must swear an oath that you'll not reveal my secret to anyone. It could destroy the Soho coven."

"We don't care about your secrets," Flynn said. "We just want to get to Maeve. Tell us about the tattoo."

"Not until you swear it," Isadora held out her hand. "A witch's oath is binding."

"Fine. We'll swear this oath." Flynn flicked a knife out of his shoe. He nicked a cut across his palm. Arthur held his hand out for the knife, but instead of handing it to him, Flynn drew the blade across Arthur's palm, leaving a cut so tiny it barely broke the skin. "You're not getting your hands on one of these until you prove you can use it responsibly, Aragorn."

Arthur grumbled something under his breath. Flynn slid the knife into my hands. I gritted my teeth as I cut across my palm, squeezing out a few droplets of blood to make the oath.

Around the circle we went, everyone nicking their hands. Isadora shook with each of us, mingling her blood with ours to bind the oath. When she got to Clara, the women clenched their jaws as they squeezed hard enough to break fingers.

Neither would flinch, and finally Ryan had to pull them apart.

The oath done, Isadora sat down at the table. She dug her phone out of her cleavage and placed it beside her, then folded her hands together. Blood smeared across her palms. "There is an ancient chivalric order that comprised many witches and fae, called the Order of Saint Lazarus. They have passed their secrets down through the generations, but since the fae had been banished, there were very few who knew of their work in hospitals and sick rooms, performing the miracles that restore the dead to life. In order to do this, they need the blood of both demon and fae, and their stores have long since run out. I am a descendant of this order. I know their secrets, but without blood, I could never perform them, not even for myself, not even when my need was great. It was during this need that I met Daigh in a salon in Paris in 1880, during the Belle Époque—"

"1880?" Flynn squealed. "But wouldn't that make you over a hundred-and-forty years old?"

"You are correct, Irishman, but pray let me continue. By this date, Daigh had amassed enough power to go on extended jaunts into the human realm. Mostly he spent his time with artists, bestowing them with gifts in exchange for their adoration. At this time, I was ill with tuberculosis. I had tried everything to acquire demon or fae blood, but those who kept a small store would not sell to me for all the money I offered, so I was without choice but to die. I raged against my coming doom. In Paris, I numbed my rage in the opium dens and drowned my sorrow in fine French absinthe. The first outward signs of my degeneration were beginning to show, and even in the gloom of the salon the other patrons sat as far from me as possible. All except Daigh. He flopped down beside me. He flattered me and bought me wine and cheese. He asked me to sit for a portrait, and like a fool I accepted. He dressed me in the finest French silks, then painted me as I truly was – the disease seeping through my body, poisoning every part of me. The portrait was hideous. I threw it into the Somme. But the fae king intrigued me. And I intrigued him."

I suspected there was more to this story than she was telling. A dark flicker in Aline's eye suggested she thought so as well.

"One night, he proposed our agreement. He knew how badly I wanted to live, so he dangled the offer of rebirth in front of me. Humans have no power over the realm of death, but the Unseelie have often made pacts with the demons there, and Daigh revealed he kept a small store of their blood. He offered some of that blood to me, but I would have to make it worth his while. So I offered him a favor he could redeem in the future."

"But if Daigh kept you alive, wouldn't that make you old and decrepit?" Flynn asked.

"That was one part of the spell Daigh hid from me. I returned, but I was never able to age. My mind grows old, but my body remains in this unmoving, immortal shell." Isadora glanced at Aline. "It is as you experienced. You did not age in your prison, and when you emerged you are the same age as when you went in. Fae magic can never fully restore human life – there is always a corruption."

Flynn balked at those words, but they filled me with hope. Even if Corbin and Maeve ended up like Isadora, if they never aged, surely it would be better than the alternative?

"The spell requires the blood of all three magical creatures, a likeness of them that shows their true nature, and an incantation. If the person is already dead, which I was not, their restoration also requires a sacrifice, for a soul must be given to the demons in their place. The more magic that is given to the spell, the more life it can bestow. Daigh performed the ritual on his own, giving me a tattoo infused with the blood of fae and demon, but he was much depleted by his presence on earth. He could only manage this bastard of a life. But it was enough for me – eternal youth has suited me well. The tattoo, as that Viking boy saw it, has been his way of communicating with me, of assurring my coopera- tion." She winced as her hand skimmed over her thigh.

"What about Aline?" Flynn asked. "She didn't have a body, and we gave her no blood, and yet she returned after twenty- one years."

"Images and portraits are part of fae magic," Isadora said. "Hence their requirement in the ritual. Their ability to create glamours and communicate through mirrors is that same kind of magic. Because of the binding, Aline's witch blood possessed fae magic, and if she stole power from Daigh in her pendant—"

"Robert Smithers was my magister, so I often gave him the pendant to wear or look after," Aline said. "I recall before the ritual, he clasped it around my neck and promised it would keep me safe."

"It kept you safe," Smithers chimed in. "Rob kept you safe."

Aline turned to him and kissed his cheek. "Did you put demon blood in that pendant for me? Did you steal it from Daigh? Is that how you trapped me inside the painting? Oh, you clever man!"

Smithers' dopey smile gave nothing away.

"Maeve's wearing that pendant now, isn't she?" Aline's eyes glinted. "That means she has everything she needs for us to restore her to life."

"She doesn't have fae blood," I reminded.

"Actually, she does," Flynn said, pulling a crumpled paper out of his pocket. "It's the DNA results Maeve sent away for.

It turns out she's got the DNA from two fathers, which is scientifically impossible even though it's right there on those squiggly graphs. Some of Daigh's DNA runs through her veins."

"Then we have all the ingredients we need to complete this spell," Clara hugged the book to her chest, her eyes glinting. "We can bring Maeve and Corbin back. But we must hurry. We'll need their likenesses. Do you have any photographs of them?"

"I've got a ton on my phone," Arthur said. "We'll have to go to that camera place in Crooks Worthy to get them printed."

"Does the painting have to look exactly like the person for this to work?" Flynn asked.

"Not in a photographic sense, but it should represent them. After all, a photograph is only an expression of light, but a painting can reveal more about a person – or the painter."

"Then I have the images," Flynn announced. "There's a painting I did for Maeve in Avebury. It'll be in her room somewhere, if it didn't get destroyed…"

"But this ritual requires a fae to perform it," Isadora said. "And considering you banished them all with the Slaugh, including the amputee, you won't find a one to help you. Not to mention the sacrifices. Which of you will offer your own life in exchange for theirs?"

"I will," said Arthur, Flynn, Blake and I in unison. My heart pattered. Tonight, we would bring Maeve and Corbin, but we would still lose someone precious. Our coven would still be broken.

"Don't be a wanker," Arthur shoved Flynn. "You're needed here. You sorted everything while I was lying in the hospital. You didn't even need me to destroy the Slaugh. I'll be a sacrifice."

"It should be me," I whispered, thinking of what Maeve said before the Slaugh, about how she and Corbin had talked about studying at Oxford together. "I willingly give my life so they will have a future."

"Boys, don't be silly." Clara touched Arthur's arm. "You are young, and you *all* have a future ahead of you. I have had many bright years upon this earth. I offer myself willingly as a sacrifice."

"Mum, no." Ryan moved in front of her, as if his body shielded her from a death ray.

"I should go," Andrew offered. "I drove Corbin away after our other son's death. If it wasn't for me he'd—"

"Oh, *please.* All this self-flagellation is sickening. The sacrifice does not have to be complicit. Do you have any enemies?" Isadora asked lazily, staring at her fingernails. "Those two police officers that were poking around earlier would make an excellent offering."

"They don't need an enemy, Isadora. They have us."

I whirled around. In the doorway stood Aline, her arm looped in Smithers'. "Between the two of us, we have all the fae magic you'll need. And we have the sacrifice, too. Rob and I will go to the underworld in exchange."

BLAKE

"It's no use trying to change our minds," Aline squeezed Smithers' hand. "We've decided. We're both two souls out of time. On this plane of existence there is nothing for us, but in the underworld there is hope. We will not truly die. Our souls will live on. It is our own second chance. Let us go to our next stage of life joyfully, knowing we saved our daughter."

"I should go," I said, with a look at Arthur. "I'm not even supposed to be here."

Flynn kicked Arthur in the leg. He winced and stepped forward. His huge, meaty hand fell on my shoulder, and a pair of ice-blue eyes blazed into mine. "Blake, you're a wanker. But this coven wouldn't be the same without you."

Does he really mean that?

I studied those eyes for any sign of a cruel ploy, but I found nothing but regret and sadness. *He means it.*

A lump rose in my throat. Weirdly, hearing those words from Arthur felt more genuine than anything Maeve had ever said to me about belonging here. I wrapped my arms around his enormous frame. He stiffened for a moment, then

245

relaxed into the hug. Flynn winked at me over Arthur's shoulder, and I reached down and pinched his bottom.

"Gor now, get off," Arthur shoved me away. "We're not Corbin and Rowan, got it?"

"We could be," I winked at him. Flynn snorted with laughter.

"So this ritual, right? What do we need to make it happen?" Arthur shoved his hands in his pockets, pointedly ignoring my comment. Something like pride brimmed in my chest. I was finally, actually, part of this world. Now we just had to get Maeve and Corbin back, and everything would be perfect.

"We'll need those two portraits Flynn made. And some candles and standard ritual supplies." Clara consulted the page of the book. "And, of course, we shall need Corbin's body."

No, please—" Bree choked out. Andrew took her by the arm and led her from the room. I heard them murmuring in the hall.

"The body is with the coroner," Flynn said. "Wallace said it would probably be available today, but it's barely even six in the morning. They won't—"

Arthur strode toward the door. "I'll make them give it to us. Blake, you're coming with me."

"Why me?"

"Because I already pulled his body off that bloody stake and carried it out of the meadow. I'm not touching it again." Arthur jangled his car keys. "Plus, you've got that whole ethereal beauty thing going for you that Officer Judge can't resist. Let's go."

～

A few minutes later, Arthur parked the car in front of the police station and shoved me toward the entrance.

Of all the times to have made peace with Arthur. Three days ago he'd never have trusted me with Corbin's body.

I pushed the door open and approached the front desk. "I'm Blake Beckett. I've come to pick up the remains of my friend, Corbin Harris. I know it's early, but I was hoping—"

The officer behind the desk raised an eyebrow. "Corbin Harris? You're in luck. I think the coroner finished with that case late yesterday. DS Judge will want to have a word with you before she signs the body over. Come through."

I was led into a small room containing a round table, four plastic chairs and a strange machine with a number of buttons and levers. The fae in me reviled against sitting on the plastic surface. At least Briarwood had been filled with sumptuous natural fabrics and wooden furniture – Daigh was right, the humans who invented plastic deserved to die a horrible, grisly death.

Officer Judge – or DS Judge now – appeared at the doorway. "Blake Beckett? Did you look into a crystal ball and see we'd finished with Corbin's body? I was going to call, you know."

I remembered that Flynn had told her we were witches. I flicked my hair over my shoulder and settled her with my dark gaze. "Actually, the tarot cards told me."

"Coffee?" DS Judge held two plastic cups under the machine and pressed a button. A sludgy brown liquid dribbled into the cups. She filled both to the brim and passed one to me. I took one sniff and pushed it across the table, as far from me as I could get. Why would humans bother inventing a machine that made dirt water? Now, a curry dispensing machine, that I could get behind.

"Does coffee interfere with your powers or something?" Judge raised her own cup to her lips and gulped back the foul liquid.

"No. It offends my fragile soul." She snorted and downed the last of her cup before moving on to mine. "You've had a promotion, I see."

"Yep, and the hours to match." She rubbed her eye. "You might wonder why I'm here so early, but the truth is, I never left the station. I haven't had any sleep since that night at Briarwood. I'm not even exaggerating. I've got a sleeping bag behind my desk and I tried to take a nap earlier this morning but Wallace was watching so I couldn't. A whole bunch of reporters came in here shouting about some spectral horses that chased them across town then vanished into thin air. I told them to jog on. We've got real crimes to solve, can't waste time with no spectral horses. Incidentally," she trained me with a fierce glance, "there aren't going to be any more spectral horses, are there?"

"I'd say you're in the clear."

She sighed with relief. "We're still taking statements from all the people in that mob. As of now, we'll be charging five people with various crimes. I imagine there will be many more. Arson, property damage, assault, manslaughter, inciting violence… you sure know how to make friends."

I shrugged. "What can I say? I'm a likable guy."

DS Judge's eyes darted to the door, then fixed on mine. She drew her phone out of her pocket and placed it on the table in front of me. "Check it if you like. It'll show you I'm not recording this conversation, Blake. There are no cameras in this room. No one is listening in. It's just you and me."

"I believe you." Mostly because I had no idea what to do with her phone.

"So maybe you can tell me why the only record I can find

about you is a death certificate from when you were only a few months old?"

"Why don't you tell me why you think I have a death certificate." I knew about death certificates from episodes of *Elementary* on the telly. It was actually kind of cool, being at the station and seeing the human justice machine clanking along in real life.

Judge tapped the edge of her phone against the table. "There were reports that one Aline Moore – that's Maeve Moore's mother, another person connected to Briarwood with a death certificate to her name – was sighted at the castle a day before this mob attacked. That's not a coincidence. I think you've been meddling with some kind of magic you don't understand."

I flashed her my winning Blake Beckett smirk. "You've got everything exactly right, and also completely backward. I'm on an urgent errand, so I can't sit here forever and chat over these delightful cups of watery grit. I do have a question, though. Does Corbin have a death certificate?"

"Not yet. You'll need to register his death. The front desk can give you a pamphlet to tell you what to—"

I leaned back in the chair. "We might hold off on that for a wee while."

She narrowed her eyes at me. "Why? You think he might be coming back?"

"I couldn't say," I shrugged again. "Incidentally, what would you do if someone you thought was dead appeared to return to the world of the living?"

"I'd have to conduct a serious investigation. If it was found that some shenanigans had taken place to waste police time, there could be serious consequences for the people involved." *Tap, tap, tap*, went her phone. "Jail time, even."

"That's fine. We can wash our hands of this and leave the next army of the dead for the law to deal with."

Judge smiled. "I like you, Beckett. I'll get the paperwork for you to fill out and you can have his body back immediately."

"Did the autopsy reveal anything?" Corbin would be proud I'd remembered the word for human scientists dissecting bodies to figure out how they died. In the Unseelie Court, dissections were usually performed while a subject was still alive, and they served no legal purpose – the Princes just found disembowelment fun.

"I'm not really supposed to share details from an active investigation. Will it help you in your, er, magic?"

I nodded.

"Corbin Harris was killed when a knife entered his abdomen, and he bled internally. His body was then thrown on a fire and impaled on a stake. We have some DNA material, but it's a mess. There's human, and fox, and some other DNA we can't identify that the pathologist believes is a corrupted sample. The fire destroyed much of our physical evidence. All we know is he had several pens and a candy wrapper in his pocket. Oh yes, and there was a metal object around his neck. It's filled with some kind of weird organic sludge the pathologist couldn't identify." She pulled out a plastic bag from her pocket and tossed it on the table.

I picked up the bag, hating the way the plastic crinkled beneath my fingers. The object rolled across my palm. It was a tiny metal vial, encrusted with rust and stoppered with a tight wooden cork. A symbol was carved into the side – the same cross I'd seen on the pages of Clara's book.

The cross of Saint Lazarus.

~

*E*ven with my paperwork, I had to sweet-talk the women at the coroner's office to get the body released. She said it wasn't normal for the family to pick up the remains. Over and over again she asked me for the name of my funeral director. "A guy named Lazarus," I finally said. "I can't remember his number. But he's going to do the ah… *funeraling* at our home, so he suggested we swing by and pick up the body. It just saves time."

The flustered secretary finally gave in, and a few minutes later I returned to Arthur's car with a large box under my arm. "That's it?" he asked, peering at the box that held the last earthly remains of a larger-than-life human. We could both tell from the shape that Corbin wasn't even whole anymore.

"That's it." I placed the box on the floor in the backseat, slammed the door, and slid into the passenger side, glad that ordeal was over. "Don't brake hard. The lid isn't exactly sealed, and I don't want bits of Corbin through my hair."

We raced back to Briarwood. On a normal day, the driveway would be choked with tourist vehicle as people showed up to get their fix of turrets and wonky stairs. But Corbin put the tours on hold a couple of weeks ago to focus on the fae. It was just as well, because two guys carrying a body in a box through the grounds wasn't going to get the castle top-rated on TripAdvisor.

Everyone was already gathered around the sidhe when we arrived with Corbin's body. Arthur placed the box under a tree on the far side of the meadow, next to Maeve's body. He kissed the tips of his fingers and placed them to her lips. I looked away, not wanting to intrude on his private moment.

Flynn, of course, had no such compunctions. He walked up behind Arthur and clamped two hands on his shoulders. "Boo!" he cried in Arthur's ear.

Arthur leapt two feet in the air, spun around, and clobbered Flynn around the head. I sniggered. Aline and Smithers may have been the ones heading to the underworld, but Flynn was the one with the death wish.

"Boys," Clara called from the sidhe. "We're ready."

I approached the mounds that formed the gateway to the fae realm, the place I'd spent my entire life plotting to escape. All this time, I had no idea that Daigh knew how to resurrect the dead. I knew then that he'd kept it secret so he could also keep his other evil deeds – such as the death of my parents – buried forever. Who knows how long he'd been planning this transition from fae to demon, this play toward dominion over life and death?

At the entrance to the mound, Clara had placed a pile of twigs and bracken. Beside it, she laid out the paintings, ready to be thrown on when the time was right. One wave of Arthur's hand and the fire caught. It wasn't a raging blaze, but it would do for our purposes.

"Are our sacrifices ready?"

Aline and Smithers stepped forward, joining hands as they faced Clara over the fire. Aline wore Maeve's pendant, and Smithers had the ampulla I'd recovered from Judge around his neck. Aline's jaw was set in a firm line, the same expression Maeve wore when she'd decided something and there was no changing her mind.

Sacrifice. It was the bond of a parent to a child – the love that defied dimensions and would bring down kings. Daigh may have raised me, but he'd cast me aside as soon as he no longer needed me. In all his plans and schemes, he'd never accounted for the fact that love could be his undoing.

And yet, my gaze fell on every face in the circle. On Rowan, who'd trusted me when no one else did. On Flynn, who'd been the first of the guys to show me what it meant to have a friend. On Arthur, who had been willing to admit he'd been wrong. My gaze flicked to the box and the body lying under the tree. I would leap into the flames for any one of them, and for the first time I didn't doubt they would do the same for me.

This is what it is to have a family.

After casting the circle with salt and fire, Clara lifted her hands skyward, indicating that we should do the same. I stood between Arthur and Kelly, who'd insisted on being involved even though she wasn't a witch. "I'll do the belief magic," she'd said. No attempt to explain that belief magic didn't work like that would dissuade her. Jane was the only one sitting out the ritual. She remained under the tree with Connor, keeping a watch over the bodies.

"The clay steals the clay," Clara intoned. "Death's wings have swept away two souls who are before their time. We humbly submit for their return, and offer in exchange these worthy replacements. Let the clay steal the clay."

"The clay steals the clay," we chanted. "The clay steals the clay."

At least our chant was in English. Apparently, Corbin usually made the coven chant in Latin or Orcish or whatever extinct language he was obsessed with that week. As I spoke the words, I focused on drawing up my spirit magic. There was precious little left after our efforts with the Slaugh, but a trickle still snaked through my veins. I hoped it would be enough. Thinking of Maeve and her bright smile, and Corbin and his sacrifice drew up a fresh burst from a source deep inside me. I forced the magic through my palms. It crackled in the air as it merged with the other witches' power, creating a great cone that extended down over our circle.

The ground shook. I dug the heels of my boots into the earth to hold myself upright, and kept pushing. I remembered Maeve's quick mind and how she stood defiant even when she was scared, how she got that authoritative tone in her voice when she lectured one of us about science, how I kissed her for the first time and it was like no kiss before that had ever existed.

Spirit magic churned inside me, pulsing against my palms as I fed it into the spell. The ground bucked and swayed, sending chunks of dirt cascading from the sides of the sidhe.

A dark crack opened in the earth in front of me, running from the top of the sidhe steps out toward Clara – a dark path none should ever follow. Black fog poured from the crack, which widened, the earth groaning as it was torn asunder.

Aline gripped Smithers' hand. "Are you ready, my love?"

Smithers' nodded.

Aline flashed him a bright smile with no hint of sadness. They broke from the circle, and together they leapt into the darkness, into their doom.

The void shuddered as the darkness embraced them. My stomach clenched as a flash of green caught the corner of my eye. A figure darted from the forest behind the sidhe, running toward us at full speed. It broke through the circle and paused on the edge of the void, white braids whipping around her face, arms outstretched, ready to jump.

"Liah!" I cried.

Her face spun toward me, her expression ice. She nodded, and dived for the void.

I surged forward and dived after her. As I toppled into the void, another body brushed against mine. Isadora's eyes met mine, her mouth curled into an O of surprise. I tried to shout at her to get back before she fell in herself, but the darkness filled my mouth with gloom. My body exploded with pain as it collided with terror itself, and the underworld swallowed me completely.

*M*aeve crackled with power. A cold glow rose off her skin, a blue flame burning bright with power. Daigh stiffened in her arms as she pressed her hand to his temples and blasted his mind with her pain. She screamed, he screamed, and the whole of the underworld groaned under their collective agony.

My breath caught in my throat. My legs froze in place. I didn't know what to do, what I wanted Maeve to do. I wanted to see Daigh suffer as much as she did, but was this the way? Was this the right way?

Maeve's eyes fluttered open and her body went slack. She tore her hand from Daigh's temple. The air whispered as her magic snapped from his mind. She stepped back. Daigh wobbled on his feet, steadying himself against the steps.

"Sorry, father," Maeve said, staring down at the blue light glowing around her hands. "I never was very good at listening to my parents. I don't want to kill you. I think we should talk."

Relief flooded me, followed by a nervous clamor. Even

after everything Daigh had done, Maeve didn't want to kill him. She'd chosen the path of righteousness, as Matthew Crawford might've said. But it was not the easy path. We still had to deal with Daigh.

What good will come of talking to Daigh? Everything he says is a lie.

Maeve flicked her gaze to me for a moment, and the flicker of a voice echoed in my head. A voice that wasn't my own.

Corbin, get the crown.

I gaped at her. How had she sent her voice into my head? She shouldn't be able to do that with a non-spirit witch. That was interesting. Were her powers somehow growing—

The crown. It's what he meant when he said there's no king to kill. That demon wasn't the king, it was a guard or something. The crown is the source of all their power. I'll distract him, and you've got to get it off him.

My eyes locked on Daigh's crown, and I immediately grasped Maeve's thinking. The bone crown on Daigh's head glowed with a similar blue light to the one that surrounded Maeve. Some of her power had been drawn into it, like a corruption of Flynn's witch statue collecting the magic of belief.

In this world of darkness, the blue aura was a way for the demons to discern the shades of witches. It would also help them to keep any visiting fae in check. The demon blood on my face was making me see it as a demon would. But the thing Maeve had to have noticed was that only the crown glowed – no other part of Daigh's body shared the aura.

Daigh wasn't fully demon, not yet. He still had little power of his own. He streamed it from the crown. If we could get that crown off his head, then he'd be powerless.

"I want to talk about you and me," Maeve started, folding

her arms. "I got the DNA test results back, and you were right – I am your daughter. It's all very strange, because the binding has made my DNA completely different from any other human."

I crept across the bridge to where Maeve stood, moving slowly and smoothly, as if my whole purpose was to stand near Maeve. Our fingers touched, and Maeve's magic sparked a memory across my mind.

It was Maeve and Rowan and I in the seedy hotel room in London, our bodies wrapped together in the heat of our love.

Daigh's eyes glittered at Maeve. "There you are, you see? Your earth science has proven what I already knew – you are mine, daughter, and you are special. The fae have been wrong to forbid bindings. You are the strongest witch of your age. What you did to me just now would have killed a mortal. It's fortunate I'm no longer a mortal."

"Indeed," Maeve tapped her chin. "It seems I've been completely wrong about magic. It's written into our DNA. It's scientifically observable and—"

I slid off to the side and crept around the dais. Daigh's eyes didn't leave Maeve's face as she waxed on about the awesome power of DNA. It was quite a speech, delivered in her best "schoolteacher" voice, the one that Flynn thought was the sexiest sound alive.

At the back of the throne, the steps were so narrow there was only enough room for the toes of my boots. I stepped up on to the stairs and peered around the side. Daigh didn't seem to have noticed me, but he'd moved back up to settle on top of the throne. That meant I'd have to climb all the way to the top.

I swung my leg up and balanced precariously on the next shelf. Even though I was a shade or something, my muscles screamed with the effort. Heat rose from the fire, burning a good twenty feet beneath me. I stretched with my hand and gripped the edge of the next step.

Almost there. Just keep him distracted a moment longer, Maeve. I've almost got him!

BLAKE

I landed hard on my side, but the pain that shot through me was oddly dulled, like I'd hit my toe instead of fallen into the underworld. I rubbed my eyes, trying to adjust to the dim light of the hallway. The palms of my hands were covered with fine dust.

A lump groaned beside me. *Isadora.* I reached out and touched her arm. She shrunk away from me like I was made of fire.

After a few moments, my eyes adjusted and I dragged myself to my knees. I was sitting in the middle of a wide hall made of black veined stone, lined with wooden doors on either side of us. Every surface was covered with a thick layer of dust.

It looks exactly like Maeve's dream.

I pulled myself to my feet and went to find the others. Aline leaned against the wall, cradling Smithers in her lap. I held out a hand and helped them both up, then turned to Isadora. She waved me off as she staggered to her feet and smoothed the wrinkles out of her dress.

"I never thought I'd see this dump again," she muttered.

She bent down and slipped off one of her stilettos, eyeing the broken heel with disgust. "What a waste of a new pair of Louboutins." She tossed the shoes away.

"What are you doing here?" I demanded.

"I'm here because you can't count," Isadora huffed. "For each soul that leaves the underworld, one must remain. And since you jumped in like a bloody fool, I had to go in after you to even up the numbers."

"No, you can't count. I was following Liah." I cast my eyes around in search of her, but I couldn't see her anywhere. My stomach churned. *Did I imagine her?* "She broke through the circle and—"

"If she is even here, she is fae. That sigil on her arm has been infused with demon and witch blood. It already carries the magic to pass between the worlds." Isadora yanked her skirt up and showed me a cross of Saint Lazarus carved into her thigh. Arthur had said the tattoo looked all diseased and bloody. But now it was dull and perfectly clean. "This was tattooed with demon, fae, and witch blood, the same as your fae friend's arm. Only mine has been weakened so much, it will not work again."

"Oh." *Shite.* "Well, thanks. You're giving up your immortality for me. That's big."

"Don't get all emotional about it," Isadora waved a hand. "It's a matter of politeness, is all. Besides, you know what they say – live well, die immortal, leave a beautiful corpse."

"I've never heard that said," I grinned.

"Shut up," Isadora snapped. "It's your fault I'm here at all. Every word from your lips should be deference to my sacrifice."

"Sexy lady with pretty ink, like a picture book with a beginning, middle, and end," Smithers sang, bending down to inspect Isadora's tattoo. She slapped him away.

"I love what they've done with the place," I said, gazing

around the dark hallway, searching for Liah in the dark corners. I remembered the commentary on the interior design shows I'd watched on the telly. "Bold color scheme, excellent use of lighting, decor a mix of minimalism and abject terror. I have one question, though. Shouldn't this place be swarming with demons?"

"It will take some time for them to make their way back here after they were hit with that belief bomb," Aline said. "For now, we've got the place to ourselves."

"Not just you," a voice said from behind us.

I whirled around. In the middle of the hall, holding a bow over her shoulder, was Liah.

The urge to embrace her itched in my arms. Being with Maeve was turning me soft. Fae didn't embrace. I walked over to her and fixed her with a nonchalant look. "So you weren't a mirage."

"I was not."

Fuck it. I wasn't fae anymore. I was a human, and seeing her gladdened my heart. I threw myself at her, wrapping my arms around her neck.

"I'm glad you're not a megalomaniac villain," I whispered in her ear.

"Get off me." Liah pushed me away, but there was a hint of softness in her cold eyes. "The humans have made you all sentimental. We don't have time for this. If you want to stop Daigh once and for all, you'd better come with me."

~

We stood at the mouth of hell – a gaping maw of darkness so dark it made the void seem like the Blackpool Illuminations. Surrounding the arch was a decorative border formed from skulls and femurs. The decor reminded me a little of the Unseelie court, except we never had doorways made of darkness so solid and oppressive it threw you away from it.

Liah took a vial from a pouch on her hip and tipped a black sludge on to her stump. A rank smell rose through the hallway. Liah rubbed her hand into the sludge, smearing her skin with the black slime. Aline shrieked as Liah rubbed the foul grease into her skin.

"Stop squirming," she commanded. "This is the blood of the demon that held me at Daigh's behest. He deserved his death. It may spoil your complexion, but it will get you through that door."

She did the same to Smithers, then approached me, her hands raised. I kept my face impassive as she slid her hand over my skin. This was no worse than some of the things Daigh had forced me to do. And if it led us to Maeve and Corbin, it was worth it.

I sniffed, and the foul shite caught in my throat and made my stomach gag and retch. Liah thumped me on the back while I struggled to breath normally.

It had better *be worth it.*

With the demon's blood smearing my face, the black doorway no longer appeared as oppressive. In fact, I could make out the faint glow of a light in the depths. I sprinted forward and passed through the darkness with ease. Nothing bit me nor snared me.

I emerged into a cavernous space, shaped like the interior of a sidhe but on an impossibly grand scale. In the center of the room stood a high throne built from a pile of bones, presiding over an enormous fire from which sulfurous flames leapt and licked. A long bridge stretched from where I stood across to the throne.

Atop the throne sat Daigh, an enormous crown with a blue aura sitting atop his head. Across from him at the foot of the throne stood a figure, her skin smeared with black sludge and her stance wide and defiant.

Maeve!

She had her hands on her hips and her head cocked to one side as she spoke. From the expression on her face, it looked like... it was impossible, but...

I stifled a laugh.

Maeve Moore was giving Daigh a *science lecture.*

Her voice reverberated from the cavernous space as she enunciated on some vital point. I caught the words 'DNA' and 'epigenetics,' but the rest of it was like a foreign language. On the throne, Daigh's mouth hung open. He tried to interject, but Maeve kept talking and talking.

"For a High Priestess, she's useless," Liah said. "She had him at her mercy, but she let him go. Now she just keeps trying to talk to him about *science.*"

"That sounds exactly like Maeve."

As I watched in fascination, trying to figure out if Maeve had a plan, a shadow moved at the base of the throne. A human arm reached up between the femurs, hauling his body up with surprising stealth. Corbin reached the next step and kept going, climbing up the back of the throne until he was so close to Daigh he could reach out and touch him.

"I don't know what he's doing," Liah said. "He's got no weapon."

But he does.

I wanted to cheer as Corbin reached the top of the throne. Daigh still hadn't noticed him, mesmerized as he was by Maeve, who was now trying to explain how the genome worked. Corbin hung off the back and pulled the knife from his side – the same knife Daigh had used to kill him. He swung around like a monkey, flying over the side of the throne. I expected him to plunge the blade into Daigh's chest.

Instead, he jammed it into the blue-eyes skull in the center of the crown.

"Ooooh," Daigh moaned. The blue aura of the crown flickered and died out. Corbin grabbed it off Daigh's head as he lost his balance on the precarious bone steps. He toppled down, down, in a whirl of pale skin and black robes. Skulls shattered as his body bounced once before sliding to a stop in front of Maeve.

Daigh's hands flew to his head. When he found it bare, he roared with anguish. The sound was music to my ears. I surged forward, my only thought on reaching Maeve.

"It's over, father," Maeve said, her hands still on her hips. "I didn't have to defeat you with magic. I've already outwitted you with science. That crown was the source of any power you had. I've destroyed it, and with it your future, as you tried to destroy mine."

I reached her side and threw my arms around her. She jumped, but relaxed into my embrace as she realized it was me. "It figures you two would defeat our ultimate enemy with a boring lecture," I grinned, my heart surging with pride and awe and love. Corbin stood over Daigh, his knife in his hand, ready to stab if he so much as fluttered an eyelash.

"Blake." Maeve nuzzled her head into my neck. She felt so good in my arms. "I trust you're our rescue party?"

I swept my arm back toward the others, who were crowding on to the bridge to embrace her in turn. "At your service. But how did you know the crown was where he was getting power?"

"Easy. When I got my DNA results back, I realized that our magic was scientifically observable. It was written into my DNA, which means it's also written into Daigh's. When he made the deal with the demon king and gave his magic, he altered his DNA. But DNA can only be altered in one of two ways – by random, spontaneous mutations, or by epigenetics, which is changes to the way DNA expresses itself, and not the actual code. Then I thought of Aline's use of fae magic after she emerged from the painting, and how you were able to perform some kinds of fae magic even though you shouldn't be able to, and it hit me."

"What hit you?" This was already over my head, but she was squirming in my arms in her excitement to explain.

"That perhaps everything we think about magic is wrong. That perhaps epigenetics is what gives us our magical specialties. We only present with one specialty, because it's better for working magic, but we actually contain the DNA *potential* to perform any kind of magic. That would mean there had to be an environmental trigger to force the change. Yours was the trauma of growing up with Daigh, Aline's was being trapped inside the painting. And Daigh's was whatever bargain he struck with the demon when he exchanged his powers."

Daigh moaned. Corbin kicked him, and Maeve continued. "And *then* it occurred to me that a demon wouldn't just allow Daigh's power to go to waste. After all, they have shades come through here, and I remembered what you told me about the human sacrifices required to raised the Slaugh, and how the demons drew the energy of their blood, of their genetic material." Corbin kicked the broken crown out of Daigh's reach. "And I realized that what we're standing in right here is the universe's most sophisticated genetics lab, and that crown was the switch. I was going to kill him, but then I realized I didn't have to. I could truly, finally, strip him of power, and to him that would be worse than death."

"Sever the crown from the king, and watch him fall." I stood on Daigh's wrist, grinding the heel of my boot into his hand until he whimpered. The sound was the purest music. "Maeve Moore, I am in awe. What are we going to do with—"

A bowstring zinged. I whipped around. Daigh groaned,

rolling on to his side. A green-tipped arrow stuck out of his abdomen, the shaft quivering.

I didn't have to trace my eyes back to know who'd taken that shot. Liah stalked across the bridge, her cold eyes narrowed. Daigh groaned and tried to climb to his knees to crawl away. Liah shoved her boot in his back and pushed him down.

He curled over, his eyes meeting hers, swimming with pain. "Your new queen had demanded mercy for me, and you disobeyed her."

"I'm not Liah's queen," Maeve said.

"I have hated you my entire life," Liah growled. She drew back her bow and aimed her arrow at his forehead. "You took away the one thing in my life that was good. You took Blake and you twisted him into a pale imitation of you, and in doing so you twisted me. This death is only the death you gave me."

"Liah, stop." I laid my hand on her arm, above the stump of her ruined hand. Her skin was warm, strong, her muscles taut. *I can't believe I'm doing this.* "He's not worth it."

Liah's eyes flicked to mine. "After everything he's done to you, you want him to live?"

I shrugged. "I want him to live as a shade, without power, without an outlet for his cruelty. He will suffer here in this halfway house of the dead far more than if he were to truly join it. Besides, why should we care about him? We've won."

It was true. Hated for Daigh had burned inside me for many years. Liah was right, he had twisted me, but not nearly as much as that rage had done. Now that he had no power over me, now that I had found my family, I couldn't bring myself to perform this one last act of cruelty. Daigh deserved death, that I would not dispute. But it would not be by my hand, or by Liah's.

Now that I knew I had a home, and Maeve, and a real family, I didn't need that hatred anymore. I let it go.

"*You* may have won, Blake. You stopped the Slaugh. You have your plan to resurrect your dead friends. You'll have a bright and beautiful future as a human." Liah's lip trembled. "I have nothing."

"That's not true. I'll show you. Let Daigh stay here with the demons. Let him be the one making deals on the crossroads. The fae need a new leader, one who thinks of more than just himself. It should be you, Liah."

She snorted.

"Blake's right." Maeve stepped beside Liah, her hand resting on Liah's shoulder. "Did you know that we made Daigh an offer? If you would lead the fae, I would make you the same offer. We destroy the gateway to Tir Na Nog and invite the fae back to the earth. You will have dominion over all the wild places. We will return to you the forests and the glades and the oceans and the rivers. And you and Blake will work *together* to preserve them, to protect the spirits of the trees from further attack. Would you accept this offer?"

Liah lowered the bow. "Yes. I will do it."

Maeve's eyes bugged out. "Seriously?"

Liah shrugged. "The fae will return to their rightful home. It is what we were supposed to be fighting for all along. We will need to negotiate something about all the iron up there, and about protection for our—"

"We can hammer out the details later." Maeve held out her hand.

Liah stared at it until I nudged her arm. "You grab her hand and shake it. It's a human thing."

"How odd." But Liah swung her bow onto her back, and shook Maeve's hand. "I accept your bargain, High Priestess. The fae shall return. We shall care for the wild places and the ghosts of trees."

Daigh burst out laughing. Blood bubbled out of the wound in his side. Red blood. Human blood. "You can't... they'll never accept you..."

"I have achieved the prize you long boasted of," Liah said, kicking him in the side until his laughter turned to a slow wheeze. "The fae will return to earth, Tir Na Nog will be destroyed, and we shall have no more bloodshed."

"I like her chances," Maeve grinned.

"Yes." Liah stood back from Daigh. She nodded at the knife in Maeve's chest. "I am sorry about that."

An apology from Liah? Wow, this really was a day for miracles. I gathered Maeve in my arms, my heart bursting.

Corbin pointed to the crown at his feet. The knife stuck out of the central skull, whose eyes flashed erratically. "What do we do with this?"

"Throw it into the flames," Maeve said.

"No!" Aline showed past me, striding up to Corbin. She bent down and picked up the crown. "If you destroy it completely, you'll bring down this whole place, and then the dead won't have anywhere to go. It must have a master, and it must be repaired."

"Than what do you suggest?" Corbin demanded.

Aline's face broke into a beautiful smile, a mirror of Maeve. She pressed her palm to the skull, which hummed in her hand as the blue light flickered inside it once more. She held up the crown, and placed it on her head.

"I will wear it," she said. "It's time the underworld had a queen."

37

ARTHUR

The void closed up with a shudder and a great rush of darkness, leaving behind a pile of slumped bodies – all that remained of those who'd entered it. I stared at the blank spots on the circle where Blake and Isadora had stood.

"What happened?" I demanded, stamping my foot down on the ground where the void had been. My boot narrowly missed kicking Blake's limp hand. "How did we lose two extra people?"

"Liah broke through the circle and leapt into the void," Flynn said, his voice uneven. "Blake followed her. And Isadora followed Blake."

"Why would Blake do something so completely fucked up?"

"We don't have time to consider it." Clara shoved her way to the center of the circle, a black bag slung over her shoulder. "Quickly now, we've got a lot of work to do to prepare the next part of the ritual. Bring all the bodies."

Flynn grabbed Blake's wrists and dragged him in front of the sidhe. Isadora was already slumped there, her arm shrunk away from me. As Flynn rolled Blake over, his glassy eyes stared at the sky, and a chill ran down my spine.

"We can bring him back too, right?" I asked Clara.

"We're going to try," she said. "If he even wants to return."

A dark rage flared inside me. She had a point. After everything I'd accused Blake of, and the way we'd all refused to trust him even though Maeve did, he might've decided it was time to switch loyalties. I thought we'd made our peace, but maybe I underestimated just how much he'd been hurting. Guilt gnawed at my gut, and my bandaged arm flared with pain.

"We'll need a likeness of Blake." Flynn pulled a ballpoint pen and one of Corbin's Post-it notes from his pocket and sat down, leaning the paper against his knee as he started to sketch.

"I'll get the others." I spun around and headed to the tree. I didn't want to think about Blake anymore.

We'd wrapped Maeve's body in a sheet, which was just as well, because if I had to look at her glassy eyes or touch her clammy skin I'd probably end up immolating her on the spot, and then we'd never get her back. I shoved my hands underneath her and gingerly picked up the stiff body, the way I'd always carried her up to bed when we'd lived at Briarwood.

"I'll bring Corbin," Jane said, reaching for the box. My chest heaved as I noticed again how small it was. I hadn't looked inside, but there was no way it housed Corbin's body intact. Could we even restore him if he was in pieces?

We're going to find out.

Goosepimples prickled across my shoulders. I glanced behind me, scanning the trees for movement. But there was nothing, because the fear was from inside me.

I shook my head. *You're being stupid. You've got goosepimples because you're carrying around your lover's body.*

I gapped it down to the sidhe. The others had dragged the

bodies into the entrance, piling them up against each other. I laid Maeve down beside Blake, and Jane placed the box beside her. "As long as some of the body remains, we'll be able to perform the spell," Clara said, stroking the end of the box. "You can thank yourself for recovering the body, Arthur. "

"Oh," Corbin's mother took in the box with wide eyes. She buried her head into her husband's shoulders. Andrew glanced across at me and nodded. I wasn't sure what the nod meant, but its significance weighed over my heart.

"We're going to have to take the lid off," Clara said gently. Andrew flinched. His wife wailed.

"Super," Flynn gulped, looking up from his drawing.

My gaze snapped to Rowan. He stared at his feet, his lips moving as he counted something none of us could see. After a few moments, he nodded. "If it will bring Corbin back, it's worth it."

"I'll do it," Clara said kindly, pulling the box toward herself and pointing to a spot on the other side of the sidhe. "You take up that position in the circle, Rowan. Flynn, you're over there. Arthur, stand between them. Andrew and Bree, you're at the back. You won't see anything, I promise. Gwen and Candice will stand beside me."

"What about me?" Kelly piped up.

"Or Ryan?" Flynn asked.

"Can't you do anything without your new boyfriend?" I shot back.

Clara waved her hand. "Ryan doesn't have a magical bone in his body."

"He changes into a fox!"

"That's not magic. No energy transforms place. It's just physiology, like a butterfly unfurling its wings. Ryan and Kelly will sit this ritual out. Witches only. Everyone link hands."

I did as she asked. Rowan's hand trembled in mine. I gave his fingers a squeeze. *Hold it together, mate. We've only got this chance now because you never gave up on Corbin or Maeve.*

If we could bring Corbin back... if we could bring them all back... even Blake...

"Our friends are now in a place where we cannot reach them with our minds. We have to trust that they will find each other in the darkness. What we need to do is create a beacon of power to light their way home. I need each of you to picture all the people in the underworld." Clara sighed. "Even Isadora. Focus on the details of their physical form – what did Maeve's eyes look like? How did Corbin's hair fall over his eyes? How did being with Blake make you feel?"

Frustrated, I thought but didn't say.

"You got to bring them to life in your minds, okay? Flynn, throw the artwork into the fire."

As I watched the flames curling around the paintings and reducing them to ash, I thought of Corbin. I remembered the first time I'd met him, when he came to speak to my lawyer on my behalf. His hair hadn't been quite as long then. I thought he'd been growing it because he liked mine. A curl fell over his left eye, and he had to keep tucking it behind his ear as he spoke. He mentioned his age – a year younger than me – but the way he held himself he seemed much older.

The first week I lived at Briarwood was... odd. Corbin clearly had no idea how to live with someone like me. He always had his nose in a book and it made me feel stupid and I got frustrated a lot and burned things. We tiptoed around each other until one day I incinerated an old book of his and we gave each other a bollocking and then we got drunk and everything was cool.

Then I thought of Blake, his stupid smirk and his black hair that never seemed to have a strand out of place. I thought of his newfound fondness for curry, and that flicker of emotion in the corners of his mouth when we'd shaken hands, or when he watched Maeve while she wasn't looking.

And Maeve... how could I ever forget what her eyes looked like? Deep hazel flecked with gold, sparkling with intelligence and mischief and kindness. Her short hair bouncing on her head. Her lips wide with laughter or curled around the end of my cock.

With her free hand, Clara flipped back the lid of Corbin's box. Even from as far back as I stood, I could make out blackened shapes wrapped in plastic. Corbin was in pieces. Heat flared into my fingers. *This isn't going to work.*

"Save your fire for the candles, Arthur," Clara said sharply. I glanced down. My pants were on fire. Shite. I sat down in the grass, stifling the flames between my arse cheeks and the dirt. Beside me, Flynn burst out laughing.

"Boys, please, if we could focus," Andrew frowned. Fire flared in my fingers again, that he dare tell me what to do when he was the one who abandoned Corbin and refused to speak to him after Keegan's death, he was the one who let Corbin go on believing his brother's suicide was his fault—

Get a hold of yourself. If I derailed this ritual, we'd lose our chance to get Corbin back, and Maeve and the others might remain trapped down there with Daigh...

I glanced down at the bandages wrapped around my forearm, recalling the cut beneath them that split through the Norse rune tattoo Corbin had translated for me. A line of neat sutures kept the wound closed, like I was some kind of Frankenstein's monster – a beast made of pieces of the dead.

"Sorry," I muttered, standing up again.

Clara lowered the tongs into Corbin's box and placed the stone on top. She scattered the smaller stones on the other bodies, placing one with each. She stood white taper candles around the bodies, and added some other stones. "Arthur, light the candles."

Grateful for a task that could siphon off some of the energy pulsing in my veins, I waved my hand and the candles flickered to life.

"Repeat the chant along with me," Clara said. "As you do, picture a cone of white light rising up from Corbin's chest and encompassing all the bodies. This cone will help the spirits find their way back inside their bodies and undo the mortification that's already taken place."

"And it will put my son back together?" Andrew said, his voice wavering.

"According to Isadora, it will." Clara glanced down at the frozen face of the Soho priestess. "Whatever happens, you must keep this vision in your mind. Let us begin." She paused, then spoke, "The clay steals the clay."

I chanted the words along with the others, forcing the power through my hands. A noxious smell wafted across my nostrils. It reminded me of the time last year when Obelix hid a dead rat in the cellar and it took me three weeks to locate the source of the stench.

This was a hundred dead rats. A thousand rotting rodent buggers, all being shoveled at my mouth. I stumbled on the words as the malodor closed my throat and poured tears from my eyes.

"Don't break the circle," Clara screamed. "Keep chanting."

"The clay steals the clay. The clay steals—" I choked as my mouth crawled with rot. The reek grew form, burrowing into every pore and soaking me in horror. I mashed my lips together in an attempt to hold out the fetid decay. If I opened my mouth again, I'd drown in it.

Keep going. I forced myself to picture that cone of power, to imagine it pulling my loved ones up from the earth. *Do it for Maeve, for Corbin, for all of them.*

I squeezed my eyes shut and tore my lips apart. Instead of being flooded by the unforgivable stench, I got a whiff of

Maeve's sweet perfume, and Corbin's leathery book smell, and Blake's crisp autumn scent.

"I can feel them," Clara yelled. Magic surged through my fingers as the cone of magic over us vibrated. "We've got them. Now, everyone, pull!"

38

MAEVE

"Why did you do that?" I gaped at Aline in horror as she ascended the steps of the throne, the crown gleaming under the flickering firelight. It sat askance on her head, too large really to fit her properly. "Aren't you making yourself into a demon?"

"I have done this because it's time the underworld stopped standing apart and pretending its problems didn't reverberate across the other realms." Aline smiled down at me. "Do not be afraid, daughter. I will draw the power I need to make change, but I will not become a creature of shadow and fear, or spirit and sorrow. I will bring so much joy to these halls that humans will find joy in death as they never had before. The same kind of joy as you have given me in death, for you reunited me with my love, and I got to see what a remarkable woman my daughter has become."

Smithers scurried over to kneel before her. "I will serve you forever."

"There will be no servants in my house." Aline reached up to the crown and wrenched free one of the horns. She placed it in Smithers' hand. "This is yours. Take its power and do good with it."

To my surprise, she turned and kicked Daigh's outstretched hand, turning it over so his palm faced up. She dropped another– much tinier – piece of the broken crown into his fingers. His eyes widened in surprise.

"What are you doing?" I moved to wrench that piece of bone from Daigh's grasp, but Aline raised her hand, and an invisible force held me back.

"More than anyone I have ever met, you have embodied true chaos," Aline said to Daigh. "I can't pretend that I haven't hated the things you've done, especially to our daughter who you professed to love, but I cannot hate you. If you rule with me, you do so because you love me, and you obey me and the rest of my harem, do you understand? In return, I will give you a small kingdom where your chaos can have free rein."

Daigh's lips moved in a silent agreement. His fingers curled around the bone. Smithers waved a hand and a jet of water shot out, breaking off the shaft of the arrow and cleaning out the wound. Daigh crawled to his knees, and came to kneel beside Smithers, his forehead touching the ground.

"I will obey you and love you," he murmured. For the first time, I detected true emotion in his voice. Defeat, yes, but also affection. Was it truly possible that even a fae like Daigh was yet capable of love? "You have always been my queen."

"This is ludicrous." Liah reached for her bow. "We've only just deprived him of his power and that witch has given it back."

"You can't do this," I cried. "He can't have power. We've seen what he chooses to do with it."

"Daigh's ruled by chaos, not malevolence," Aline said. "It's only when the emotions he learned from my dear Smithers have clouded his thinking that he has enacted his terrible crimes. You yourself said that hate is only the other side of love. Here, in this place, I can give him the love that will sustain him. It is my sacrifice to you, daughter. I will love the man you cannot, and in this way, we will keep the worlds in balance."

"But I don't want any part of anything he touches influencing the world!"

"Does not the world need his chaos? Do you remember one night at Briarwood, when we were talking about predestination, and you said the way I described it reminded you of chaos theory – that within complex and chaotic systems were underlying patterns, repition, and self-organisation. Daigh is that chaos. He's as much a part of the world as earth, air, water, fire, and spirit."

I rubbed my temples. My own mother was throwing mathematical theory back in my face to justify this? I hated her for it and yet my logical mind ticked through her points and remembered that a small change in state in a deterministic nonlinear system can have a huge and unknown impact in a later state. And I knew she was right.

I don't understand a word you just thought, Princess. Blake said inside my head. *Are you actually talking about letting her keep Daigh, and letting him keep that piece of the crown?*

"What do you think?" My mother stood and beckoned me to climb her throne. "I loved these two men once, and our love produced you. No matter how many evil things Daigh has done, I can't forget that. Together, I believe we will be just what the underworld needs. I will take inspiration from you and have my very own harem. At least, if Isadora will join us?"

She tossed another piece of the crown across the room. It sailed through the air before it was ensnared in Isadora's talons.

"I accept," she said, sashaying toward the throne. I noticed that the first thing she did as she grasped that power in her hand was sculpt herself some new red pumps.

Aline grinned at me, her arms wide. "Like mother, like daughter."

"If Daigh truly has no power without you now," I said, "I think this could work."

I allowed Aline to embrace me. She held me for a long time. I tried to imprint her body on my mind. She felt so familiar, and yet completely foreign. I never knew her as a mother, but I knew now I could count her as a friend. Her lips pressed against my forehead, warm and still tingling with residual magic. "Keep a mirror with you always, so I can check in on you from time to time." She glared at Blake and Corbin. "Just don't put it in your bedroom. There are some things a mother doesn't need to know."

"Deal," Blake grinned.

"Uh, guys?" Corbin held up his hand. His forearm was still solid, but his fingers had faded into black tendrils. "I think it's time."

I knew the guys would find a way!

I hopped down from the dais and ran to Blake and Corbin. They caught me in their arms and the three of us huddled together, gasping and exclaiming as the black tendrils appeared from thin air to wrap around us. Where they touched my skin, they tickled, and the tickle became an itch, and as the darkness wrapped around my torso and breasts and crept toward my chin, the itch became an all-consuming roar of pain – a thousand tiny needles all piercing me at once. I opened my mouth to scream, but the darkness filled it, stinging my tongue so that it puffed up and closed my airway.

With the last dim light of vision, I caught Aline waving at me. "Bye bye!"

"The dove flies the nest," called Smithers, his voice muffled as the darkness stuffed my ears. "Fly little dove!"

"This won't be the last we see of each other, dear daughter," Daigh coughed out, his rough voice turning into a dull ring as the darkness consumed me utterly.

~

*M*y eyes fluttered open.

I lay on my back on rock hard earth. Orange fire streaked the horizon. My throat burned. Fear leapt into my chest. *The world's been irradiated. Daigh's vision came true—*

"Maeve." Warm arms wrapped around me, tugging me into a sitting position. A dark curtain fell across my face, obscuring the burning sky. Hot kisses trailed along my neck as a familiar smell of herbs and flour filled my nose.

Rowan.

"Why is the sky on fire?" I choked out, every word tearing at my raw throat.

"It's not on fire," Rowan stroked my cheek. "It's sunrise, Maeve. It's the first day of a new world."

My breath caught in my throat as the brilliance of the cosmos streaked across the sky. Atmospheric molecules scattered the cool blue light, leaving us with the majestic stripes of red and orange. I drank in its beauty, more touched because it was a sunrise I'd never thought I'd see.

"I did it," I sighed into Rowan's shoulder. "I scienced my way out of Hell."

Rowan's rich, hearty laugh filled me with a joy so deep and rich it seemed impossible it could belong to one person. My palms itched with magic, and I sent some out into him, giving him back some of the warmth and light he'd given me.

"Oh, Einstein, it's you, it's you." Flynn planted a million

slobbery kisses on my face, his eyes dancing with delight. I ran my fingers through his wavy red hair, relishing that cheeky smile I'd missed so much.

Flynn's head flopped to the side, and I glimpse a wide forehead, deep-set eyes as still as glaciers, and a thick, wild beard. *Arthur.*

"You're alive," I breathed, my heart welling.

In reply, Arthur crushed his lips to mine, his kiss leaving me gasping. There was no better way to be brought back to the world of the living.

I broke the kiss, laughing as I wiped a strand of blond hair from his eyes. He gazed at me with awe, like he couldn't breathe without me. *My viking warrior.* Tears streamed down my cheeks. *I almost lost you.*

"Don't cry," he said gruffly, and a single tear leaked from his eye and spilled down his cheek, catching on the end of a beard hair like a tiny snowflake. "You'll set off the whole bloody lot of us."

"Come here, big guy." Blake threw his arms around Arthur's shoulders and planted a wet kiss on his cheek. Arthur stiffened for a moment, then he put Blake's head into a pretend headlock and rubbed his fist on his head, mussing up Blake's perfect hair.

"Hey!" Blake yelped, scrambling to escape Arthur's hold.

Warm lips grazed my cheek. I turned to meet Corbin's gaze, and another surge of emotion opened my heart. His eyes blazed with gentle warmth, his dark hair whipped around his face, his skin was streaked with foul demon blood. I traced his cheekbone with my fingers, savouring the warmth of his skin. He'd gone to hell for all of us, and we'd brought him back. There was no love in the universe that was greater than that.

We all fell over each other, crying and laughing and hugging and kissing, relishing the warmth of living skin.

Rowan and Corbin locked lips in a kiss that seared with passion. Only when Corbin pulled back did his parents manage to elbow their way into the fray to envelop him in a fierce hug. His mother whispered a long string of words into his ears that made his whole face light up with happiness. It was the most beautiful sight I'd ever seen.

"I knew you'd kick some demon arse, big sister." Kelly and Jane squashed me between them. I kissed them both.

"Nice use of arse, little sister," I teased her.

"I know," she beamed. "I've been practicing."

Kelly and I gazed at each other, a million unsaid things flickering through our eyes. *I forgive you*, and *I love you* being the two that mattered most. I knew that one day, when I was ready, I would tell her that I saw our parents in the Slaugh, and that it was her words that stopped me from using my magic for murder. *I won't have any more secrets.*

We fell in the grass together, laughing and talking over each other as we watched the sun pierce the sky. Flynn had his phone out and he was trying to convince the guy at the local curry house to deliver a big order of food right to the field. Blake and Arthur got into an argument about Sherlock Holmes and Arthur put Blake in another headlock. I laughed until my sides ached and my tears dried into sticky trails down my cheeks.

Love swelled in my chest as I observed my big, messy, perfect family. My five broken boys who had faced their own demons in order to save the world and to unite us again. The people who had believed in us, even when we didn't believe in ourselves. My sister, who had lost so much and yet kept on smiling. And behind them, the blackened walls of Briarwood, broken too, but still fighting, still working their own magic on us all.

*A*s the sun fell behind the horizon, streaking blood red light across the sky, we took up our positions around the sidhe. It was two weeks after we returned from the underworld, and Liah and I had finally finished negotiations for the treaty between humans and fae. I raised my hands and called on the elements, the words of our coven rituals now committed to memory. Magic hummed through my veins, rising like a cone through my body, spurred on by the excitement that marked today as a turning point in the future of fae/human relations.

Two months ago, I'd never heard of witchcraft outside Harry Potter films and my parents' Sunday sermons. I thought my future was lined up in a neat row of boxes I could tick off. I'd never traveled outside my country, never set foot inside a real castle, I never even had a real boyfriend. Now I was the head of the most powerful coven in the world, I was rebuilding a medieval castle, and I counted five remarkable men as my lovers and my partners in life.

(Rowan would call us all soulmates, but... I was still me. No soulmate talk around the scientist, thanks.)

And tonight... I would mark my first public action as High Priestess of the Briarwood Coven, and it would change the future of what it meant to be a witch, and a fae.

I raised my arms and addressed the equal numbers of witches and fae who made up the circle. Behind them, more ranks of bystanders – fae legions, and witches from our allied covens – came together to witness this historical event. "Liah, step forward."

The queen of the fae glided out of the circle and faced me across the sidhe entrance. The fae had bedecked her in their finery – a gown of green silk spun with shimmering veins, garlands of flowers in all the colors of the rainbow cascading from her neck and waist, and her white hair piled on top of her head and woven around her dramatic crown of vines.

"Today, Liah and I make a pact. Witches and fae are no longer enemies. We now share this world. The fae will reclaim their roles as guardians of the wild places, and we witches make it our responsibility to protect them. In return, the fae will revoke their right to lie. They are now bidden to tell the truth in all dealings with humans, witches, demons, or their own kin."

A gasp rocked the crowd of fae and witches. I grinned, pleased with the contract Liah and I had reached. I hoped this provision would prevent another Daigh from rising again.

Liah raised her hand to mine, to show she agreed. "We agree to this provision. In turn, the witches will not raise their hands to use their powers or ours against us. We fae will mete out justice to our own kind. We are not to be inter-fered with."

"We agree." Liah and I shook hands. Together we faced the entrance to the sidhe and raised our clasped hands. Magic poured into me from my magisters and the other witches present, zipping along my skin and pooling in my hand. I drew it in, focusing on the invisible gateway that existed over the sidhe, the gateway that led to the prison that had kept the fae for centuries.

Corbin stepped forward and directed his palm toward the entrance of the sidhe. His voice rang loud and clear across the meadow. "With air, I break this prison."

The sidhe rumbled, and a clot of dirt fell from the roof and burst on the stairs.

A rush of heat burned past my face. "With fire, I break this prison," Arthur said.

The air misted with droplets as Flynn said, "With water, I break this prison."

My ankles rolled as the earth rocked again. Rowan blinked. "With earth, I break this prison."

"With spirit, I break this prison," Blake said, his eyes warm as they fixed on Liah.

Together, Liah and I *pushed*.

Magic streamed through my fingers, mingling with Liah's power and becoming an unstoppable ball of opposing forces. As that power crashed into the entrance to the wormhole, it fractured something beyond the earth.

Smoke appeared at the edges of the sidhe entrance. A wave of energy flared out, shoving against my body. I pressed against it, but something told me to let it come. I relaxed my body and a great shockwave sailed up the steps, swiping my feet out from beneath me. I fell hard on my back, my breath knocked out of me. The energy flowed over my head, out of the circle. Trees fluttered as it soared into the wood and disappeared.

Beside me, Liah clambered to her feet and crawled forward. She thrust her hand through the entrance of the sidhe. I expected to see her hand disappear into darkness, but instead she waggled it around, a grin spreading across her stony features. "The gateway has been destroyed," she declared, offering me her good hand. I took it and allowed her to help me up.

"Welcome back to the earth," I said. "I hope with your help, we'll take better care of it."

Cheers rose up from the ranks of the fae and witches. Sprites darted through the air, chittering and flicking their wings together like a hundred tiny Blood Lust drummers. Far Darrig's clattered their bone blades together in a jangle of cacophonous delight. The court fae loosed fire-tipped arrows into the sky. The arrows burst into colorful fireworks that rained over us, speckling our flesh with crystalline light.

My coven cheered also. Corbin thrust his fist in the air. Arthur spun his sword around in one hand, a broad smile breaking his stern features. Rowan's grin lit up the evening. Flynn grabbed Blake and forced him to dance an Irish jig.

"We call upon the earth and the stars as our witness," I said, to complete the ritual. "This barrier is broken. The fae are welcome back into the wild places of the earth. No witch or human or other magical creature will stand against them. Both sides will abide by the accord set forth on this day."

Liah held out the papers we'd drawn up, detailing the treaty between fae and humans. I was quite proud of it. Corbin helped a lot, putting his quick mind to use thinking of new scenarios and clauses that would protect both sides long into the future.

Arthur waved his hand, and the treaty burst into flames. I tossed it onto the steps, and a new cheer rose up as the flames devoured our careful words, binding us with air and fire. Liah and I had copies, of course. But by burning the papers, we gave the words back to the earth. The trees would see the accord was kept.

The Avebury coven had insisted we celebrate the union in true Druidic form – with a feast. Liah had shown Rowan how to bake honey cakes and other traditional fae fare. Now they were no longer banished, both fae and humans could break bread together. Arthur rolled out two barrels of his best mead, and across the meadow we toasted our new alliance.

Flynn spread out a picnic blanket under a tree, and the six of us crowded together, passing around plates and drinks. Obelix waddled between us, picking scraps of chicken off our plates. "What now, Princess?" Blake asked, biting into one of Rowan's meat pies.

I glanced over to Corbin, and he nodded. "I guess now is as good a time as any to talk about it. Corbin and I would like to do something that impacts the future of the coven. We think it's going to be a good thing, but only if you guys agree. We'd like to apply to study at Oxford."

Rowan's eyes lit up. He pounced on us, knocking us back with the force of his embrace. "That's amazing," he breathed. "You *have* to do it."

"I knew you two brainiacs wouldn't be able to rest on your arses like the rest of us," Flynn grinned as he stroked Obelix's fur.

"So this is it, then." Blake's eyes blazed. "You guys leave Briarwood, and then what? We all go our separate ways?"

"Don't be ridiculous," I jabbed him in the arm. "We're not breaking up the team. Oxford is only an hour away on the train. We'll come home for weekends and holidays, and you guys can come visit during the semester. It'll be hard, but we *did* just defeat an army of resurrected shades and brokered peace with the fae, so I think we can handle a long distance relationship for a few years. Plus, I imagine you'll find something here to occupy you."

Blake's eyes widened. "You want... you want me to stay at Briarwood?"

"Of course. I mean, if that's what you want to do—oof!"

This time it was Blake bowling me over, his lips finding

mine, locking me in a deep, sensual kiss. Behind us, Arthur whistled. Obelix let out a satisfied "meow!"

When we came up for air, Flynn punched Blake in the arm. "You didn't think you'd escape us that easily, did you? I need all hands on deck for rebuilding my workshop. I'm going to need the space to produce enough work to keep the gallery full."

"Gallery?"

"Yeah." Flynn's ears flared red. "I've been thinking about using the old servant's quarters to open a gallery shop for the tourists. They'll be able to buy my paintings and sculptures and maybe some of Rowan's preserve. That is, if it's okay with you, Maeve? It is your castle, after all."

"Briarwood is not my castle. It's ours. I want everyone to do something that lifts them up, that makes them happy." I pulled out a pamphlet from my bag and handed it to Blake. "Speaking of which, I thought you might like to have a look at this."

Blake held up the glossy booklet. "Police Academy?"

I nodded. "Since you read all those Sherlock Holmes stories, I thought maybe you'd like to be a real detective. I bet if you spoke to DS Judge, she'd give you a recommendation, along with some training tips."

Blake tucked the pamphlet into the pocket of his coat. "I'll give it some thought," he said mysteriously. His smirk tugged at the corner of his mouth. He loved the idea.

Someone slid down beside me. Kelly held up a glass of mead and I toasted her. "This stuff is delicious," she beamed at Arthur as she drained her glass. "You should go into business."

"Thanks," Arthur beamed, lifting his goblet to her. "There's plenty more if you want it."

"That's actually not a bad idea, Arnold," Flynn said, his eyes dancing as he considered the possibilities. "We could sell your mead in our shop – for the real castle experience. I could draw you a fancy label. It'll be complicated applying for the license, but I reckon—"

Arthur shook his head. "I don't think people will really want to buy my mead."

"I agree. It's totally disgusting." Kelly grabbed his full goblet from his hands and handed him hers, which was now empty.

"Sure they will," Flynn put in. "We could have a whole range of flavors. Maybe some cider in the summer. Oh, and I bet we could even buy a still and do some honey whiskey."

I snorted. "With you around, whiskey would never make it to the shop!"

"What shop?" Kelly asked.

"We were just talking about the future of Briarwood. Flynn's going to open a gallery shop for his artwork, and Rowan's going to sell some of his preserves and other things."

"Let me guess, you're going to braniac space school back in America?" Kelly said, her words slurring a little as she sipped her mead.

"Actually, I thought I'd apply somewhere closer to home." Kelly's face lit up as I told her about Corbin and I studying at Oxford, and the others staying on at Briarwood to manage the place. "You're welcome to stay here, too – you and Jane and Connor. There's room for everyone."

"Thanks for the offer, Einstein, but I've decided to go traveling."

"You have?" I tried to keep the incredulity out of my voice.

"Don't look at me like that," Kelly exclaimed as she took my full goblet of mead from my hand and exchanged it with Arthur's goblet, which was also now empty. "I came over to England to be a backpacker, and I did buy that new back-pack, so I should get some proper use out of it. Jane has some money saved up, and she's always wanted to see Europe, so we're going to do it. We're leaving for Paris next month."

"What about Connor?" Surely, Kelly hadn't forgotten Jane's adorable young son.

"He's coming with us, of course," Kelly grinned. "It's going to be a bit ridiculous backpacking with such a tiny baby, but Jane's read some websites and she reckons we can do it. She's already found us an old postal van, and we were gonna ask Flynn to help us fit a mattress and some shelves and a fridge into the back."

"Happy to help," Flynn beamed. "I'll even make Connor the cutest wee foldaway crib."

"That sounds awesome," Arthur grinned.

"It does, doesn't it?" Kelly beamed. She grabbed Arthur's arm. "Hey, Aragorn, do you fancy escorting two awesome ladies and a cute wee baby around Europe? We could do with a handsome pack mule."

"Fuck no," Arthur touched the bottom of his spine. "I'm going to be seeing a chiropractor for *months* after humping your backpack around London."

Kelly laughed, a sound I'd heard too little of ever since she'd arrived in London. I wrapped my arms around her. "I'm going to miss you."

"Me too, but we've only a short train ride or flight away, and we can talk on the phone all the time. I'll come visit you in Oxford once Jane gets sick of me."

Jane waved at Kelly from across the field. She was sitting with Liah and a bunch of her court fae. I smiled and waved back. I could see Jane and Liah getting along. They both had that no-nonsense nature about them. *Kelly's going to drive her up a wall, but she'll never get sick of her.*

Kelly left me and ran over to join them. I watched her bend down to kiss Jane on the cheek and scoop Connor up into her arms. Kelly had a girlfriend and a little boy she was crazy about. A month ago, I never would have imagined the scene. Now, it felt like the most natural thing.

So much can change when you least expect it. I leaned against Arthur's shoulder, letting his bulk reassure me. My hand traced the length of his cut. We still had a lot of healing to do. But we could do it together, as a family.

MAEVE

THREE MONTHS LATER

"Just a minute!" I yelled. A heavy fist pounded on my door. I shoved my physics textbook under the pillow of my bed and grabbed a trashy science fiction novel by some new writer called S C Green. I fluffed my hair and threw open the door.

Corbin stood on the landing, wearing his leather jacket and dark jeans and a smile a mile wide.

"You were studying, weren't you?" he teased.

"Who, me?" I raised an innocent eyebrow as I held up the novel. "No, no. I was just so immersed in this steampunk book I didn't hear you knocking—"

Corbin pushed past me and made for my bed. He slid his hand under the pillow and pulled out my textbook, which he waved in my face. "Maeve Moore, you *promised* me. No studying today. We're officially on holiday."

"Give me that." I grabbed for the book, but Corbin held it out my window, waving it over the courtyard below. "I can't help it that astrophysics is so interesting."

"That novel is about dinosaurs and steam-powered robots

duking it out in 19th century London. It's way more interesting than astrophysics."

"Says the guy who spent our Friday night date reciting Farsi declensions under his breath. What are you doing here, anyway? We said we were meeting outside the Ashmolean—"

"Hey, could you two lovebirds give it a rest? Some of us are weary after climbing your stupid university's seven million stairs."

"Omigod, Flynn!" My Irish artist stood in the door of my room, wearing his signature wicked grin and a long green trench coat splattered with paint. I flung my arms around him and he spun me in a wild circle. My leg flew out and knocked over my chair. Oxford college lodgings for undergraduates were little more than closets.

They also didn't have elevators inside the medieval college buildings, so anyone who wanted to reach my room had to climb an uneven wooden spiral staircase. I'd already lost three pounds just lugging my books home at the end of the day.

"Hey, I climbed the sodding stairs, too. Why does he get the first hug?" Arthur grumbled from behind him. I let go of Flynn and allowed Arthur to crush me in an enormous bear hug. I peered behind him at Rowan and Blake, both wrapped up warm in their winter clothes. Rowan's smile was radiant and Blake's wicked smirk made heat pool between my legs.

Flynn flopped down on my bed, peering at the NASA photographs and tutorial schedules above my desk. "Love the decor, Einstein. What happened to that painting I did for you? Do they have a rule at this posh university that you're only allowed to put brainiac stuff on the walls?"

I pointed up to the ceiling, where Flynn's painting hung from a low beam, along with a collage of photographs from Briarwood Castle I'd stuck up there. "I like that you guys are the last thing I see before I go to sleep. Speaking of seeing you, what are you all doing here? Corbin and I were going to meet you later. We had it all planned out, because—"

"Because you were going shopping for pre-Christmas gifts for all of us to say you're sorry you've been gone for so long?" Flynn lifted an eyebrow. "We *know*. Corbin let it slip. We thought we should come and remind you that our High Priestess is the only gift we need."

"We couldn't wait to see you," Rowan explained. He stepped across the threshold of the room. I noticed that his lips didn't move in his silent incantation. He'd been seeing a cognitive behavioral specialist about his OCD and anxiety for the last two months, and it had already done wonders for him. "We wanted to help you start your Christmas holidays right."

"I'm glad you're here. Maeve needs to learn a lesson about how to relax." Corbin tossed my book to Flynn. "I caught her reading this."

"Tut tut, Princess," Blake grinned, wrapping his arms around me and breathing his words against my ear. "You promised our friend Corbin here, no studying. Do we get to claim a reward on his behalf?"

My boys. I'd missed them so much. We normally went home to see them every week, but as our first semester exams loomed, Corbin and I needed every spare minute to study. It had been five weeks since we'd last touched or spoken in person, and even our phone calls had been cut off quickly by my need to study. No wonder they couldn't wait half a day to see us.

Blake scraped his teeth along my ear. Flynn bolted off the bed and claimed my mouth, his tongue entwining with mine. Heat surged through me as they sandwiched me between them, their hands roaming over my body, lighting up desires I'd been suppressing for five long weeks.

"You've forgotten all about physics now, haven't you,

Einstein?" Flynn murmured against my lips as his fingers scraped over my nipples, which stood erect through the fabric of my merino sweater.

I ground my ass against Blake's hips in response, moaning as his hardness dug into my thigh.

"Looks like she missed us." My heart skipped as Blake's hand slid under my shirt. He flicked open my bra with one hand, and rolled my hard nipple around in his fingers. Flynn moved to nibble my earlobe, while Arthur – never one to fuss about – claimed my lips with his. Beside us, Corbin and Rowan locked lips. Corbin got me all the time, so he didn't mind playing with Rowan while the others had their fill.

Arthur's intense kiss left me breathless, hungry for more. I slid my fingers across his chest, relishing his hard muscles responding to my touch. I grabbed his t-shirt and dragged it over his head. He crushed me against his bulk, my breasts filling his big hands.

"No fair. Arthur's hogging," Flynn stuck his lip out in a fake pout. But Blake wasn't waiting for permission. He tugged at my wool-lined leggings, pulling them down to reveal my new g-string, covered with cute dancing snowmen.

"Christmas is coming early," Flynn grinned when he saw them. I groaned. Arthur pretended to smack him around the ears.

The boys shuffled me over to the bed. Arthur sat on the edge, dragging me down so I straddled his hips. Blake stood behind me, kissing along my collarbone as he rolled and pinched my nipples. I leaned my head back and kissed him, the angle bringing new sensations as the tops of our tongues rolled together.

I lifted my hips so Flynn could tug off my boots and roll down my leggings and socks. "I was all ready to go out..." I moaned, but my words fell away as Flynn and Blake took my nipples into their mouths. Without breaking our kiss, Arthur tugged down his pants and settled me back on top, his enormous cock twitching in anticipation.

I sighed as I slid down on Arthur's shaft, filling my body with his warmth. I'd been aching with need all through exams and now I could sate myself with their bodies and hearts. As I ground my hips to drive Arthur deeper, I realized that all those weeks of waiting and thinking and sending filthy text messages had been worth it, for this moment right here. For Arthur buried inside me, his icy-gaze fixed on me. For Blake and Flynn's hands roaming over my body, for Rowan and Corbin breaking their kiss to nuzzle and nip at my neck.

Arthur held my body rigid as he bucked his hips up into me, his features set in an intense stare as he poured out his heart to me through our bodies. Together we slaked our dark thoughts in the heat of our bodies, burning our flames out in each other's light until we were glowing embers.

A wet, lubed finger drew down my spine and slid into my ass. Flynn? I turned my head, and my cheeky Irishman grinned at me. Each time I slammed down on Arthur's cock, Flynn pushed his finger deeper, giving me a taste of what might come over my vacation, of how much I needed to escape from the university and relinquish my control and my rules and my desire for perfection and just *be*.

"That's it," Blake purred, his teeth digging into my earlobe. "All that exam stress, all those late nights studying, give it all to us, Princess."

"Yes," I breathed as Blake's lips claimed mine and I had three of my guys inside me, and my body shuddered with a cosmic orgasm.

Through heavy-lidded eyes, I could make out Rowan sitting on my desk chair. Corbin was bent between his legs, his mouth wrapped around his cock. As he moved his head in a steady rhythm, Rowan's head tipped back, his dreadlocks spilling down the chair as he dwelled in his own ecstasy.

"We're going to be late," I murmured, thinking that we could stay in this state, this passion, this healing, all afternoon and long into the night. There was still so much of ourselves to explore and open up.

"They'll wait for us," muttered Arthur through gritted teeth. His muscles tensed, and he sped up his strokes. He was almost there. I leaned back, pressing my body harder against Flynn's finger, and claimed Rowan's mouth in mine. He moaned and pushed Corbin's head away, wanting to save his pleasure for me. I had to admit, I was glad of that. I wanted to have them all first. It was my right as High Priestess.

I locked my eyes with Arthur, and something in that look must've sparked inside him, because at that moment he lost control, his jaw clenching, his hands digging into my thighs as he released weeks of tension in one great, glorious bellow.

We fell back onto my narrow dorm bed. Blake crawled up beside me and flipped me over, sliding me up against my pillows and diving between my legs, not caring that I was now sticky from Arthur's load. His tongue pressed against my clit and in moments a second orgasm washed over me.

I was still shaking from my orgasm when Corbin and Rowan climbed onto the bed with us. Rowan slid along my body, our skin already slick with sweat. He tangled his lips in mine as he rolled a condom down his cock and entered me.

His kisses were soft and sweet and buttery, like the baking he was so well known for. His body came undone around me, his nakedness revealing more than just his skin. His struggles over these past weeks, living without Corbin and I, dealing with the intensity of his therapy, scarred him still. I took those scars into myself, giving him only peace and love in return.

Behind him, Corbin stroked his cock as he watched us. I

stretched out a hand to Flynn and gripped his cock in my fingers, stroking him hard. My Flynn, who'd found in himself a strength he'd never seen before, who'd discovered a passion for entrepreneurial pursuits that fueled his artwork. In his hands, Briarwood would flourish.

Flynn's eyes fluttered closed, his long eyelashes tangling together as he sank into this moment with me. His lips opened, but not a single pun or awful joke passed through them. Only one word, my name, over and over.

"Maeve, Maeve, Maeve..." The sweetest sound from my sweetest boy.

In those moments, I lost track of who entered me, of whose lips were on mine and whose cock was in my hands. The six of us moved together as one, seeking our solace and strength in each other. Our bodies rippled and writhed as we drowned in our need. Magic sizzled through the room, peeling the photographs off the walls and causing a fine mist to form on the windows. I wouldn't need to put the heat on.

Finally, we collapsed in a pile, our bodies slack and exhausted, our hearts full. I lay back on Rowan's chest, my gaze flicking over Flynn's painting and the photo collage on the ceiling. I'd even pinned up Kelly's postcards from her travels. Her latest one was from Santorini. The month before that was Romania, and then Prague and Budapest. Apparently Connor was having a great time, and Jane hadn't killed her yet. Kelly had even purchased a new, more sensible backpack.

Arthur's strong arms fell across my chest, and my heart soared. With everything that had happened since I first came to England, it seemed impossible that we were all here now, happy and in love and leading somewhat normal lives without the fate of the world resting on our shoulders. It wasn't easy. Corbin and I missed the guys, and Flynn wasn't exactly the most serious castle manager, but every minute we were together was a gift.

Corbin sat up, his brow furrowing as he noticed the clock above my desk. "Shite. We really are late."

We untangled ourselves and scrambled into our clothes. I ran a comb through my hair, but it was beyond saving, so I just pulled on my thickest wool beanie and left it at that. I'd dyed my bangs a variety of rainbow colors a few weeks ago to join Corbin in a campus queer event, but the dye didn't take and now it was just a mess of orange streaks. Oh well, at least I looked like a real freaky witch.

After pulling on my thick coat, scarf, and gloves (I was discovering just how bitter cold English winters could be, especially when you lived in a medieval building) I led the way down the winding staircase and out into the quadrangle. Outside the college gates, we hopped on the bus out to the suburbs. Oxford's "dreaming spires" gave way to modest Victorian townhouses and the rolling Cotswolds hills beyond. The bus dropped us off on a suburban street lined with identical brick semi-detached homes, and we followed Corbin to the house.

Four pairs of boots – one with striking spiked heels and pointed toes that looked like it was straight off a Paris runway – were lined up next to the usual family sneakers and sparkly Wellingtons. I pushed open the door. Laughter burst from the kitchen. Aline, Isadora, Daigh, and Smithers sat across the table from Corbin's parents, sipping from mugs of steaming tea while my mother regaled them with some recent story of their underworld rule.

My heart surged. I spoke to Aline every couple of weeks in my bedroom mirror, but it wasn't the same as being able to embrace her. But she now carried witch, fae, and demon essence inside her, which meant she could travel between the worlds whenever she wanted, although bringing her harem with her sapped much of her energy. Thankfully, the young demon she'd recently taken into her harem wasn't able to leave the underworld, so at least we didn't have to eat our Christmas feast with a creature of nightmares. Aline still wore her scary crown, which Corbin's sister Tessa kept trying to steal.

It took some time to get through the greetings and hugs before Bree and Andrew ushered us all into the reception room and found enough seats and teacups for everybody. My heart soared. I loved having everyone together, talking over each other and fighting over the Christmas cookies (*biscuits*, I had to keep reminding myself). Smithers sat by the window and sang to himself under his breath. Aline's powers had restored much of his cognition, but he still had a strange way about him.

"I wanted to tell you all something," Aline said. She set down her cup and stretched her hands in front of her, her lip trembling a little, as though she were nervous. Smithers took her fingers in his, knitting their digits together. On her other side, Daigh patted her hand like he was indulging a puppy.

"What is it?" I asked, hoping like hell it wasn't some problem that would derail my vacation.

"I'm pregnant," she purred, touching her smooth stomach. "Maeve, you're going to have a baby sister."

That was *not* what I'd expected. But at the news, my heart soared. A new baby, born of a union like mine – a binding of magic – would be a welcome joy, and it would cement Aline's rule over the dead and ensure her good work continued long into the future.

It was odd to think that I'd be watching Aline raise my baby sister when she was really no older than me. I'd be more like an aunt than a big sister. I thought I could deal with it. I couldn't help but wonder about all the interesting epigenetic possibilities.

"That's wonderful. I'm so happy for you." I hugged her and Smithers. Daigh put out his arm for me, but I backed away, shaking my head. I'd gotten myself to the point I could be in the same room as the guy without tearing his face off, but I'd never be able to embrace him as an ally. Not when my parents' bodies still burned between us.

My parents taught me that Jesus forgave, but that didn't mean I could forget.

"What about you?" Aline asked me.

"What about me?"

She batted her eyelashes. "Are you ever going to give me a grandchild with one of those strapping lads of yours?"

Behind me, Arthur choked on his biscuit. Corbin coughed, and Flynn burst out laughing.

"Mother!"

"What?" she grinned. "I'm allowed to ask sometimes."

"I guess so," I smiled. "Right now I'm just focusing on college. Or university, as they call it in Jolly Old England. But I'm definitely up for babysitting duties whenever you need me."

"And me!" Flynn piped up. "I love little babies."

"I may just take you up on that," Aline smiled, touching her stomach again. "It will be good for your sister to learn about life without demons trying to stick pitchforks in her little bum."

After a delicious dinner, we said goodbye to Corbin's parents, and to Aline and her harem, and piled into cars. Simon had driven Clara down from Crookshollow for the occasion, so between Ryan's fancy Bentley and Arthur's heap of junk, we had enough space for all of us. Three guesses which car I chose.

As Simon drove through the center of Crookshollow. I peered out the window at a construction sight – "What's that?"

"The Halt Institute," Clara answered from the front seat. "It's a new arts and culture building that will offer local artists, writers, and performers space to showcase their work. The bottom story will house a witchcraft museum, with exhibits that chronicle the history of the village as well as witches in popular culture. There will even be a witch-themed bookshop."

"A witchcraft museum? The town hasn't revolted?"

"They begged for it," Flynn beamed. "We had a public meeting and there was so much enthusiasm. I've already got ten volunteer docents lined up and the museum hasn't even opened yet."

"Things are changing around here," Clara said. "People are realizing that witches are part of Crookshollow's history, and they might even play a role in the town's future."

"I love it." We passed by the village green, and I saw the witch statue in the center had acquired a friend – a half-man, half-wolf rearing up to reveal enormous paws and sharp teeth. Two kids chased each other around the statues while their parents looked on. "But where did the money for this art institute come from? Last I remember the village didn't even have the funds to repaint the kindergarten."

"A certain reclusive artist may have had a hand in it." Clara lifted an eyebrow. Flynn grinned. *So that's what Ryan did with the money from the witch painting.*

It was only a few minutes later when Simon rounded the last bend in the drive and slid to a stop on the gravel in front of the inner gatehouse. I gasped at the changes to my beloved castle. The curtain wall and the front-facing battlements had been scrubbed clean of soot and repainted. They looked like they'd been built yesterday. Flynn had the carcass of the Victorian stables demolished and the area cleared. He and Ryan had been working together to create a new design, and then they'd have to apply for a building permit, which Flynn had said could take a while because of the castle's status as a listed building. In the meantime, a small portable pod had been set up there, and Flynn had covered all the external walls in bold paintings. Obelix luxuriated along the apex of the roof.

I climbed out of the car and linked arms with Flynn and Blake. The others crowded around me, and we gazed up at the castle. Behind the walls, I could see the tower and internal courtyard were still in a bad way. The ticket office was still out of commission, and the portcullis hadn't been replaced yet. One of the walls on the eastern wing had collapsed, and although there was a makeshift wall in place to keep the building watertight, rubble still littered the ground in front of it.

"I hate how broken she looks," Corbin whispered, squeezing my hand.

"She's not broken," I said, my fingers grazing Arthur's scarred arm as Rowan rested his head on Corbin's shoulder. "She wears her scars proudly. They make her stronger."

Briarwood castle had stood for centuries. Its foundations were strong. Stones could be re-cut, walls rebuilt, flagstones re-laid, tapestries replaced by Banksy-esque graffiti art. But the true Briarwood wasn't the stones or the beams or the uneven staircases. It was the people who dwelled within her walls, the scarred souls held strong and fast and who fought for what they believed in – the hearts that dared to love against impossible odds.

As long as we had each other, Briarwood Castle would always stand.

THE END

∽

Can't get enough of Maeve and her boys? Get *The Summer Court* – a Briarwood short story – for free in *Cabinet of Curiosities*, a Steffanie Holmes compendium of short stories and bonus scenes. To get this collection, all you need to do is sign up for updates with the Steffanie Holmes newsletter.

He's an arrogant, reclusive artist, and a complete and utter prick. So why can't she get him out of her head? Fall into Ryan and Alex's story in Art of Cunning, *book 1 in the Crookshollow Gothic Romance series, free from your favorite store - READ NOW*

(Turn the page for a sizzling excerpt).

EXCERPT: ART OF CUNNING

ALEX

"James Alexandra Kline!"

I cringed as my full name reverberated off the hallway walls. Through the glass wall in my office I could see Matthew storming toward me, his round face puffed up like a pimple about to burst. Across the hall, Tara – the visiting collections curator – looked up from her desk, her face alight with the promise of intrigue.

Matthew was mad. Which meant only one thing. He'd found out that—

"James Alexandra! The Raynard exhibit is opening in two weeks. Where the *fuck* are my paintings?"

I sank down lower behind my desk, wringing my hands in my lap. I'd known this confrontation was coming. In my head, I screamed at him that they weren't "his" paintings. Matthew Callahan was the director of the modern art department at the Halt Institute, a prestigious art gallery in the heart of Crookshollow village. He could no more paint an exquisite work of art than he could recognise one. He didn't even really *care* about art. He had only one trait that made him a competent curator: he was loud and bolshy and could usually get his way. Except, of course, when his assistant curator messed things up.

The assistant curator being me, although judging by Matthew's voice, probably not for much longer.

"Well?" Matthew loomed in my doorway and barked. "Do you have anything to say for yourself, *James*?"

"No," I muttered, staring at my knees. I hated it when Matthew used my real first name. He only did it because he knew it made me uncomfortable, and Matthew loved making people uncomfortable. Silently I cursed my parents for naming me – their only daughter – after James Fauntelroy, my famous male ancestor. *Who does that?*

But now wasn't the time to be thinking about my parents, especially since that usually brought up some tough memories. I had a bigger, angrier problem hurtling through my office door.

A thousand excuses loomed on my lips. It wasn't my fault the paintings were late. The Halt Institute won the contract for one of the most anticipated exhibitions in the entire country. The artist, Ryan Raynard – despite being one of the darlings of the modern art scene (and my favourite English artist) – was a recluse. He lived in his family's crumbling manor not far from my own flat in Crookshollow, but he hadn't been seen outside the manor walls for at least ten years. Despite never having exhibited, never doing press, and never schmoozing with the rich collectors who made the art world go round, Raynard was one of the most sought-after artists painting in the modern impressionist style. Buyers snapped his pieces up as soon as they hit the auction houses. His paintings leached into the market through his secretary, Simon Host, who was the man I had been dealing with over Raynard's first-ever public exhibition.

Everything had gone well initially, until I needed to have the paintings shipped to the Institute. Despite numerous calls, emails, and even a drunken attempt to smoke signal from the pub last night (courtesy of my flatmate Kylie helping me drown my sorrows) to Simon's office, I'd heard not a single reply about the delivery of the paintings.

Of course, Matthew didn't care about any of that. All he saw was a big gap in the warehouse where the Raynard paintings should've been, and a staff photographer getting paid to Instagram pictures of his nostrils.

Matthew leaned against the doorframe and scowled at me. He'd curled the ends of his moustache with wax, so it looked as if he was smiling and frowning at the same time. "Gareth isn't working this weekend. If those paintings aren't here by tomorrow, the photographs don't get shot until next week, which means the advertisements don't get to the printers on time, the *Guardian* hold back our editorial, and I start wondering why on earth I hired someone so goddamn incompetent."

I gritted my teeth. "I know all this, Matthew. Raynard's office is being difficult, but I've got it under control."

"Tomorrow, then. On your head be it." Matthew shot me a final, deadly stare, and continued down the hall to harass another curator.

I rose and shut the door, turning the key in the lock so Matthew couldn't walk in again. Across the hall, Tara – another curator – waved at me through the glass. I glared at her and pulled down the shade, hoping she hadn't noticed my red face and shaking hands.

I slumped back into my chair, rubbing my fingers against my throbbing temples. I didn't need Matthew to tell me that the artwork was going to be late. I *knew* it was going to be late, if it even showed up at all.

What I didn't know was what to do about it.

Two years ago, I'd landed my dream job as assistant curator here at Halt, off the back of a successful kinetic exhibition I'd curated for the Tate Modern. But compared to some of the other curators – who'd been working at Halt so long they remembered when Warhol was just an upstart young commercial illustrator with a canned foods fetish – I was green. I'd been astounded when Matthew shoved a thick file on my desk two weeks ago and announced that it was my job to co-ordinate the exhibition details with Raynard.

My astonishment quickly turned to dread when I realised Raynard wasn't going to be easy to deal with. Despite his absurd insistence on an opening only a month away (most of our exhibitions at this scale were planned a year in advance) he refused to even get on the phone to discuss a single detail, and he had a list of demands rivalling that of a rock star. He knew no gallery would turn down his wishes, and he was clearly a man of some considerable ego. Even though I greatly admired his work and I'd never even talked to the man, I was beginning to hate Ryan Raynard more and more each day.

Right now, my fear of losing my job boiled that hate over into seething, unadulterated rage.

Calm down, Alex. You have to think. I wiped my sweaty palms against my wool skirt. Perhaps Simon Host was just busy with other preparations for the exhibition. The exhibition was to be his client's first public showing in ten years, after all. It was likely Simon was in his office right now.

I dialled the number I now knew by heart, after calling it twenty times already today. While I listened to it ring I refreshed my browser. No new emails. The phone rang and rang... ten times... twenty times... Raynard's secretary still wasn't answering, and there was no way to leave a message.

What am I going to do?

This was the first major exhibit Matthew had entrusted me with. If I messed this one up, I'd be back to doing administration and running the children's gallery talks. If I had any hope of becoming a serious curator one day, I had to figure out a way to solve this.

My stomach churned. My pulse throbbed in my ears. I gulped down the urge to throw up. Panicking wasn't going to get those paintings to the gallery. I stared at my car keys on the table. There was nothing else to do.

I was going to talk to Ryan Raynard and make him hand over the artwork, even if it meant breaking into Raynard Hall itself.

CHAPTER TWO

ALEX

I sped out of the Halt Institute car park, and straight into a
line of cars waiting to turn onto the high street. The radio
blared out a news report about another hiker who'd been
attacked by a rabid fox while walking in Crookshollow
forest. That was the third such incident this month. *Must be a
global warming thing,* I thought, flicking the radio over to the
local indie station. Greenies blamed global warming for
everything, from unseasonably warm summers to lines at the
supermarket.

I tapped my foot impatiently on the pedal, in my mind
seeing Matthew's red face and curly moustache as he chewed
me out. It was nearly 4 pm., and traffic was starting to pick
up for the afternoon, especially now that the tourist season
was closing in. I needed to get across town to Raynard Hall
as quickly as possible, so I could catch this Simon Host
before he left the estate for the evening.

Like Salisbury and the Fens, Crookshollow Village and
the surrounding forest was one of those English landscapes
known for its ritual significance throughout history. There
were several Neolithic henges and other ancient religious

sites scattered across hilltops and hidden in the dense forest groves. Witches used to gather in the trees to dance naked and take part in ritual orgies – that was, until the witch finders swept in and put a stop to that. More than 200 convicted witches had been burnt in the market square at the opposite end of the high street, or at least that's the story they tell at the local medieval torture museum. It's said that the witches left their imprint in the landscape – that they transferred their spirits to their animal familiars, and their magic still dwells within the wild cats and foxes and deer and birds of Crookshollow Forest.

Growing up in the village, I was thrilled by these stories. They filled my imagination with enchanted worlds of witches and werewolves and fairies, right there in the forest on my own back doorstep. I was the weird loner kid, the strange girl who drew pictures all the time and sucked at playing cricket. After enduring days at school where kids either ignored me or threw things at me, I would take my paints and my camera and hike for miles into the gloom, stopping to draw fantastical scenes of witches dancing by the stream and half-human, half-crow creatures flying between the towering oaks. The forest fuelled my art and held together my soul.

But small towns were hell for kids like me, so I moved to London as soon as the final bell rang, eager to get away from the bad memories and embrace my art. I studied at the Wimbledon College of Arts, where I spent four blissful years painting and sculpting and attending political rallies and poetry readings and pretending to be a lamppost with eccentric performance artists. I lived in squalour and survived on white rice and kebabs. They were the best years of my life.

My carefree student days had to come to an end, and not just because my parents were killed in a car accident during my final year. I emerged a fresh-faced artist trying to establish myself right in the heart of the Global Financial Crisis. No one was buying art, especially not from an unknown like me. After six months of slogging my paintings around every independent gallery in London, my landlady threatened me with eviction if I couldn't come up with the two months' rent I owed her.

I had to grow up and face facts: being an artist wasn't a viable career. I hadn't even been able to pick up a brush since my parents died. What kind of an artist was I, if I couldn't even paint through my pain? I had to find a real job.

Luckily, I was still in contact with my old professors, and through one of them I landed a paid internship at the Tate Modern, than was offered a full-time position as a professional ass-kisser and errand-girl. I traded my paint-stained trackies for pencil skirts and pumps. My landlady stopped bugging me.

In the four years I worked at the Tate, I barely created any artwork, and I never hiked off into the wilderness. Even though I had a great job many people would've killed for, I felt like a failure. I wasn't turning into the person I always imagined myself to be. My kind, supportive parents who I usually turned to for advice were now just cold stones in a cemetery.

Still the forest had called me back. When Halt offered me the job, I accepted without a second thought, packed up my apartment and moved into the tiny two-bed semi I shared with my friend Kylie, a pudgy calico cat named Miss Havisham and several recalcitrant mice. Our tiny back garden backed onto the forest edge.

I even started drawing and painting again, although I was woefully out of practice. Even though I lived near my parents' old house and all their memories, I felt calmer than I had in a long time. Except for today. Today I was so far from calm I couldn't see it if it were driving toward me in a Panzer tank.

I leaned on my horn as a woman wearing a kaftan covered with moon symbols stepped out from a candle shop and wandered across the street in front of the car, staring at her smartphone screen and completely unaware of the fact I'd had to slam on my brakes to avoid hitting her. It was all just another summer's day in Crookshollow.

Because of its significance as an ancient religious land-scape, as well as being the site of numerous modern tales of hauntings, Crookshollow was a popular destination with free spirits and new-age pagans, all of whom were apparently on the road at *this very moment*, taking things as slowly as their pot-addled brains allowed. The centre of Crookshollow was a hodgepodge of occult stores, artisan candle makers, and alternative record shops, attracting a crowd with a particular disregard for traffic rules. The Halt building – a gleaming, modern installation of steel and glass, housing the art galleries, the witchcraft museum and some bank offices – loomed over the quaint high street, a constant reminder that corporate power still reigned supreme.

Eventually, I escaped the tangle of the high street and was speeding out toward Raynard Hall. Despite being back in Crookshollow for nearly two years, I hadn't traveled out near the crumbling manor since my childhood. I'd grown up in a small bungalow nearby, on Roundoak Drive, and the grounds of Raynard Hall were as familiar to me as my own childhood home.

Back then, the manor had been in the hands of Alistair Raynard, Ryan's father, who lived somewhere up in the Scottish mountains but kept on a few servants at the manor to maintain the estate. They never did a very good job. Overgrown and decaying, the manor had been a popular place for local kids to play, daring each other to approach the windows and peer in at the drab, empty rooms. It's dark stone façade, high gothic windows and sinister gargoyles lining the edge of the roof made it a popular source for local legends of ghosts and strange sightings. One of the most oft-told stories was of a younger Alistair Raynard – when he still lived in the Hall – hunting deer in the night and coming across a coven of witches in the forest. He was said to have chased them off his land with his rifle before they could complete their ritual and so they'd cursed him with some kind of affliction, and that was why he'd fled to Scotland.

I pulled into Holly Avenue. Raynard Hall dominated the view – its towering grey turrets and black-shuttered windows casting a dim shadow across the bright townhouses that lined the street. A couple of tourists had parked their bikes at the gates and were snapping pictures of the famous artist's home, but they quickly moved on when they saw my car approach. I parked the car outside the heavy iron gates and stared up at the gothic manor, my breath catching in my throat. I'd walked past Raynard Hall hundreds of times as a kid, even sneaking into the grounds at night and peeking in at the grimy windows to see what ghosts might lurk inside, but it had never looked so menacing before.

I sucked in a breath. *You've got to do this, Alex. You need to call on all your hidden powers of persuasion and allure, and get inside that house. Or you can kiss your career at Halt goodbye.*

I leaned out the window and pushed the button on the intercom. It buzzed impatiently. My mind went completely blank. *What am I going to say? Ryan Raynard hasn't opened these doors to anyone else in ten long years. What will possibly make him open them for me?*

The intercom crackled, as if urging me to speak. I took a deep breath, then said, "Hello, Mr Host? Mr Raynard? I need to talk to someone about the exhibition—"

"Go away," a voice crackled on the other end. "This is private property."

I bristled. Who did this guy think he was? The haughty tone of Simon Host – coupled with my agitation at having being forced to stand outside the manor at all – made me snap back. "I'm parked on the road, *sir*, which is *not* private property at all, so I'd thank you to lose that tone and let me speak uninterrupted. I'm James Alexandra Kline, from the Halt Institute. I need to know when Ryan Raynard's paintings are being delivered. They should have arrived on Monday and we have a photographer waiting—"

"No one by that name lives here. Go away."

Now I was getting angry. "Do you think I'm an idiot? We've talked on the phone several times already. Besides, who are you trying to fool? Ryan Raynard may be an artistic genius, but he's a idiot if he thinks he's flying below the radar living in a manor that would make the Addams Family jealous. How many gargoyles have you got on that façade? One... two... three..." I counted them aloud. "*Fifteen* gargoyles. I mean, that's *obviously* the aesthetic choice of someone who wants to stay hidden away. I'm being sarcastic, in case you can't tell."

"I did ascertain that, thank you." The voice on the other end sounded faintly amused.

"Listen, Mr. Host, I know Raynard is inside that house, and I need to talk to him about the exhibit, and he's left me no other way to contact him. So either you let me in, or I cancel the exhibition. It's that simple."

My heart pounded against my chest. I hadn't planned to say all that. I'd got angry and it had all just slipped out, and now I wished I could take it back. I was taking a huge risk. Raynard could simply decide to cancel the exhibition, and my career would be over before it had even begun.

The intercom crackled. "What did you say your name was?"

"James Alexandra Kline. But people just call me Alex—"

"Very well. Drive up to the doors."

The gate creaked open, and I slammed down on the accelerator, careering up the cracked concrete drive before the voice on the end of the intercom could change his mind.

"Woah." I gazed up at the imposing façade. Up close, the manor appeared even more sinister. It didn't look as if Ryan had done any upkeep on the place since he'd moved in. Weeds snaked across the drive from the wild, overgrown flower beds. Vines twisted around the columns flanking the main entrance. The glass on several windows was cracked or missing, and most were covered with thick, soiled drapes.

The dark oak front doors swung open, revealing a willowy man with beady eyes and a few wisps of grey hair, wearing an old-fashioned black tailored suit. He signalled to me to park off to the left, and follow him inside.

"I'm Alexandra Kline," I said, extending my hand to him. He merely stared at my outstretched digits, nodded, then walked silently through the lofty foyer. My cheap M&S pumps *clack-clacked* against the polished marble floor, and I couldn't help but glance around at the expensive, but dusty, furnishings and bland portraits in gilded frames that dominated the space.

The man led me down a wide hall, its vaulted ceiling painted with hunting scenes and framed by geometric designs. On the walls hung traditional portraits and hunting trophies – not the decor I'd expect from one of the foremost modern artists in Britain, whose paintings burst with light and movement and colour. I peered into the open rooms as we passed them, seeing some furnished with dark wood and thick velvet, others packed with boxes and furniture covered in white dust sheets, like silent ghosts of the manor's past.

This was the home of the great Ryan Raynard? It just didn't fit.

At the end of the hall we stepped into a cold drawing room, furnished with the same dark wood and heavy velvet drapery as the rest of the manor. It looked as if no one had used it for a long time, judging by the layer of dust covering every surface, and the spiderwebs clinging to the stag antlers hanging over the fireplace. The casement window was broken, and a chilly breeze blew from the overgrown garden behind the house and swirled around the room. I covered my bare arms with my hands, trying to keep them warm.

I turned to Raynard's lurch, not certain what I was meant to do. "Where's Ryan?" I asked.

"I'll get you some tea," he croaked in reply, then shuffled away. I recognised his voice instantly. That was Simon Host.

Well, isn't this a walking bloody cliché? Raynard's secretary was also his butler. I perched gingerly on one of the grimy chairs, half expecting a bat to fly down from one of the darkened corners and materialise into Ryan Raynard before me. I pulled at a loose thread on my skirt, wishing I'd thought to go home and change into something smarter. My stomach twisted into a knot. I was about to meet the man whose art career I'd followed religiously since college, a man whose work made me see the world in new and exciting ways, who made me feel that wanting to make art was a perfectly legitimate and wonderful thing to do…

I heard footsteps down the hall, and a deep voice calling out to the butler, who croaked out "James Kline awaits your audience," from somewhere deeper in the house. The footsteps slowed as they approached the door, and the voice said, "Sorry about the wait, Mr Kline. I've been busy in the studio. You know artists, always forgetting the time—"

Ryan Raynard stalked into the room, and I got my first glimpse of my artistic hero. He appeared younger than I expected, his unkempt red hair and stubbled chin at odds with the stiffness of the home around him. Deep, intelligent brown eyes flicked from object to object, unfocused, still lost in the world of whatever he'd been creating. He wore black jeans, a black vest pulled tight across his toned, sculpted chest, and heavy black motorcycle boots that clomped against the marble floor. All three of these items were splattered with paint.

Holy smokes. He was, in short, quite simply the most attractive man I'd ever laid eyes on. A strange shiver ran through my body, spreading from my head right down to my toes.

When Ryan finally looked up, his eyes met mine, and his whole body froze. The stiffness ran from his feet, right the way to the top of his head, as if someone had suddenly shoved a giant popsicle stick up his ass, forcing him upright. He opened his mouth as if to say something, but nothing came out.

I stood, my heart pounding, "Alex Kline," I said, outstretching my hand toward him, trying to keep my voice steady. "I'm from the Halt Institute. It's a pleasure to meet you, Mr Raynard. I'm a huge fan of your work—"

Ryan Raynard stared at my hand hanging there in the space between us, with a look of such utter horror I had to turn it over to ensure it wasn't covered in grease or something.

"You... you're a woman?" he whispered, his eyes boring into mine. The muscles in his face twitched, and I could see the veins in his neck standing out. Something was really wrong here.

"Last time I checked." My hand still hung awkwardly in the air. Ryan tore his gaze from mine, physically wrenching his body away from me. He backed away toward the door, his handsome face shot now with panic.

"Simon!" he yelled into the hall. "Come here, *now*!"

The butler rushed into the room, a tea tray clattering in his shaking arms. "Sir?"

Raynard was inching toward the door, his hard eyes glaring at me like I was a bug he wished to be squashed immediately. "Why did you let this... this...*woman* into my home? You know I don't want to be disturbed."

"You told me I could let her in, not five minutes ago, Mr Raynard. She needs your paintings for the exhibition."

"You told me her name was James!"

"That's what she told me, sir—"

Ryan Raynard whirled around and faced me, his eyes burning. "You said your name was James."

I bristled, a sure-fire sign I was about to say something inappropriate. But he was acting like a jerk, so I allowed my voice to drip with scorn. "Forgive me; I didn't know my birth name had to be approved by the great Ryan Raynard. I was named after an ancestor on my mother's side, James Fauntelroy. Apparently, he used to help women accused of witchcraft in the village escape before they were trialled—"

"While I'm really enjoying this *fascinating* history lesson," Ryan faced into the hall so he didn't have to look at me. "You need to leave."

I shook my head, a stupid gesture, since he couldn't see me. "I can't leave until we've cleared up a few details for your exhibition. Where are the paintings? I know you've never done an exhibition before, so maybe all this organising is new to you, but if you want this one to go well, you need to co-operate with me. If I don't get those paintings to Halt tomorrow, the exhibition can't go ahead."

His shoulders sagged. I observed the movement with interest. It seemed the exhibition meant more to him than his attitude had led me to believe. "Simon, show Mrs Kline—"

"*Ms* Kline," I corrected him, cursing myself inwardly as I

felt a blush appear on my cheeks. Luckily, Ryan was still avoiding my eyes, so he didn't see.

"—to the painting hall. Answer all her questions. If you want me, I'll be in the studio, but don't bring her in there. Please deal with Ms Kline on all aspects concerning the exhibition, and make sure she understands that even though my paintings will be available to the public for the first time, I will not. *Don't* let anyone else in."

Without even another glance in my direction, Ryan Raynard slipped back into the hall and disappeared. The clomp of his boots faded away into silence.

Simon inclined his head toward me, indicating I should follow him. Picking myself up, I followed the butler out of the cold drawing room and back down that drab hall, through another dark, gloomy sitting room, and along a narrow corridor.

My whole body buzzed with a strange energy. It must've been the surge of righteous anger. *How dare he treat me like... like I wasn't even a person, like I didn't even deserve his eye contact? No wonder he hides from the world, if he doesn't even have the decency to act pleasantly to those helping him. I can't believe that's the same guy who created all that beautiful art.*

"Is he always so... abrasive?" I asked Simon, by way of making conversation. "How do you stand it?"

"Mr Raynard has his proclivities," the butler replied, his drawn face indicating he thought he might have said too much.

"And what's his problem with women? This isn't the bloody stone age. Does he think the art world is only for straight, white, rich men like himself?"

The butler didn't reply.

We walked on in silence through the dark, drab hallway, Ryan's ancestors staring disapprovingly down on me. All the while I replayed the meeting with Ryan Raynard over in my mind – his handsome face hardening to stone when he realised I was female, his body going rigid like a statue, his aversion even to meet my eyes. The way he swaggered in, those gorgeous curls flopping in his eyes, his shoulders bulging from that black vest...

I shook my head. Hot artistic visionary or not, the man was a complete tosser. It wouldn't do for me to dwell on his looks.

We stopped in front of a heavy steel door – at odds with the drab wood panelling that surrounded it. Simon hunched over the lock, keying in a complex combination. The door clicked open, and I was greeted with a sight that took my breath away.

A long, white room stretched in front of me, the other end a distant blur on the horizon. Rectangular skylights flooded the space in natural light, and after the gloom of the house, the light, airy space made me feel giddy, almost drunk. Simon flicked a switch, and rows of low-hanging spotlights flickered on, illuminating the artwork hanging on the walls. Every spare space on the walls was taken up with paintings – a hodgepodge of different styles and eras, all chosen with the keen eye of someone who understood colour and light and beauty. I noticed what looked like a Banksy print to the left of the door, butted up next to a Chagall. I turned, dizzy with the splendour of it all, and came face to face with some of Monet's water lilies, the beauty of the lines leaping from the canvas, pulling me into the gardens of Giverny, filling my nostrils with the scent of spring. I turned again, and this time my eye fell upon a Cézanne still life, the repetitive, exploratory brushstrokes creating a dramatic tension between the objects.

Nestled amongst these great words were pieces I recognised as belonging to the hand of Raynard himself. Impressionistic views of forests – great oaks with branches twisting, birds flying in lazy circles over a foggy grove, deer drinking from the brook. A beautiful red fox frolicking between the trees. I stepped closer, admiring the dappled light streaming from the gaps in the leaves, touching the fox's fur.

I glanced at the title. *Vixen.*

"Why isn't this painting in the exhibition?" I breathed. The title wasn't on the list Simon had given me. Ryan's exhibition was called *The Hunt,* and his images, we'd been informed, took inspiration from the animals in Crookshollow Forest as they went about their nocturnal wanderings. This remarkable piece should have been the focal point of the room.

Simon shook his head. "He will not part with that one for anything," he said. "And don't you even ask. Come, I have packaged up the ten pieces for the exhibition. Three of them are quite large, and I shall help you carry them to your car."

TO BE CONTINUED

He's an arrogant, reclusive artist, and a complete and utter prick. So why can't she get him out of her head? Fall into Ryan and Alex's story in Art of Cunning, *book 1 in the Crookshollow Gothic Romance series – READ NOW*

WANT MORE STORIES FROM THE
WORLD OF CROOKSHOLLOW

Haven't read the Wolves of Crookshollow series yet?

Sink your teeth into the hot werewolf paranormal romance from *USA Today* bestselling author, Steffanie Holmes.

Anna

It's been five months since my boyfriend was tragically killed in a climbing accident. I didn't think I was over him … until Luke walked on to the archaeological site.

Tall, dark, sexy, tattooed, funny, dangerous. Everything I want in a man.

But he's hiding something. He acts strangely in the moonlight. He won't tell me anything about his life. And I caught him trying to destroy an important find.

My body aches for him, but my heart tells me I'm not ready to make myself vulnerable again, especially not for a guy who isn't being straight with me.

If only …

Luke

Anna Sinclair – archaeologist, geek girl, totally and utterly delectable.

I knew from the moment her intoxicating scent wafted across my wolf senses, she's meant to be mine.

And that knowledge is *terrifying*.

The last thing I expected was to find my fated mate on an archaeological site. Whenever I'm near her, all I want to do is claim her.

But she's broken. The last thing she needs in her life is a werewolf out for revenge. I'm here to destroy the site, to keep my family's past buried forever.

If Anna finds out the truth, she'd never speak to me again.

But I can't deny the bond between us. **I'll do anything to make her mine.**

Digging the Wolf is a standalone paranormal romance by USA Today bestselling author Steffanie Holmes. Read if you love archaeological mysteries, badass wolves, a broken heroine, and a hero so hot he'll have you howling for more.

ABOUT THE AUTHOR

Steffanie Holmes is a *USA Today* bestselling author of paranormal romance, urban fantasy, and supernatural mysteries. Her books feature clever, witty heroines, dark and haunted settings, cunning witches, and a dash of sadistic humor.

Before becoming a writer, Steffanie worked as an archaeologist and museum curator. From Dark Age Europe to crumbling gothic estates, Steffanie is fascinated with how love can blossom between the most unlikely characters.

Steffanie lives in New Zealand with her husband, a horde of cantankerous cats, and their medieval sword collection.

STEFFANIE HOLMES NEWSLETTER

Can't get enough of Maeve and her boys? Get *The Summer Court* – a Briarwood short story – for free in *Cabinet of Curiosities*, a Steffanie Holmes compendium of short stories and bonus scenes. To get this collection, all you need to do is sign up for updates with the Steffanie Holmes newsletter.

Come hang with Steffanie
www.steffanieholmes.com
hello@steffanieholmes.com

COME HANG ON FACEBOOK!

Thank you so much for reading and enjoying the Briarwood Reverse Harem series!

I've got a super-active reader group on Facebook. Join BOOKS THAT BITE if you want to talk about the series, get exclusive previews and bonus content, and meet some other awesome readers! I've love to see you there!